PRAISE FOR *FEBI*

Lefty Finalist for Most Humorous Mystery

"The best outing yet for Mira!"

—*Kirkus Reviews*

"Lourey skillfully mixes humor and suspense . . . and the mile-a-minute pace never falters. Another excellent addition to Lourey's very entertaining Mira James mystery series."

—*Booklist* (starred review)

"[An] incredible series . . . [*February Fever*] is a charming story with great dialogue, [and] there are more months coming, so readers definitely have something to look forward to."

—*Suspense Magazine*

"I can't wait to see what Mira does next."

—*Crimespree Magazine*

PRAISE FOR *JANUARY THAW*

Lefty Finalist for Most Humorous Mystery

"Who can resist a mystery that includes a daredevil octogenarian sidekick; a flashy, plant-whispering mayor; some really bad villains; and a little girl ghost?"

—*Booklist*

"Those looking for an engaging, multigenerational small-town mystery that tackles contemporary issues can't miss with this entry."

—*Library Journal*

"Good, high-calorie fun!"

—*Mystery Scene*

"Lourey has successfully created an independent, relatable heroine in Mira James. Mira's wit and fearlessness enable her to overcome the many challenges she faces as she tries to unravel the murder."

—*Crimespree Magazine*

PRAISE FOR *DECEMBER DREAD*

Lefty Finalist for Most Humorous Mystery

"Lourey creates a splendid mix of humor and suspense."

—*Booklist*

"Lourey, who keeps her secrets well, delivers a breathtaking finale."

—*Publishers Weekly*

"Lourey pulls out all the stops in this eighth case."

—*Library Journal*

PRAISE FOR *NOVEMBER HUNT*

"It's not easy to make people laugh while they're on the edge of their seats, but Lourey pulls it off, while her vivid descriptions of a brutal Minnesota winter will make readers shiver in the seventh book in her very clever Mira James mystery series."

—*Booklist* (starred review)

"Clever, quirky, and completely original!"
—Hank Phillippi Ryan, Anthony, Agatha, and Macavity Award–winning author

"A masterful mix of mayhem and mirth."
—Reed Farrel Coleman, *New York Times* bestselling author

"Lourey has successfully created an independent, relatable heroine in Mira James. Mira's wit and fearlessness enable her to overcome the many challenges she faces as she tries to unravel the murder."

—*Crimespree Magazine*

"Lourey's seventh cozy featuring PI wannabe Mira James successfully combines humor, an intriguing mystery, and quirky small-town characters."

—*Publishers Weekly*

"Lourey has a knack for wholesome sexual innuendo, and she gets plenty of mileage out of Minnesota. This light novel keeps the reader engaged, like one of those sweet, chewy Nut Goodies that Mira is addicted to."

—*The Boston Globe*

"Lourey has a talent for creating hilarious characters in bizarre, laugh-out-loud situations, while at the same time capturing the honest and endearing subtleties of human life."

—The Strand

PRAISE FOR *AUGUST MOON*

"Hilarious, fast paced, and madcap."

—*Booklist* (starred review)

"Another amusing tale set in the town full of over-the-top zanies who've endeared themselves to the engaging Mira."

—*Kirkus Reviews*

"[A] hilarious, wonderfully funny cozy."

—*Crimespree Magazine*

"Lourey has a gift for creating terrific characters. Her sly and witty take on small-town USA is a sweet summer treat. Pull up a lawn chair, pour yourself a glass of lemonade, and enjoy."

—Denise Swanson, bestselling author

"A fun, fast-paced mystery with a heroine readers will enjoy."

—*The Mystery Reader*

"With just the right amount of insouciance, tongue-in-cheek sexiness, and plain common sense, Jess Lourey offers up a funny, well-written, engaging story . . . Readers will thoroughly enjoy the well-paced ride."
—Carl Brookins, author of *The Case of the Greedy Lawyers*

PRAISE FOR *MAY DAY*

"Jess Lourey writes about a small-town assistant librarian, but this is no genteel traditional mystery. Mira James likes guys in a big way, likes booze, and isn't afraid of motorcycles. She flees a dead-end job and a dead-end boyfriend in Minneapolis and ends up in Battle Lake, a little town with plenty of dirty secrets. The first-person narrative in *May Day* is fresh, the characters quirky. Minnesota has many fine crime writers, and Jess Lourey has just entered their ranks!"
—Ellen Hart, award-winning author of the Jane Lawless and Sophie Greenway series

"This trade paperback packed a punch . . . I loved it from the get-go!"
—*Tulsa World*

"What a romp this is! I found myself laughing out loud."
—*Crimespree Magazine*

"Mira digs up a closetful of dirty secrets, including sex parties, cross-dressing, and blackmail, on her way to exposing the killer. Lourey's debut has a likable heroine and surfeit of sass."
—*Kirkus Reviews*

PRAISE FOR *THE TAKEN ONES*

Short-listed for the 2024 Edgar Award for Best Paperback Original

"Setting the standard for top-notch thrillers, *The Taken Ones* is smart, compelling, and filled with utterly real characters. Lourey brings her formidable storytelling talent to the game and, on top of that, wows us with a deft stylistic touch. This is a one-sitting read!"

—Jeffery Deaver, author of *The Bone Collector* and
The Watchmaker's Hand

"*The Taken Ones* has Jess Lourey's trademark of suspense all the way. A damaged and brave heroine, an equally damaged evildoer, and missing girls from long ago all combine to keep the reader rushing through to the explosive ending."

—Charlaine Harris, *New York Times* bestselling author

"Lourey is at the top of her game with *The Taken Ones*. A master of building tension while maintaining a riveting pace, Lourey is a hell of a writer on all fronts, but her greatest talent may be her characters. Evangeline Reed, an agent with the Minnesota Bureau of Criminal Apprehension, is a woman with a devastating past and the haunting ability to know the darkest crimes happening around her. She is also exactly the kind of character I would happily follow through a dozen books or more. In awe of her bravery, I also identified with her pain and wanted desperately to protect her. Along with an incredible cast of support characters, *The Taken Ones* will break your heart wide open and stay with you long after you've turned the final page. This is a 2023 must read."

—Danielle Girard, *USA Today* and Amazon #1 bestselling author of
Up Close

PRAISE FOR *THE QUARRY GIRLS*

Winner of the 2023 Anthony Award for Best Paperback Original

Winner of the 2023 Minnesota Book Award for Genre Fiction

"Few authors can blend the genuine fear generated by a sordid tale of true crime with evocative, three-dimensional characters and mesmerizing prose like Jess Lourey. Her fictional stories feel rooted in a world we all know but also fear. *The Quarry Girls* is a story of secrets gone to seed, and Lourey gives readers her best novel yet—which is quite the accomplishment. Calling it: *The Quarry Girls* will be one of the best books of the year."

—Alex Segura, acclaimed author of *Secret Identity*, *Star Wars Poe Dameron: Free Fall*, and *Miami Midnight*

"Jess Lourey once more taps deep into her Midwest roots and childhood fears with *The Quarry Girls*, an absorbing, true crime–informed thriller narrated in the compelling voice of young drummer Heather Cash as she and her bandmates navigate the treacherous and confusing ground between girlhood and womanhood one simmering and deadly summer. Lourey conveys the edgy, hungry restlessness of teen girls with a touch of Megan Abbott while steadily intensifying the claustrophobic atmosphere of a small 1977 Minnesota town where darkness snakes below the surface."

—Loreth Anne White, *Washington Post* and Amazon Charts bestselling author of *The Patient's Secret*

"Jess Lourey is a master of the coming-of-age thriller, and *The Quarry Girls* may be her best yet—as dark, twisty, and full of secrets as the tunnels that lurk beneath Pantown's deceptively idyllic streets."
—Chris Holm, Anthony Award–winning author of *The Killing Kind*

PRAISE FOR *BLOODLINE*

Winner of the 2022 Anthony Award for Best Paperback Original

Winner of the 2022 ITW Thriller Award for Best Paperback Original

Short-listed for the 2021 Goodreads Choice Awards

"Fans of *Rosemary's Baby* will relish this."
—*Publishers Weekly*

"Based on a true story, this is a sinister, suspenseful thriller full of creeping horror."
—*Kirkus Reviews*

"Lourey ratchets up the fear in a novel that verges on horror."
—*Library Journal*

"In *Bloodline*, Jess Lourey blends elements of mystery, suspense, and horror to stunning effect."
—*BOLO Books*

"Jess Lourey writes small-town Minnesota like Stephen King writes small-town Maine. *Bloodline* is a tremendous book with a heart and a hacksaw . . . and I loved every second of it."
—Rachel Howzell Hall, author of the critically acclaimed novels *And Now She's Gone* and *They All Fall Down*

PRAISE FOR *UNSPEAKABLE THINGS*

Winner of the 2021 Anthony Award for Best Paperback Original

Short-listed for the 2021 Edgar Awards and 2020 Goodreads Choice Awards

"The suspense never wavers in this page-turner."
—*Publishers Weekly*

"The atmospheric suspense novel is haunting because it's narrated from the point of view of a thirteen-year-old, an age that should be more innocent but often isn't. Even more chilling, it's based on real-life incidents. Lourey may be known for comic capers (*March of Crimes*), but this tense novel combines the best of a coming-of-age story with suspense and an unforgettable young narrator."
—*Library Journal* (starred review)

"Part suspense, part coming-of-age, Jess Lourey's *Unspeakable Things* is a story of creeping dread, about childhood when you know the monster under your bed is real. A novel that clings to you long after the last page."
—Lori Rader-Day, Edgar Award–nominated author of *Under a Dark Sky*

"A noose of a novel that tightens by inches. The squirming tension comes from every direction—including the ones that are supposed to be safe. I felt complicit as I read, as if at any moment I stopped I would be abandoning Cassie, alone, in the dark, straining to listen and fearing to hear."

—Marcus Sakey, bestselling author of *Brilliance*

"*Unspeakable Things* is an absolutely riveting novel about the poisonous secrets buried deep in towns and families. Jess Lourey has created a story that will chill you to the bone and a main character who will break your heart wide open."

—Lou Berney, Edgar Award–winning author of *November Road*

"Inspired by a true story, *Unspeakable Things* crackles with authenticity, humanity, and humor. The novel reminded me of *To Kill a Mockingbird* and *The Marsh King's Daughter*. Highly recommended."

—Mark Sullivan, bestselling author of *Beneath a Scarlet Sky*

"Jess Lourey does a masterful job building tension and dread, but her greatest asset in *Unspeakable Things* is Cassie—an arresting narrator you identify with, root for, and desperately want to protect. This is a book that will stick with you long after you've torn through it."

—Rob Hart, author of *The Warehouse*

"With *Unspeakable Things*, Jess Lourey has managed the near-impossible, crafting a mystery as harrowing as it is tender, as gut-wrenching as it is lyrical. There is real darkness here, a creeping, inescapable dread that more than once had me looking over my own shoulder. But at its heart beats the irrepressible—and irresistible—spirit of its . . . heroine, a young woman so bright and vital and brave she kept even the fiercest monsters at bay. This is a book that will stay with me for a long time."

—Elizabeth Little, *Los Angeles Times* bestselling author of *Dear Daughter* and *Pretty as a Picture*

PRAISE FOR *SALEM'S CIPHER*

"A fast-paced, sometimes brutal thriller reminiscent of Dan Brown's *The Da Vinci Code*."

—*Booklist* (starred review)

"A hair-raising thrill ride."

—*Library Journal* (starred review)

"The fascinating historical information combined with a storyline ripped from the headlines will hook conspiracy theorists and action addicts alike."

—*Kirkus Reviews*

"Fans of *The Da Vinci Code* are going to love this book . . . One of my favorite reads of 2016."

—*Crimespree Magazine*

"This suspenseful tale has something for absolutely everyone to enjoy."

—*Suspense Magazine*

PRAISE FOR *MERCY'S CHASE*

"An immersive voice, an intriguing story, a wonderful character—highly recommended!"

—Lee Child, #1 *New York Times* bestselling author

"Both a sweeping adventure and race-against-time thriller, *Mercy's Chase* is fascinating, fierce, and brimming with heart—just like its heroine, Salem Wiley."

—Meg Gardiner, author of *Into the Black Nowhere*

"Action-packed, great writing taut with suspense, an appealing main character to root for—who could ask for anything more?"

—Buried Under Books

PRAISE FOR *REWRITE YOUR LIFE: DISCOVER YOUR TRUTH THROUGH THE HEALING POWER OF FICTION*

"Interweaving practical advice with stories and insights garnered in her own writing journey, Jessica Lourey offers a step-by-step guide for writers struggling to create fiction from their life experiences. But this book isn't just about writing. It's also about the power of stories to transform those who write them. I know of no other guide that delivers on its promise with such honesty, simplicity, and beauty."

—William Kent Krueger, *New York Times* bestselling author of the Cork O'Connor series and *Ordinary Grace*

FEBRUARY
FEVER

OTHER TITLES BY JESS LOUREY

MURDER BY MONTH MYSTERIES

STEINBECK AND REED THRILLERS

THRILLERS

The Quarry Girls

Litani

Bloodline

Unspeakable Things

SALEM'S CIPHER THRILLERS

Salem's Cipher

Mercy's Chase

CHILDREN'S BOOKS

Leave My Book Alone! Starring Claudette, a Dragon with Control Issues

YOUNG ADULT

A Whisper of Poison

NONFICTION

Rewrite Your Life: Discover Your Truth Through the Healing Power of Fiction

FEBRUARY FEVER

JESS LOUREY

THOMAS & MERCER

Text copyright © 2014, 2018, 2025 by Jess Lourey
All rights reserved.

No part of this book may be reproduced, or stored in a retrieval system, or transmitted in any form or by any means, electronic, mechanical, photocopying, recording, or otherwise, without express written permission of the publisher.

Published by Thomas & Mercer, Seattle

www.apub.com

Amazon, the Amazon logo, and Thomas & Mercer are trademarks of Amazon.com, Inc., or its affiliates.

ISBN-13: 9781662519413 (paperback)
ISBN-13: 9781662519406 (digital)

Cover design and illustration by Sarah Horgan

Printed in the United States of America

For Bob Harris, a kindhearted gentleman I was lucky to know

Chapter 1

The upright bass strings resonated, the notes deep and husky. In the background, the finger snapping began. Peggy Lee's voice threaded over the top of the rhythm. It was playful, hot, and full of delicious promise. She was doing her best to convince me that I couldn't possibly know the depths of her love, could never understand how much she cared.

Johnny noted my delighted expression when I placed the lyrics, and he smiled. He was standing over me, backlit by a crackling fire, naked from the waist up. His Levi's hung low on his lean hips, and the shadows from the fire played off his soft blond curls, the marble cut of his biceps, and the strength in his hands, which hung loosely at his sides.

The chorus of the song scorched out of the speakers.

Fever.

Believe me, I felt the heat.

Johnny had removed my blindfold moments earlier. I'd been wearing it since he'd surprised me at the Battle Lake Public Library thirty minutes earlier. Of course I'd protested—I'm not a woman whose boyfriend shows up at her work on a random Sunday afternoon in February with a bouquet of tangerine-colored tulips, a blindfold, and a whispered promise that makes her blush in her most private parts. Heck, I'm not the gal who usually even *has* a boyfriend, and when I do, he's more likely the type to regard dental floss and socks as "fancy-shmancy" (yes, Bad Brad, I'm talking about you) than to surprise me with an every-minute-planned evening.

Johnny was different.

Johnny was love and rockets and romance and sweetness. We'd officially been a couple since December, not even two months, but we'd casually dated before that. That's how I was gonna tell the story, anyhow. Another person might interpret my "casual dating" as more like "neurotic socializing," with me constantly worrying what a great guy like Johnny was doing with someone like me, and subsequently doing everything I could to sabotage our budding relationship.

You see, I'm a little messed up.

I'm an only child, the daughter of an alcoholic who died driving drunk the spring of my junior year of high school. He'd killed someone else in the accident, and I became a pariah in my hometown of Paynesville, Minnesota. By the end of my senior year, I was only too happy to skedaddle from that tiny spot on the map.

Ink not even dry on my high school diploma, I took off for the Cities. I did all right for a while. Earned my English degree from the University of Minnesota, waited tables at a Vietnamese restaurant on the West Bank, hit the bars—but only on weekends. Once I graduated, however, I quickly discovered that an English bachelor's and four dollars will buy you a medium latte, a license to critique the punctuation on the Caribou Coffee specials board, and not much else. (I can see why the English Department left that out of their advertising materials.)

After taking a couple years off from college to find myself (i.e., pay off some loans and check out what life is like when you're *not* going to school), I enrolled in a master's program in English and began hitting the clubs in earnest. Eventually, I found myself attending more bars than classes, dating Bad Brad, and wondering if this was what my alcoholic dad's life had looked like in his twenties. I didn't like the direction—or lack thereof—I was headed.

Last April, I received a shittily wrapped gift when I was flashed by an unhoused man while crossing the Washington Avenue Bridge and then, shortly after, caught Brad cheating on me. Nothing like stumbling across two out-of-place penises in one day to crowbar you out of a rut, you know what I mean?

When my friend Sunny called soon after the doubleheader and asked me to take care of her dog and cute little prefab home on the most gorgeous hundred acres in all of Minnesota, I didn't so much leap at the offer as trust fall into it. The gig was only supposed to last April through August while Sunny explored Alaska with Rodney, her unibrowed lover, but late last summer, the couple landed a year-round job on one of the fishing boats, and here I was, an unofficial Battle Lake resident for coming up on a year.

The Battle Lake Public Library head librarian had hired me as his assistant within a week of my moving to the tiny northwestern Minnesota town, followed immediately by me scoring a supplemental job as a freelance reporter for the *Battle Lake Recall*. The newspaper editor, Ron Sims, had been so impressed with my work (read: no one else would do it) that he'd assigned me a recipe column, which I'd named Battle Lake Bites.

Admittedly, the title had been passive-aggressive. You see, it took me a second to reacclimate to living in a small town, a community so tight-knit that if your car slid into a ditch, somebody'd be there to pull you out within five minutes. Within ten, the rest of the population would know you'd gone off the road, and it'd be twelve more minutes before they began speculating on whether you'd been drinking, whether the interior of your car was messy, and whether you'd ever find love or were biologically doomed to a life of spirited Hallmark-figurine collecting.

I imagine I'd have fallen into the small-town rhythm sooner—I'd been born and raised in a little burg, after all—if not for the dead bodies popping up. As in, regularly.

One corpse a month, every month since May, matter of fact.

A guy I'd been dating here, a statue thief there, and pretty soon, it added up to me stumbling over nine murders in as many months. I didn't like to speculate on that record, because when I did, I inevitably came to two conclusions:

1. I was jinxed with the mother of all cooties: dead-body magnetism.
2. It had been twenty-three days since I'd slid over a frozen corpse on West Battle Lake. I could almost hear the clock ticking down on February. When and where would I find the next murder victim?

Because of this propensity, I decided to become proactive back in November and began pursuing my private eye license. (When life hands you corpses, you make lemonade, I always say.) Still and all, I didn't like the countdown to the next dead body. The waiting was making me jittery.

On good days, I told myself my run of bad luck *had* to be over and I was crazy for jumping at shadows. On bad days, I'd returned to sleeping under my bed, empty cans stacked inside my bedroom door so I'd wake up if anyone tried to sneak in. It made dating a healthy, open guy like Johnny . . . interesting. He'd borne it like a champ, but I found myself watching him closely, waiting for the day when he said, understandably, "Hey, I was thinking I might like to try dating a woman who doesn't trip over dead bodies like other people find pennies. Your thoughts?"

Many times I'd caught myself trying to pull the trigger first. You know, dump him before he inevitably ran out on me. I'd fabricate a fight, or decide he hadn't called in two days because he was cheating on me, and then, when he did call the third day, I wouldn't pick up. *Sigh*. I was a lot of work. Johnny had been true-blue through all of it, though, and my walls were crumbling, brick by precious brick. It was terrifying to be slowly revealed and made vulnerable.

Terrifying, but also exhilarating.

These were the thoughts I juggled on an average day.

But today was no run-of-the-mill day. Today, I'd been blindfolded and brought to Johnny's living room, where a fire crackled and I was alone with the cutest boy on earth. As he eased closer to me, Peggy Lee melting the speakers with her velvety tones and my blindfold dangling from his jeans pocket, my fears began disintegrating. There simply wasn't enough blood in my northern hemisphere to maintain a facial expression, let alone a coherent thought.

When he stood only inches away, his body heat coursed over my flesh like a lovely wave. I reached for his abdomen, longing to touch one of my favorite spots: the point where his hipbones carved a line into his sculpted ab muscles. He grabbed my hand just short of his tempting skin and, in a masterful move, wrapped one end of the silk blindfold around my wrist.

I glanced up at him, caught off guard. I was still sitting, which was a delicious angle. It put my head level with his belly button. Everything from that point up was sleek, strong, and staring intently at me. The blue of his eyes was as dark as storm clouds.

I knew that look, and it gave me the most exquisite shivers.

I offered him the other wrist, but he shook his head, his lips quirking up. I began to ask him what the plan was, but he stopped my words by leaning over, taking my face in his free hand, and kissing me, deep and long.

Peggy Lee was right: this was indeed a lovely way to burn.

I reached for him again, but he still had my right hand wrapped in the silk blindfold. He pulled back from the kiss and tugged my Henley over my head. He had to string it along the blindfold until it was free. As he tossed my shirt behind the couch, my smile of anticipation melted to horror when I realized I was wearing my plan B bra—i.e., the one so puckered and ratty that it served as backup birth control. I'd never have worn it if I'd known this was where I'd end up tonight.

Curse words!

He noticed the direction of my glance and put his finger under my chin, forcing me to stare into his eyes. I immediately forgot what

I'd been worrying about. He was stunning, open, honest, and in love with me.

The soundtrack he must have created for the evening switched over to Bill Withers's "Use Me." It was brighter than Peggy Lee, but no less seductive. Johnny reached over and behind me. A cork popped and flew dramatically across the room. Next came the golden glug of champagne being poured into a flute. When he handed me the glass, the firelight reflected off the sparkling, honeyed bubbles.

I was technically free to move around, as he'd dropped the other end of the blindfold to remove my shirt, but I remained still, hypnotized. He put the glass to my lips and I drank, spilling only a little. He set down the flute and kissed the wet spot on my chin and, quick as a blink, maneuvered me so I lay on my back on the couch. He grabbed both wrists, pulled them over my head, and used the blindfold to tie them to the table next to the sofa.

This pure hotness took all of three seconds.

I tugged at the binding, not wanting to escape but curious if I could. The knots were pleasantly tight. I smiled. I'd never been tied up before, but it had always been a fantasy. I figured it was a command to be lazy. Who doesn't like someone else doing all the work during sex? Bring on the Nut Goodie ice cream, and you'd have three of my favorite things. Johnny had also tucked a pillow under me when he'd leaned me back, which meant my head was higher than my waist and my A-cups hadn't completely disappeared.

Double good!

Johnny looked me over from tip to toe as I lay on the couch wearing only a bra and jeans, my hands tied above my head. He let his eyes travel up and down me like hot fingers, and it took every ounce of self-control for me not to beg him to kiss me. When he placed his hand on his flat, muscled stomach—a move he did unconsciously but that I loved—I almost squealed. He continued to study me as if deciding whether to remove my pants.

He hadn't spoken a single word since we'd entered his house.

For my part, it was all I could do not to make every stupid joke that crossed my mind, as I do when I'm excited and/or nervous. (Allow me to be a cautionary tale: turns out "pull my finger" jokes are *not* an aphrodisiac.)

Apparently deciding to leave my jeans on for the time being, he ambled over to the fireplace and removed a candle from the mantel. Watching him move made me squirm, in a good way. His broad shoulders served as a stunning counterpoint to his narrow waist, and I still had the smell of him on me—clean and spicy, like cinnamon. He returned and held the candle above my stomach, one eyebrow raised. I responded by shrugging, at least as much as I could with my arms tied over my head.

He dropped a single dot of hot wax onto my stomach. It was an intense, momentary sting, followed by warmth. I closed my eyes and smiled. He leaned down and kissed the spot just above my belly button where the wax had hardened. He made three more dots, leading up from the original spot toward my neck. He kissed each after it cooled.

My shady spots tingled with delight.

When he reached my neck, he set the candle on the table and began kissing me in earnest in the sensitive valley where my throat met my collarbone. His hand was on my inner thigh, kneading. Chris Isaak took over for Bill Withers, telling me about a bad, bad thing. I was ready to commit a crime myself if it meant Johnny would lie on me. I bucked my hips, but he pushed them down, moving his hot mouth to mine.

He was the best kisser I'd ever had, full, strong lips, never too wet, tongue just right, but tonight he was outdoing himself. I moaned. He finally eased on top of me, his knee between my legs, his weight hovering just above my body. I thrust again, but he wouldn't put his weight on me.

He moved his mouth toward my ear, his tongue tracing the ridges, his breath hot. I shivered. I loved it when he talked dirty, and I could tell I was about to get an earful. His voice, when it came, was deep and growly with desire.

"I have to go to Portland."

Huh?

I relaxed into the couch and blinked once. Twice. With my bachelor's in English and a handful of master's classes in the same, I felt fairly confident with most of my native language, including innuendo. But this "going to Portland" euphemism was new to me. Oh well, I could roll with it. I got back into character.

"Portland would be happy to host you for as long as you can *come*," I whispered back, grinding underneath him.

He tensed slightly.

Shoot. I must have read this one wrong. Did it refer to gastrointestinal distress?

I pitched my voice into what I hoped was a sympathetic tone, any hint of disappointment erased. "That's OK, honey. Sometimes we all have to go to Portland."

He pulled back completely, sitting on the side of the couch, his warm hand still on my hip. I could see laughter warring with something else on his face.

"No, Mira, I feel fine. I meant the city of Portland. In Oregon? I've been offered an environmental science internship at Portland State. I found out this morning, after I'd planned this whole evening. I was going to wait to tell you until"—he made a gesture to indicate me, who, for the record, was beginning to feel pretty dang foolish with her arms tied over her head and her white bra glowing like the eyes of a nervous cave creature—"after we made love, but I can't go through with it. It seems dishonest. Sorry to spring it on you like this."

Ah, that was more like my luck. As sucky as this was, at least I felt on familiar ground. When had things ever worked out for me? "For how long?"

He ran his hands through his hair. "Through the end of the semester. I'd be done in May."

My stomach dropped, but I fought to keep my face neutral. "When do you leave?"

8

"Wednesday morning, if I accept." He leaned over to untie me, and I sat up next to him, rubbing my wrists. Our hips were barely touching.

"They gave you not even two days to decide?" Shoot, that sounded like whining.

He nodded. "Someone else dropped out from the program, opening up a spot. It's a once-in-a-lifetime opportunity."

I took a deep breath. "Why Portland?"

He kneaded one hand with the other. "It was one of the master's programs I applied to." His voice grew quieter. "Before we started dating."

My heart constricted. I knew Johnny had big life plans. He'd earned an undergraduate degree in horticulture, which was another thing I loved about him. It meant he was green and cared about something bigger than himself. He'd planned to go straight on to grad school, but when his dad had developed cancer late last summer, he'd come home. And then, after his dad passed, he'd taken a year off to look after his mom, which I loved even more. It had felt so good to build a life with him in Battle Lake that I'd kind of forgotten it was temporary.

"What if you like it, and they like you?" I asked.

He glanced back at me, cupping my cheek with his warm, strong hand. The storm was gone from his eyes, replaced by a blue so pure that I could almost see waves. "Then we have some talking to do."

Chapter 2

Johnny had been wise to tie me up before he sprang the Portland news. How mad could a chick get wearing her plan B bra with her hands lassoed over her head? Plus, I was charmed that he'd been too honest to go any further in our boot-knocking without telling me he'd be leaving in less than three days.

And in the end, what could I do? He really had been offered a rare opportunity. I'd be a hagasaurus to stand in his way. Still, it hurt. What if he met someone new? Worse, what if once he got far enough away from me, he realized how ludicrous it had been to date me in the first place? Me, carcass-finding, killer-dad-having, life-never-quite-together Mira James?

Sigh.

"Someone poop in your coffee?"

I was standing outside the door of the Battle Lake Public Library with the key in hand, cold February wind licking at my exposed face, lost in thought.

I hadn't heard Mrs. Berns crunch up behind me.

"Morning," I said.

"Morning, Eeyore." Mrs. Berns wore a quilted winter coat and a knit cap designed to look like a grumpy penguin squatting on her head. Her mittens matched. She crossed her arms and studied me. An errant snowflake drifted past her face. "Hey, you know what's worse than a moping woman who won't tell you what's bothering her?"

"What?"

"Nothing." She scrunched up her nose. "There is absolutely nothing worse."

It was enough to tug a smile from me, but she didn't let my changed expression slow her down. She grabbed the key from me, unlocked the door, and walked in without holding it open for me.

Through the glass, I watched her flip on the lights and stride to the front desk computer to boot it up before removing her coat. She wore a modest outfit, overall: white tennis shoes, fuchsia jogging pants with a matching windbreaker, her perfect white hair dyed a light apricot shade. Her choice of accessory was what separated her from the herd. She'd slung a gun belt around her hips, a silver cap pistol resting in each holster.

My smile grew wider.

I'd first seen her packing last July, when she'd kidnapped an Indian impersonator from the Chief Wenonga Days parade and disappeared with him for two days. Not bad for a woman who'd recently turned ninety. I entered the library, leaving behind the snapping February wind.

"I see you're armed today," I said as I entered the library, removing my down-filled coat and hanging it on the rack by the front door.

She shrugged and strode over to turn on the public computers. I'd hired her as my assistant a few months earlier (actually, she'd hired herself), and this was more work than I'd seen her do in that entire time.

"Felt like a gun-toting sort of day," she said. "You gonna tell me what's got your face upside-down?"

I sighed, brought back into the moment. "Johnny is going to Portland for three months."

She whipped around on her heels. "What?"

"Johnny. Oregon. Three months."

"Yeehaw! I can't wait!" She yanked a gun from her belt and pointed it in the air, firing off several rounds. The salty-egg smell of sulfur curled toward my nose.

That was *not* the reaction I'd expected. "What?"

By way of answer, she holstered her gun and ran over to me, trying to pick me up. Since she was four inches shorter and sixty-one years older, she had little luck. "Portland! That's the city of the future. I was just reading about it in *AARP*. Senior discounts up the ying-yang, pot brownies served right next to the croissants at the coffee shops if you know who to ask, and one-point-five single men for every single woman."

If anybody could figure out what to do with one and a half single men, it was Mrs. Berns. She had a sex life at ninety that I couldn't approach in my twenties. But that was hardly the point. "I said *Johnny* is going to Portland. You and I still have to work. Here. In Battle Lake."

She looked down her nose at me. "Have you ever heard of a vacation, baby? We're due!"

We weren't, actually. We'd been given mandatory time off in December because the city didn't have the funds to keep the library open over the holidays. That situation corrected itself after I'd agreed to take a significant pay cut in my insignificant salary—a town needs its library—but since Mrs. Berns and I were the only library employees, there was no way we could both leave. All that was true, and valid, but it was not the argument that escaped my mouth. "I can't fly."

It was a fact. Even if I could afford a vacation, had the leave to do so, and there was someone to cover for me, there was No Way I was stepping on a plane. I hadn't left the ground for more than three seconds in my entire life, and that was back when I was a kid who liked to jump. I had no intention of breaking that streak.

"You don't have to fly, loser." She flapped her arms. "They have planes to do that."

I shook my head. "No way. Not getting on an airplane. Being airborne is for birds and people who like to die. I am neither."

She planted her hands on her hips and looked at me as if I'd just told her that I wanted to be a pink monkey when I grew up. "You've *never* been on an airplane?"

"Never."

"How do you get around the country?"

"I don't. Everything I need is in Minnesota, or at least within driving range of it."

"That's stupid."

"Maybe. But even if it weren't, I can't go to Portland. I don't have the money or the time. I have a library to run." Why couldn't I have started with the sane arguments? Story of my life. Luckily, at that moment, the library doorbell bonged, indicating we had our first patron and saving me from further pointless argument with Mrs. Berns.

Two kids rolled in, nearly unrecognizable in their winter gear. Because it was early in February, the weather still hovered barely above zero, which turned most Minnesotans into layered creatures who waddled around because they were nearly as wide as they were tall. Fortunately, I spotted a lock of red hair sticking out of the ski cap of the bundle walking toward me.

"Sierra!"

She attached herself to my leg. I picked her up, runny nose and all, and hugged her. It was the weirdest thing. If you gave me a choice between bearing my own child and getting hit by a car, I'd need to know how fast the car would be going before I decided. Running the children's reading hour at the library was a whole different animal, though.

I'd inherited the job from the previous librarian. He'd liked it about as well as I'd figured I would, which had translated into him putting out kid books and tiny boxes of raisins every Monday at 10:00 a.m. My first Monday on the job, I referred to the raisins as ogre boogers, which earned me a sea of rolling giggles from the four kids who had gathered.

I'd found my people.

Since, I'd quadrupled the number of attendees. These days, between sixteen and twenty kids came by every Monday morning. I read to them, and we colored, crafted sock puppets and then put on shows, mixed no-bake treats, and generally partied like it was 1999. Their moms and dads got a welcome break to read a book or magazine uninterrupted, and I got my kid time.

"What are we gonna do today?" Sierra begged.

I reached for a tissue from the front counter to wipe her nose. On second thought, I grabbed two. "We're going to read *Insectlopedia*, make insect art with finger paints and tissue paper, and write our own poems about them!" I didn't have to feign excitement. It sounded like a kick-butt morning.

"Whee!" Sierra said. Once I had her coat off, she ran over to Joshie, her little brother, and caught him with a flying kick. Fortunately, he was still swaddled in his snowsuit and didn't feel a thing. Or, if he did, he responded to pain by giggling. Either worked for me.

Sierra and Joshie's mom, Becky, watched the exchange impassively. I looked at her, really looked at her, for the first time since she'd walked in the library. Her face was pinched, her eyes swollen.

"Can I pick them up in an hour?" she asked without glancing at me.

The rule was that parents had to stay in the building with their kids at all times, but this was a special case: I knew that Becky's husband had run out on the family recently. "Sure. I'll take care of them. No worries."

She looked grateful enough to cry. She kissed her kids on the head and disappeared.

I leaned down to help release Joshie from his coat, snow pants, hat, mittens, and scarf. "You want to be an insect today, buddy?"

"Gun!"

He wasn't quite two and knew only a handful of words. Because this was Otter Tail County, "gun" was one of them. "No, sweetie. No guns. Insects don't need them. They have other skills."

"Gun!" He pointed behind me with his chubby little finger.

I turned to see Mrs. Berns at the computer, her cap pistols catching the light. "Ah, I see. No, hon, those are *her* guns. Not our guns."

He didn't know a lot of words, but he knew "no," and it crushed him. Literally. He went from perfectly content to no-bones on the floor, all his energy focused on wailing at the unfairness of life. Kids are strange that way.

"Ignore him," Sierra said, only four and already so wise. She stepped over him and walked toward the stack of new arrivals, all glossy picture books.

Unfortunately, I didn't have the luxury of ignoring a screaming child. I'd promised his mom that I'd take care of him. "I'll be back, Joshie. You just hang on."

He either didn't hear me or didn't care. I walked over to the computers and tapped Mrs. Berns on the shoulder. "Hey, see that suffering kid back there? He wants your guns."

She didn't bother looking up from the screen. "He can't even touch 'em, and here's why: it's good practice for life. Who ever gets what they want?"

My shoulders tightened. "Could you at least hide them until kid time is over? It'd make my life easier."

She rolled her eyes. "You can't coddle them. Then they just grow up to be men who don't pick up after themselves and never read fiction."

"I don't see the connection."

She harrumphed. "Probably because you're too busy coddling boys."

I blew air through my mouth, loudly. Was it *really* going to be one of those days? "Please. I just found out my boyfriend is leaving the state, and I'm pretty sure it won't take more than a day away for him to realize it was a mistake to ever date me. I have a toddler who's sure he's going to die if he doesn't get your guns. Oh, and it's winter, which means I can't garden, so my stress has no outlet. So can you just do this one favor for me?"

Mrs. Berns made a show of blinking rapidly and shaking her head. "Sorry. I fell asleep somewhere in the middle of that. What were you saying?"

I threw up my hands and returned to Joshie. Despite the impressive decibels of his howls, I had to admire how fully he was throwing himself into the role. I pitched my voice so he could hear it over his screaming tears. "Hey, Joshie, you want some ogre boogers?"

He immediately paused his crying and squinted at me out of the corner of an eye. "Ooger oogers?"

I smiled. See how quickly little people can win you back? They're too dang cute. "Yup. A whole box of ooger oogers. I have them in secret storage. Want to check them out?"

"Don't fall for it, Joshie," Sierra called from a nearby table, where she was flipping through an issue of *Ranger Rick*. "They're raisins."

Man, if that girl were twenty-five years older, we'd have been hanging out. I didn't know if she was looking out for her little brother or camping on the side of general fairness, but I couldn't deny the truth of her words. "Sure, they're raisins, but they're *special* raisins. Want to go see them?"

He did. He held his hands up to me, and I hoisted him onto my hip. We strolled to the back room, where I grabbed a not-too-old box of raisins from the bulk the previous head librarian had purchased. Joshie calmed, and I got to finish prepping.

It was a good thing, because the little ones started rolling through the door in earnest soon after Joshie fisted his box of ooger oogers. The house was packed, and children's hour went off without a hitch. I noticed partway through the poetry composing that Mrs. Berns had disappeared, but that wasn't unusual.

Once it was over, I helped parents with the arduous task of repackaging their kids into their winter gear. By eleven thirty, all the children were gone, even Sierra and Joshie. I had cleaned the stickiness from the kids' area and reshelved all the books and magazines they'd played with. Only a handful of patrons grazed in the aisles. I was feeling the exhausted afterglow of a job well done when the front door burst open—no small feat, considering it was pneumatic. I glanced over, hoping to see Mrs. Berns returning for the rest of her shift. I had some ideas for rearranging the reading tables that I wanted to run by her.

"Mira!"

Jed Heike blew into the library. He was dressed in an oversize khaki parka, bright ski cap with a ball on the top, and enormous mittens. I couldn't read his expression. It was either sad or worried. That in itself was odd. Jed was a Shaggy from *Scooby-Doo* sort of guy: curly headed and laid-back, perennially happy, in his early twenties, artistic and aimless, and in possession of some of the finest weed in the county, if the rumors were to be believed. I'd never been a smoker, but he was so genuine that we'd become fast friends.

"Jed! How've you been?" I hadn't seen him in nearly two weeks. That wasn't unusual, but the way he was carrying himself set off my radar. Something was definitely up.

He glanced behind, as if to check whether he was being followed, then scuttled toward me, breath coming fast and quick. "I gotta get something off my chest, and you're the only one I can tell."

Up close, it was easy to see he was shaken. His face was hollowed out, as if sleep had eluded him for days. I immediately thought of today's date, and how it was just about time for me to discover my next dead body. Had Jed uncovered a snow-shrouded corpse when he was out blowing snow for the neighbors? Gone to check on a mysteriously empty icehouse in front of his parents' resort and discovered two dead lovers, as cold and lively as Popsicles? Or maybe he'd witnessed a murder when he'd gone out for the daily paper? None of that would be any weirder than what I'd stumbled across in the last nine months.

My tongue felt like chalk, but I squeaked out the words anyhow. "What is it?"

Chapter 3

Jed leaned toward me, his face drawn.

He smelled like fresh winter and two-stroke exhaust, probably from one of his side businesses. He'd been an odd-jobber as long as I'd known him, fixing engines here, patching a roof there, but his main income came from helping his parents run their business. The Last Resort was seasonal, open May through October, but regular business had slowed down, and I knew they were considering winterizing the cabins before next fall to see if they could catch some of the cross-country skiers and snowmobilers. His parents loved flying south for the winter, and that's where they were now. It'd be hard for them to give that up.

"Is it something at the Last Resort?" He split his time between an apartment in town and his bedroom in the resort's main house. "Your parents?" *Or superdead bodies in an empty cabin—a cult killing, perhaps?*

He shook his head. His mouth opened. Nothing came out.

"Jed." I grabbed the fuzzy neck of his coat and pulled him in close. I couldn't conceal my neurosis any longer. "Have you found someone who's been murdered?"

His eyes widened. "No! Did you?"

I didn't realize how tense I'd been until I relaxed. "No." *Not yet.* "So what's wrong?"

The tightness returned to his face. "I dunno if I can say it."

I began to understand how Mrs. Berns must have felt when she'd found me moping outside the library this morning. An upset person who doesn't spill quickly becomes an annoying person. "You don't have to tell me if you don't want to."

"It's just . . ."

He was about to give me the inside scoop, it was obvious, but he turned away when the door opened. In sauntered Mrs. Berns, penguin cap perched on her head.

Jed's face lit up. He loved her almost as much as I did. "Hey, Mrs. Berns!"

She ignored him and walked straight up to me. She slapped an envelope on the front desk. "We're going to Portland."

I felt my blood drain, partially due to the brain bends from switching topics so quickly, partly from the thought of stepping onto an airplane. "I told you, I don't fly."

She tapped the paper with her pointer finger. "Train tickets."

Jed grabbed them. "You guys are going to Portland? Do you know what kind of snowboarding they have there? Man! Can I come with?"

I held up my hands, palms facing forward. "Slow down, tigers. Mrs. Berns and I are *not* going to Portland, so there's nowhere to come with *to*, Jed."

She laid a sheet of paper atop the envelope. INTERNATIONAL PRIVATE INVESTIGATOR CONFERENCE was splashed across the top. Below that was a date for this coming weekend, and underneath that: PORTLAND, OREGON. She stared at me, wearing a smug expression, as if the flyer explained everything.

I simply gaped.

"If we travel to Portland for a PI conference, it's a tax write-off," Mrs. Berns said, speaking slowly, as if language were the barrier. "I've already registered us for the conference, booked the hotel, and bought the train tickets—my treat. All you have to do is say yes."

I couldn't process the information she was throwing at me. Also, I couldn't believe how organized she'd suddenly become. This was a woman who didn't make her bed because she would just mess it up again that night. "Why do you want to go to Portland so bad?"

She scowled. "Why do you want to *not* go so bad?"

Jed raised his hand. "I want to go!"

"Shh," I told him. My head hurt. Mrs. Berns had an ulterior motive, clearly, but she wasn't going to reveal it with Jed here. I could tell by the set of her jaw. That was just fine. I wasn't going anyway.

"First, this is happening too quickly." I slid the envelope and flyer back toward her. "Second, I won't even consider going to Portland with you if you don't tell me why you want to go so badly. Third, I can't let you pay for me to leave the state. And fourth, even if I were OK with you paying, we can't both leave the library. Who'll run it?"

Exactly on cue, the front door opened.

I turned.

My face dropped to the floor.

The last twenty-four hours had just gone from too-small-hotel-room bad to bedbugs-and-mystery-stains bad.

Chapter 4

Kennie Rogers—former Battle Lake beauty queen, current mayor, and perennial over-dramatizer—sashayed through the door. She wore a surprisingly sedate button-down peacoat over a black pencil skirt, black nylons, and high-heeled black pumps. (How she walked in those in the winter was a mystery for the Sphinx.) Her frosty-platinum hair was pulled back into a bun. Chunky black glasses dominated her face.

She almost looked like popular culture's idea of . . .

Oh, sweet Jesus, no. I sucked in my breath as the realization smacked me upside the head: she looked like a sexy librarian.

"No way," I said to Mrs. Berns.

"Hear me out—"

She didn't have a chance to finish. Kennie's perfume of yeasty gardenias engulfed me as she tossed her coat into my arms. "I am *so* looking forward to getting to know the little people of Battle Lake as I take over the library so you can travel."

I raised an eyebrow. No matter how much time I spent with her—and believe me when I tell you it was as little as possible—I never got used to her faux southern accent. "When you say 'the little people of Battle Lake,' do you mean the readers?"

"Exactly!" She clapped her hands. "So what does a librarian do all day, anyhow? Dust? Look for funny kitty photos online? Do tell."

For the record, I was not an official librarian. I didn't possess the required degree or experience. When the librarian who'd hired me disappeared under unsavory circumstances last May, I'd stepped in as an emergency and temporary replacement. The city had tried to hire a real librarian since then, but thanks to the piddly salary and some light sabotaging from me, the position remained unfilled.

Still, even though I wasn't the real deal, I'd already heard more than enough stereotypes about what librarians did all day. People thought it was a walk in the park. It wasn't. I had to appease the city board as well as my patrons, stock the latest books on a shoestring budget, clean the space (including the bathrooms), schedule community activities outside of regular library hours, lead the children's story time, stay current on legislative issues affecting library funding and contact my representatives when necessary, complete research, lead computer classes, locate books, shelve books, and so on and so on.

Running through the list, I felt the smoke building behind my ears. "There's actually a lot more to being a librarian than sitting at the front desk."

Kennie smiled condescendingly. "I'm sure there is, dear. I just need to know enough for the week, though, don't I? Now be a sweetheart and show me how to run the computer, and then beat cheeks."

I felt the ground begin to slip under me. "You can't just take over the library." Johnny leaving, Jed's still-unknown secret, Mrs. Berns with train tickets. It was too much. I wasn't going to surrender my refuge, too. Not the library. "You can't steal my job for a week."

"I can. In fact, I have to." She pulled a sheet of paper from her purse and slapped it on the front desk. I was getting mighty sick of that trick. "The city bylaws require that the library have at least two full-time employees. You have exceeded the six-month period in which to find a second full-time worker. Mrs. Berns and I together can count as one, but only if I put in some seat time. Soon as you return from Portland, you better start hiring, you hear? We'll find the money somewhere, at least until I can get that bylaw changed. In the meanwhile, I have to work sixty hours in the next seven days, or you will have to pay back some funding."

My legs went out from under me. Fortunately, I fell into the front desk chair. "There's nothing to give back. Why didn't anyone tell me?"

She shrugged. "Bureaucracy. Be glad I'm telling you now. So, your choices are to stay behind and work with me, or you can go on an all-paid vacation to Portland. You pick."

My stomach gurgled unpleasantly. But when she put it like that . . . wait. A thought wiggled its way to the front of my brain. "Why would *you* help *me* go to Portland? And help the library keep its funding?"

After all, Kennie was the woman who put the *I* in "selfish." Since I'd met her last May, she'd had a series of ill-fated start-ups, including a coffee table that could be used as a coffin once the owner died, a home bikini-waxing service, and a refurbished marital aids company called Come Again. She was the epitome of the lone-wolf entrepreneur, always looking for her angle, always putting herself first.

She winked. "Us girls got to stick together."

I started to reevaluate my image of her. The process made a grinding noise. Fortunately, she saved me from having to try for long.

"Oh," she continued, glancing down at her bloodred nails, "coincidentally, I also have a package I need you to deliver to my friend Carlos. He lives in Seattle. You'll pass right through it on your train trip."

"Aha!" That offer had the stink of Bad Idea over it, a smell somewhere between the odor of tequila shots and the scent of fresh tattoo ink. "You want me to do something for you. That makes more sense. Why can't you mail it yourself?"

"I could. It's biggish, though. Expensive to mail."

The Bad Idea smell grew stronger. "What's in the package?"

"None of your beeswax."

I glanced from Mrs. Berns to Kennie. They both shared a smug expression that I didn't like, and it triggered a realization. "Wait wait *wait* a minute. You two are the most disorganized people I've ever met. How did you manage all this—booking a train trip, library staffing—in the span of a few hours? And Mrs. Berns, why aren't you worried about transporting a mystery package for Kennie?"

Mrs. Berns held her hands in the air, the picture of innocence. "I follow the don't ask, don't tell policy. Kept me out of jail more than once. As for going to Portland, there's not much I won't do for one point five men."

Kennie nodded. "We're women of the world, Mira. We act when it's important. And don't you worry about your house or animals, either. Johnny's mom is going to take in Luna and Tiger Pop. Says she'll be lonely without Johnny anyway. And Gary said he'd run by to make sure your pipes don't freeze."

I tried to swallow my own spit but started coughing instead. "You asked the *chief of police* to check on my place?"

Gary Wohnt and I had a complicated relationship. As in, he was perpetually gunning to arrest me and I wanted to stay out of jail. It made small talk tricky. "And Johnny's mom knows about this Portland plan? Does that mean Johnny knows, too?"

Mrs. Berns and Kennie nodded in unison, both sporting cat-who-got-the-mouse expressions. They genuinely thought they were doing something nice for me, and getting something good for themselves out of it. That's why they'd moved so fast on this. I couldn't fit it all in my brain.

"Think of it this way," Jed said, trying his best to look thoughtful. It was a hard expression to hold for someone who'd smoked as much pot as he had. "If you leave Battle Lake with us, you might not find a dead body this month!"

"With *us*?" I asked. "You just heard about this ten minutes ago, and *you've* already made up your mind to come along?"

He nodded happily. "Sure. Then I can tell you my secret on the train and get in some kick-butt snowboarding at the end of the trip. Woo-hoo!"

Sigh. I couldn't fight all four of them.

I was going to Portland.

I just wish Jed had been right about me not finding a dead body if I left Battle Lake.

Chapter 5

I used all of Tuesday night to say goodbye to Johnny in a way that I hoped would keep him warm for a while. I'd be in Portland for only a few days, and there was no guarantee we'd get much time to spend together there before I had to return home.

Turned out two could play the tie-up game.

His mom and I drove him to the airport early Wednesday, and I spent the rest of the day training Kennie at the library—not as bad as I thought it'd be, once I got it through her head that yes, there were people in Battle Lake who really did read for pleasure, and no, I'd so far never been called on to fulfill librarian fantasies during my tenure, but she was welcome to wear what she wanted while working.

After closing up the library Wednesday afternoon, I spent the evening prepping my house and animals for my eight days away. Though I was going to miss them, I felt good dropping off Luna, Sunny's sweet German shepherd mix, and Tiger Pop, my sassy calico kitty, at Johnny's mom's house Wednesday night. Mrs. Leeson was so grateful for the happy bodies to keep her company. She was going to miss Johnny just as much as I was, and watching Tiger Pop curl around her leg, and her delighted smile, made me feel better.

Come Thursday, it was weird to wake up in a quiet house. It made me feel hollow. Then I remembered that my furry friends were in good hands and that I was going on a train trip with Johnny at the end of it. That lonely spot began to warm, then started to buzz. I was going on a train trip! Mrs. Berns had booked the last sleeper car available, meaning Jed would have to sleep with the masses in coach class. (She'd agreed to let me pay her back on an installment plan. No way could I let her foot the entire bill.)

I'd researched the sleeper cars on the Miss–Sea route of the AmeriTrain, the only passenger-class rail system in the country, and that was a big part of my excitement. The cars looked roomy, with two comfy chairs that transformed into a bed as well as an overhead bunk that served as a shelf until it was time to sleep. There would even be two tiny bottles of champagne waiting for us!

The world would fly past outside our wide windows, and we'd be tucked safe inside, reading, talking, and exploring the rest of the train. I had to admit, for someone who normally balked at traveling, I was beginning to look forward to it. That is, I *had been* looking forward to it right up until Mrs. Berns made a small confession on the drive to the Detroit Lakes train station.

"There's a little thing I forgot to tell you."

She, Jed, and I were squeezed in my Toyota, pulling into the station on the north end of a town fifty miles north of Battle Lake. Her words struck me with the same foreboding that I imagined General Custer must have felt when his scout said, "Sir, I think we may have underestimated."

"What little thing?" Trying to quell the sudden greasy feeling in my stomach, I steered the car into the last open slot, tucked in the rear next to a mountain of plowed snow. I turned off the ignition and gave her my full attention.

"You know how there was only one sleeper car left, and Jed was lucky to even get a ticket in coach class?"

Jed and I both nodded.

"It's because this is a special train."

I cocked my head. Maybe this wouldn't be bad news. "Like the Polar Express?"

She looked thoughtful. "Hmmm. More like a seventies-era Studio 54 on rails."

"Rock on, dude," Jed chimed in from the back seat.

I didn't think he was familiar with the famous bacchanalian New York nightclub. He must have just liked the sound of *the seventies*.

"The AmeriTrain?" I asked, doubtfully. "I went to their website yesterday. If it came out of any decade, it was the eighties."

"Did you look up the specialty trains?"

My stomach dropped. I had a feeling I was about to find out why Mrs. Berns had been so eager to head to Portland that she'd moved heaven and earth to make it happen. "No."

She handed me a circular. Typing up bad news was apparently the latest, coolest way to deliver it. The paper was dotted with pink and red hearts designed to look like they were exploding from a heart-shaped box of candy. The chocolate inside the box was arranged to spell out the words "Valentine Train." Underneath:

> Join us on AmeriTrain's first annual Valentine Train! Singles encouraged. Guests will have the opportunity to meet and mingle during onboard dances, classes, and experiences!

> Book your seat now. Filling fast.

Below that were limited routes and dates. The February 11 Miss–Sea we were about to board was one of them.

"You knew about this before I even told you about Johnny going to Portland," I accused. My throat was tight.

Mrs. Berns patted my hand in a pitying gesture. "Mira, Mira, Mira. You think the Fates would have thrown this all together if we hadn't been meant to go? I've been working for weeks on a way to get you on this train with me, and Johnny plopped it right into our lap. How could we resist such a set of bee's knees?"

"Wow, man," Jed said from the back seat. "That is wild, if you think about it. It's like you were *meant* to go to Portland."

"And Kennie's *package*?" I stabbed my thumb toward the trunk, where a squarish bundle wrapped in butcher paper lay. It was the size of a small microwave, about as heavy, and neither ticked, meowed, nor smelled of marijuana. I thought those were fantastic qualities in baggage. Still, I didn't feel good about transporting it, especially with Kennie unwilling to let us know what was inside.

"Right?" Jed said, missing my sarcasm. "Kennie's package, too. Dude, the Universe wants you to go to Portland. It's a good thing you're listening."

I almost rolled my eyes but didn't want to squelch Jed's eternal optimism. It wasn't his fault that I was not a social person, that the phrases "Valentine Train" and "meet and mingle" made my ovaries shrivel. I was in a relationship, so it wasn't the fear of rejection. Rather, it was the safe knowledge that every time I interacted with a new person, it was one more chance to put my foot so deep down my mouth that the appendage ended up where it had started.

The library job required me to host events for the public, and I loved Johnny and my tight circle of friends, but beyond that, I was a loner—which was best for everyone involved.

Case in point: the New Year's Battle Lake Budget Bash (I didn't name it) had been held at the library a few weeks earlier. I'd played host, sticking to the perimeters, making sure drinks were filled and the cheese tray didn't run low. The one time—the one time!—I was called on for extended interaction was when Chris Schaefer, head of the chamber of commerce, brought over the owner of the new gift shop for introductions. It went something like this (it went exactly like this):

Chris: *Mira, have you met Jared? He's the new owner of the Battle Lake Framing, Tanning, and Canoe Rental Shop. Across from the apothecary?*

Me: *No, but I noticed you from across the room. You've kept your winter coat on all night! What are you, armed?* (I might have wink-winked here. I'd read somewhere that gregarious, normal people wink when they say funny stuff, and that this behavior sets others at ease. I was trying really hard to pretend I was normal.)

Chris (suddenly pale): . . .

Jared: . . . (Hurries away with flushed cheeks.)

Me (horrified): *Oh no! Did I say something?*

Chris (more horrified): *You asked him if he's* armed. *The man. Has. A fake. Arm. He's self-conscious about it, so he wanted to keep his jacket on, at least until he got a chance to meet everyone.* (Turns on heel, storms off to follow Jared and hopefully tell him I have some sort of medical disorder.)

See? I was not someone you wanted to encourage to "meet and mingle" on Valentine's trains. In fact, I probably should have looked into getting my groceries delivered to cut down on my need for public interaction.

Mrs. Berns patted my arm. She knew me well. "I won't let you embarrass yourself too much, baby cakes. Think of it this way. It'll be good practice. Light conversation is something all of us could get a little better at."

Her words would have landed better if she hadn't then pointed at me, aggressively nodded, and mouthed "really, just her" to Jed.

I breathed out deeply. Well, I was this far, so I might as well make the best of it. Come to think of it, I bet I wouldn't even need to leave our cute little cabin. Heck, I could catch up on my reading and drink tiny bottles of champagne for twenty-four hours straight if I really wanted to. That thought visibly brightened my mood.

"Fine," I said. "Let's get this show on the road."

We climbed out of the car and stepped into the frosty air of a February afternoon. The day had been sunny as a lemon, which meant it was frigid this time of year. It was the kind of atmosphere that'd freeze your outer nostrils to your septum if you inhaled too quickly. It was also as beautiful as a diamond field, with the sun glinting off the sharp flakes of snow that had been plowed into piles.

Jed had strapped his snowboard to the car roof, so he got busy removing that while Mrs. Berns and I unloaded our suitcases, our carry-ons, Kennie's package, and Jed's duffel bag. We all finished at about the same time and made our motley way to the station platform. My excitement ramped up as I spotted the crowds waiting for the train. It was supposed to arrive at 5:40 p.m. We were a half an hour early, as were approximately thirty other people, plus those who had come to see them off.

We rounded the back of the station, and my heart opened as I spotted the silver AmeriTrain sitting still and quiet. "Hurry! The train is already here! It might leave without us."

"No rush," said a man in a blue cap and matching jacket, the pocket of which was embossed with AMERITRAIN in gold thread. He was on his way to the station as well but turned to toss me a smile. "She's early. We won't leave until it's time."

"Phew." I hadn't known exactly how excited I was for this trip until it had almost been taken away from me.

"I'm going to wait inside the station," Mrs. Berns said, tipping her head toward the large brick structure. The building looked exactly like a turn-of-the-century train station, so it was probably the original. The roof had a generous overhang held up by columns to keep the elements off passengers and visitors.

"I'm going to hang outside for a bit," I said. "We'll be indoors plenty once the train leaves."

The full truth was a little more complex. First, the inside of the station looked packed to capacity with travelers escaping the nippy February air. Second, it felt more immediate and exciting to mingle in the elements with the other waiting folks. Third, and most importantly, I really, really wanted to see the smoke up close when it roared from the top of the train. *Toot toot!*

"I'm gonna wait outside, too," Jed said, grinning at me. "But I'm going to see what those guys are up to." He pointed at three men in their early twenties with ski bags slung over their shoulders.

"Fine by me," I said. "You can leave your luggage here. I'll keep an eye on it."

Jed walked one way and Mrs. Berns another, and I began people-watching with the enthusiasm of a lifer. That's the plus side of being socially awkward: you take great pleasure in studying strangers and making up their life stories. The jammed train station and platform offered a buffet of possibilities.

My eyes were immediately pulled three feet to my left, where a woman wearing a fluffy faux-fur coat dragged a box of wooden matches from her pink purse. The matchbox was full-size, the kind you'd find on a fireplace hearth. Next, she fished for a pack of generic cigarettes, 100s, tapped out a smoke, and balanced it on her lip. Finally, she withdrew a match and scraped it along the box. The flame unfurled, and I inhaled deeply of the fire scent.

Matches always smelled better in the winter.

"Smoker?" she asked.

I averted my gaze. I didn't know I'd been watching her so obviously. "Not really. It's the scent of fresh-lit matches that I love. Don't know why."

She didn't return my tentative smile. I put her in her early sixties but hanging on to her youth with dyes, creams, and soft lighting where she could find it. She offered her free hand, pink purse straps balanced across her forearm. "Susan Wrenshall."

I took her hand. It was weighted with glittering baubles over thin leather gloves, though her left ring finger was bare. For a moment, I had a vision of her fishing one of those Natasha-from-*Bullwinkle* cigarette holders from her purse and puffing elegantly on it. "Mira James. You're boarding here?"

She let out a mixture of cigarette smoke and cold air, shaking her head. "Taking a break. I've been on since New York. Haven't gotten a wink of sleep since then. The train is so cramped it's like traveling cross-country in a porta-potty, not to mention the bumpiness. If that's not bad enough, the porter's checking up on me at all hours. As soon as I get so much as thinking about sleep, there he is. 'Knock knock. Everything OK, Ms. Wrenshall? Anything I can get for you, Ms. Wrenshall?'"

I didn't like the stain she was painting on my train ride. "He checks up on you at night?"

She leaned in conspiratorially. "I think he has a thing for me." She smelled like an ashtray up close.

"Well, it *is* the Valentine's train."

Her laughter turned into a cough. "I didn't get on this train to find love."

There was an unexpected suggestion in her words. She'd gotten on the train for *something*.

"What did you get on for?"

She shrugged, all hint of mystery gone. "It's a way to travel."

"Is this your first train ride?"

Her eyes grew distant. She was done with the conversation. "And last, if I have any say in it. You'll excuse me?"

I nodded. She walked three more feet away from me, but not to talk with anyone else. Her sudden change in mood was perplexing. I ran through our conversation. Had I done it again? Said something heinous when I thought I was being polite? I couldn't recall anything, but then again, if I recognized social impropriety, I'd avoid it in the first place. I sighed and returned to my people-watching.

The rest of the crowd appeared to be standard Minnesotans, vastly different from the bright and eccentric Ms. Wrenshall. They wore parkas zipped up to their necks, an array of caps, and fur-lined boots. Judging by their chafed cheeks, I guessed they wished they were inside or, better yet, already on the train. The station must have been even more crowded than it appeared from the outside.

I noticed a couple on the perimeter of the crowd, he in a lined denim jacket and she in a puffy yellow parka, doing the "let's pretend we're not arguing" dance. Their tight faces, mouths snapping open only long enough to deliver a tense word or two, and the way they stood physically close but turned away from each other gave them away. I couldn't leave our luggage, so I craned my neck to see if I could lip-read what they were fighting about.

A bump from behind pushed me off-balance. I caught myself and turned.

"Excuse me."

The woman speaking had her head down, long brown hair obscuring her face. She was the only person at the station not wearing a cap. As she spoke to me, she glanced at a little girl whose hand she held. She wore a purse slung over her shoulder but carried no other luggage.

"I didn't see you," she continued, still not looking directly at me.

"That's OK." I stepped aside so she and the girl—who must have been her daughter—could pass. As they moved through the crowd, the little girl turned and waved at me. I noticed her heart-shaped face and the doll in her hand in the same moment.

Recognition hit like an electric jolt.

Noelle.

Chapter 6

I hadn't thought of Noelle in a decade. She'd been my best friend the summer I turned five, back when my parents lived within the Paynesville city limits. Noelle's family moved into a house on the opposite side of Koronis Park from me, which was the other end of the earth in my five-year-old mind. Back then, kids of all ages played in the streets until dusk, people smoked cigarettes in movie theaters, and no one worried about predators or seatbelts.

Noelle and I met on the playground in June, shortly after her family moved to town. I liked her the moment she appeared on the edge of the sand and walked up to the monkey bars like she owned them. She set her Velveteen Rabbit doll on the ground, clambered up the worn metal bars, and started penny dropping like a pro.

Watching her, I knew instantly that I wanted to be her friend. I'd been trying to nail a penny drop for *days*, and here she waltzed in, making it seem as easy as breathing. I was a cool cat, though. I hung out on the swings and spied on her from behind my bangs, posing so she could see the new and highly fashionable rainbow tank top I was wearing and maybe, just maybe, if she was studying me as hard as I was pretending *not* to study her, she'd see the new hair ties my mom had twisted in, each sporting two pretty red plastic marbles.

Chuckie Greaves, who earlier in the summer had landed a butterfly net over my head and tried to pull down my shorts, begged me to play tetherball with him, but I would have none of it. I swung higher and higher, trying to impress the girl doing the penny drops, but she was either way better at bluffing disinterest than I was or couldn't have cared less about me.

Four minutes into this one-sided dance, I was ready to give up. If my bejeweled hair binders and splendorous tank top weren't good enough for her, tough noogies. I'd been swinging alone all my life. What was a few more months?

That's when, for I'm sure the first time in his life, Chuckie Greaves saved the day.

Bored with trying to get my attention, he sneaked over and flashed the new penny drop girl his butt. She fell to the ground, her balance shot, grabbed her Velveteen Rabbit, and hid under the slide. I marched over and told Chuckie that the police could measure butt waves and knew he'd just mooned someone.

The Law is on its way, and you will be arrested forever, I said. (If you want to be good at anything, let's say lying, I recommend you start young.)

After he ran home, I hauled myself up on that metal bar just like I'd seen the girl do. I hooked my legs over it, hair and hands hanging. I knew she was watching me. I also sensed, using my five-year-old-girl jungle gym instincts, that she needed to come to me if this friendship was gonna have legs.

I started swinging my hands, building momentum. Back and forth, back and forth, the upside-down world becoming a blur.

When I felt like I had enough force, I unhooked my legs, propelled them under me, and landed on my feet like a gold medal gymnast.

At least, that's what I did in my head.

In reality, one of my legs stuck while the other flew free, which meant I flailed through the air like a starfish before landing on my stomach. The air knocked out of me in a *whoof.* I tasted blood and dirt.

I sprawled there for several seconds, the world a pinhole of light, wondering where I'd gone wrong. Somewhere deeper, I might have also wondered whether this was a harbinger of how the rest of my life would go. (It was.)

"You have to swing higher so you can let both your legs go at the same time," the girl called out from under the slide. "Otherwise you'll just land on your face every time."

Bingo.

Her name was Noelle, it turned out, and she took her Velveteen Rabbit everywhere. His name was Rabbie. Her parents had moved to Paynesville, Minnesota, from somewhere exotic, like Saint Cloud, Minnesota. Her dad was the new high school math teacher and her mom was a nurse. She had two younger sisters, both of them "dumb and stupid," according to Noelle (only she said it "dumb and thtoopid," because her two front teeth were missing).

I never did master the penny drop that summer (or since), but the two of us were inseparable, me an only child with a mercurial homelife, her with two annoying younger siblings stealing most of their parents' attention. We explored every nook and cranny in that playground, learned how to sneak cookies without our parents knowing, and could giggle until our sides felt like they were being unzipped.

It didn't take long to discover that Noelle was a risk-taker, and she was mischievous, once she had an ally.

For example, she had it in for Chuckie Greaves, working every angle to get revenge for his butt reveal. She finally figured out how in mid-August, when it was almost time to start kindergarten.

We were wild things by then, all dirty faces and uncombed hair, and populating an imaginary world that we ruled from sunup to sundown. We'd been working on Chuckie for two weeks. Noelle said he had to think we were his friends for her plan to work. Finally, after many cookie bribes, we convinced him to invite us into his house.

As soon as we were inside, I distracted him while she pretended to use the bathroom but instead robbed the piggy bank he'd been bragging about all summer long. Once she had the money, she found me in the kitchen, gave me the signal (touching her pointer fingers together in front of her nose), and we ran out of the house, laughing so hard we could hardly speak.

We kept running until we reached the slide in Koronis Park, where Noelle pulled out our ill-gotten gains. Chuckie had saved almost seventeen dollars, and we knew exactly what to do with it.

We were walking back from the Ben Franklin when the car pulled up. Back then, seventeen dollars bought you a literal wagonload of candy, and our red Radio Flyer overflowed with Dots, Marathon bars, Pixy Stix, Red Vines, and caramel corn. Rabbie was perched on top of the treasure like a king. Our mouths ringed with red sugar circles from our Blow Pops, we were laughing about a knock-knock joke that was all the funnier because neither of us could recollect how it ended.

I remembered all those details as if a movie were playing in front of my eyes.

What I could never remember, what would wake me up in shuddering tears as recently as ten years ago because I could not recall it, was what the vehicle had looked like.

The police asked me afterward, of course. They were at first kind, then desperate.

I was five. It was a car, and it was silver, and it was as huge as a boat. That's all I remembered. But I could tell them what happened *after* that big silver car pulled up:

The passenger door opened.

Inside, a man leaned over, smiling at us. His dark hair was laced with gray. I didn't recognize him. His smile made my stomach hurt.

"What are you girls going to do with all that candy?" His voice was pitched, that babyish "I'm talking to a kid now" tone that some adults think makes children like them more.

Noelle stood straighter and jutted out her chin. She was that kind of girl. "It's *our* candy. We bought it with *our* money."

The man chuckled, but only with his mouth. His eyes stayed on Noelle like two black flies. "I'm sure you did, baby girl. Isn't all that candy heavy?"

Noelle glanced at the red Radio Flyer, then at me, then back at the man. "Naw. We have a wagon."

His voice dropped. "You are such pretty girls. Where do you live?"

I wasn't even aware I was pointing toward my house until I saw the flash of pink to my right and realized it was my own arm. I flushed. I didn't understand the shame, but it burned hot. I wished that we could return all this candy and Chuckie's money. I wished that I'd never wanted to do a penny drop. I wished that my mom were here.

"And I live over there." Noelle pointed toward her house. "We're not sisters, if that's what you're wondering."

The man looked around, nodded. "You want to go for a ride?"

I didn't know the model of his car, or the color of his clothes, but I would forever remember the trapped-animal terror those words struck in me. My heartbeat pounded in my ears, and my vision narrowed. I wanted to cry, but I was a frozen doll.

"Sure," Noelle said. Her face grew pale. She was as scared as I was, but an adult was asking us to do something. We needed to do it.

She was closer to the car. If I'd been nearer, I would have led the way.

She walked toward the open vehicle door. His eyes were hungry, his smile tight and mean. She wore her favorite white socks, the ones her mom had sewn plastic beads around the edges of, and they made a tiny clinking sound as she stepped away.

I let the handle of the wagon drop to the sidewalk. It clanked.

I knew we'd lost the candy, everything. No point in looking back. I followed Noelle.

To an adult who wasn't there—even to myself all these years later—it's impossible to understand the awful tractor beam that pulled us toward that vehicle. The man was confident, and he was a grown-up, and he spoke in a way that left no room for argument.

Even so, if we hadn't just stolen Chuckie's money and bought all that candy, if we weren't so weighted down by guilt and sure we deserved to be in trouble, I don't think we would have walked to the car. That's something that's stuck with me, even after the nightmares finally began to ease off: our own bad choices, mine and Noelle's, had in some way made the horrible moment possible.

Noelle slid into the car. She had to put her hands on the seat to hoist herself up, and then one knee followed by the other, because she was just a little girl. I was right behind her, close enough to smell cigarettes and something sour, like old chicken noodle soup.

The tears were coming, yet I followed.

She was perched on the leather seat, and I was just about to crawl in next to her. She turned to look at me, her skin ashen, her eyes as large as plates. She was weeping, too, now. The man stared at her, the smile erased from his face.

I would soon be sitting next to Noelle, and the man would be staring at me instead of her, and then he'd close the door, and he'd drive away like the Child Catcher in *Chitty Chitty Bang Bang*, and we'd never see anyone who loved us again.

"Mira!" The voice was far away, but it was my mom's.

I felt God breathing on me. There's no other way to describe a relief that elemental.

It broke the spell. I could think clearly.

My mom loves me. She wouldn't want me to go with this man. She might be mad about the money and the candy, but she loves me and I don't have to do this.

My heartbeat receded and my vision cleared. I turned toward my mom's yelling, then back to Noelle. Her face was hopeful. She'd heard my mom, too. She knew my mom wouldn't let anything happen to us. We had our own adult now and so didn't have to listen to this one. I held out my hand to help her from the car.

She was sliding over, reaching toward my outstretched palm, when the man with eyes like flies leaned across her, slammed the door shut, and sped away. The last things I saw were the whites of her eyes, her expression so far past scared that she looked like she was wearing a Halloween mask of herself.

The air moved like fire through my lungs. The car turned.

Which direction?

I don't know.

I was burning from the inside.

You didn't see at all?

I couldn't move. The vehicle disappeared.

You sure you can't remember?

I stood there until a woman came out of her house across the road. It felt like hours. It was probably less than a minute. My mom was racing across the park, but I wouldn't register that until later.

"Are you OK, honey?" the woman said. "Did you know that man?"

I shook my head. I was so hot. My tears felt like steam. I was inside an oven. How could I breathe in an oven?

She called the police.

The rest was a blur. I was asked questions, and with each one I couldn't answer, I fell deeper into myself. My mom cried a lot. My dad looked angry.

Weeks later, Chuckie came by with a bag of caramel corn. He told me he didn't mind that I'd stolen his money. Said he'd saved up to buy me more caramel corn because it seemed like I really liked it.

He said he'd always make sure I had caramel corn, if I wanted it.

Noelle's dad didn't start teaching that fall. A For Sale sign appeared on their lawn.

My parents moved us to the country.

Noelle.

Chapter 7

Of course the girl clutching the Velveteen Rabbit at the Detroit Lakes train station wasn't Noelle, and the doll wasn't Rabbie. Noelle would be my age, if she were still alive. My eyes grew tight at the thought. I'd never pictured her as alive or dead. My brain had always been fixated on that last terror-filled image of her face and all the ways I'd let her down.

I should have looked at the license plate. I knew my letters and numbers. I could have looked, and I could have remembered, and I could have saved her if I'd been smarter and braver.

The sound of the train whistle startled me back in the moment. I was surprised at the hot tears pushing against my eyelids. I blinked them away and waved back at the little girl who'd sparked the whole memory. Her face lit up with a gap-toothed grin. Beyond the missing front teeth and the Velveteen Rabbit, she really didn't look much like Noelle. My friend had been blonde, and this girl was brunette. Noelle had been petite, with a pointier chin.

And she'd been so courageous, so beautifully perfect and bossy and bold.

I tried to catch a last look at the girl's mom, the woman who'd originally bumped into me, but she was moving fast. Even so, I could make out a little of her profile. I was struck by how little mother and daughter resembled one another.

Oh well. I didn't look much like my dad. Kids didn't always resemble their parents.

"Mira! The train!" Jed yelled into my ear. "The train!"

I jumped, thinking of *Fantasy Island*. Jed was too young to know who Tattoo was, so I spared him the rerun memories. The train was indeed firing up, a silver behemoth with smoke unfurling from its chimneys. The whistle blew again, and the crowd began to shuffle like anxious cattle. I struggled to push away thoughts of Noelle, but remembering her had dusted me with sadness.

"You stay by the luggage, and I'll grab Mrs. Berns," I said.

Jed nodded happily, perched on his tippy-toes to get a better view of the train. He was as excited as I'd been earlier. My heart warmed a bit. He was such an amazingly upbeat person that he elevated the mood of everyone around him.

I located Mrs. Berns toward the rear of the station, which was easier to navigate now that everyone was crowding outside. She stood near the pop machine, a red-and-white, bubble-shaped, old-fashioned appliance that still dispensed glass bottles.

It was in keeping with the style of the rest of the station, which was somewhere between "cool retro" and "college boy's basement apartment" in both appearance and smell. Plywood walls had been erected to create a corner office in what was otherwise an open space rimmed with benches, the walls lined with maps and schedules.

"Mrs. Berns!"

She glanced over. That's when I saw that an older gentleman was talking to her. It was funny because she usually went for the younger guys. This one was white-haired, pushing eighty at least. Maybe she knew him from Battle Lake? She gave me the *just a minute* look, so I pretended to read the WHY TRAIN TRAVEL IS BETTER poster while she finished her business. I stood there for all of two minutes before she appeared at my side.

"Time to go?"

I glanced over at her, surprised she'd reached me so quickly, then looked back toward the soda machine. The old guy was still standing there. "That was fast," I said. "Do you know him?"

"Name's Morris, he's traveling to Missoula, widowed, and wants to get in my pants."

I raised one eyebrow. "You guys covered a lot of territory."

"The important stuff, anyhow," she said, shrugging. "But he's not my type. They get to be that age, once you get to the bedroom, it's like trying to stick an oyster in a slot machine." She pointed toward the door. "We better hop on that train. It's not gonna wait for us."

She turned on her heel without giving me time to process her comment. It was probably just as well. The less I thought about her sex life, the better, especially since it was often more interesting than mine—recent events being the notable exception.

I caught up with her near Jed. I balanced my suitcase in one hand and Kennie's package in the other and led the way to the back of the line. People moved forward fluidly. When our turn to board came, I started to pull out my driver's license before I mounted the stepping stool.

"What're you doing?" the porter asked. He was in his late thirties, I would guess, and looked tired or strung out. His blue uniform was wrinkled, though his porter's hat was crisp.

"Getting my identification."

"Just get on the train."

His rudeness gave me pause. "Don't you even need to see my ticket?"

"We get that once the train is moving."

That seemed like incredibly lax security—anyone could get on or off at a stop—but I supposed it was their party. I held up Kennie's package. "I'm transporting this for a friend. Where's the best place to store it?"

He stared over my shoulder like I was wasting his time and jerked a thumb toward the rear of the train.

"There's a storage area in back?" I asked, glancing behind me. The line wasn't that long. We had plenty of time to board and still be ahead of schedule.

"Next!" he said, trying to push me up and into the train.

"Wait," I said, anger burbling. "I need to store this package. Can you tell me where to go with it?"

He sighed as if I'd asked him to donate his spare kidney. "What's your seat number?"

Mrs. Berns popped her head up, inserting herself into the conversation. "We're in Sleeper Car Eleven, Room Two, you rude bastard." She employed the same even tone she used to discuss the weather or order a meal. I still wasn't accustomed to a friend who spoke her mind, but boy, did I enjoy it. "If you'd just answered her question like a normal human being, we'd already be out of your hair."

The porter's eyes widened, and he had the good sense to take her words as the wake-up call she'd intended. "Sorry, ma'am. I'm pulling a double shift. The Car Twelve porter is sick, and so I haven't slept in twenty-eight hours."

She held eye contact.

He grew paler, if such a thing were possible. "But that's no excuse, of course. Here. Let me take your package. I'll see that it gets to the storage car. Sleeper Car Eleven, Room Two, you said?"

"Yup, and that's more like it." Mrs. Berns stuffed a five-dollar bill into his hand. Her creased face was lit by the most beautiful smile. "Buy yourself a shave and keep the champagne coming. I'm here to have a good time!"

The people in line behind her cheered.

I grinned. You would have, too, if you'd been there.

Chapter 8

"Did we accidentally get on the 'It's a Small World' train, rather than the 'Normal Human Proportions' train?" Mrs. Berns asked, incredulous, on the threshold of Sleeper Car 11, Room 2.

I had to agree.

We'd jostled our way through three different train cars, all set up the same: two rows of comfy-looking chairs on one side, two rows on the other, and storage racks over both. It was promising, especially compared to airplane travel—at least, what I knew of it from second-hand descriptions. The coach seats reclined to almost a forty-five-degree angle, at which point a footrest sprang up. They each also had a dedicated table and cup holders, and several of them had outlets.

We'd dropped Jed off at his seat in Car 8 before heading back. When we reached Car 11, the aisle narrowed. Rather than running straight through the center, the hall veered off to the right, leaving only windows on the right side and rooms on the left. A refrigerated cart stacked with mini champagne bottles stood at the head of the aisle.

Mrs. Berns grabbed four tiny bottles with her free hand. "Stuff some in your pockets."

"You don't have to tell me twice." I managed to juggle seven of the teensy bottles.

And then we made our way to our room.

And Mrs. Berns slid open the door.

"It's bigger than a bread box," I offered helpfully.

She turned to glare at me. The room wouldn't even be considered big for a *closet*. About five feet wide, it contained a single window that displayed the industrial park of Detroit Lakes. Over the window a bunk held a thin mattress, pillow, and blanket. Below that were two reclining chairs similar to those found in coach class. They faced each other, the footrests almost touching. A table was attached to the window's bottom sash.

A bathroom the size of a cupboard was to our left, and to the right, a storage cupboard half that size.

"I can't sleep here," Mrs. Berns said. "Jesus H. Christ, Superman couldn't even *change* in here."

I let out a long breath. "I love it."

I wasn't lying. The room appeared cozy and safe, with a clear exit. What more did a person need? Sure, maybe the fact that I'd barely survived a serial killer's attack in December and had taken up sleeping under my bed since had colored my perspective, but dang if I didn't want to marry this room. Hanging out here would be like playing fort with your best friend, crossed with all the greatest parts of a road trip and none of the downsides. A wide grin cracked my face.

I opened the storage cupboard and tried to slide my small suitcase in. It wouldn't fit. Undeterred, I plunked it onto the overhead bunk. I took Mrs. Berns's luggage and did the same, and then, with only a little huffing and elbow grease, maneuvered our small carry-ons into the cupboard. There also wasn't room for our winter coats, so I flung those over the backs of the reclining chairs, along with our purses.

"After you," I said, indicating the chairs. I had to suck in to give her enough room to pass. She dug an elbow into my stomach before plopping into a chair.

"I better get started on the drinking," she said, pulling a miniature bottle from her tracksuit. "It'll take five of these to even catch a buzz."

Great plan. I dropped into the chair across from her. "One bottle each, and then we explore!"

She grimaced before taking a deep swallow. "Why are you so excited? This room is like a sardine tin, and we'll be as lucky as Larry if it smells that good come Portland."

I opened my own bottle, savoring the tiny pop as the miniature cork flew to the ceiling and ricocheted off the walls. "It's an adventure! We can try new food while the world whisks by, we can play hide-and-go-seek, and"—my heartbeat picked up—"think of the people-watching!"

Train travel was right up my alley. Who knew?

I was taking another swig when a commotion erupted outside our door. It sounded like a scuffle, followed by a shrill voice: "You didn't clean my room? Why not?"

I peeked my head out, which I could do while still seated. Two people crowded the aisle. The high-pitched speaker was smoking Susan Wrenshall in her faux-fur coat, clutching her pink purse. She was cornering the porter Mrs. Berns had given a talking-to. The man appeared resigned to his fate, so I guessed this wasn't his first rodeo with her.

I cleared my throat. "It looks like we're going to be neighbors."

I indicated the open door of the room they stood in front of. I didn't want to focus Ms. Wrenshall's frustration on me, but I'd found that distracting a person having a hissy fit was often the best way to defuse a situation. Maybe I could divert her long enough for the porter to escape. He wasn't my best friend, but I'd worked my share of service jobs and recognized a soul in need when I saw one.

Her jaw clenched, and she appeared unwilling to give up haranguing the cornered man. I didn't look away. She finally had to acknowledge me.

"He said he'd clean my room," she said by way of explanation.

The porter shook his head vigorously. "I'm sorry, Ms. Wrenshall, but that's not true. The porters make your bed in the morning and turn it down at night. I explained that any maintenance beyond that is your responsibility. I'm afraid I've been called on to help in the dining car besides taking over another sleeping car, so we're tremendously understaffed at the moment."

I'd gone from thinking the guy was a jerk for how he'd treated me when I boarded to feeling sorry for him.

"How messy can your room get?" I asked her lightly. "My refrigerator is bigger than these cabins." I stood to peek into hers, but she backed into it like a hermit crab and tugged the door tight around her so I couldn't see in.

"Sorry," she said. "I'd let you look in, but you can't trust anyone these days."

It was an odd statement, and even more peculiar was her expression as she said it—as if she were scared.

I felt a familiar sensation, a heated weight dropping into my stomach, and it meant only one thing: something was not quite right with Ms. Wrenshall.

Chapter 9

Once the train started moving, at the porter's advice, Mrs. Berns and I settled into our chairs and read the materials describing the amenities available to us on our journey. Suddenly shy, I reached back and grabbed my purse.

"I got you a present. You know, to thank you for setting all this up." Probably she'd lost any rights to it by tricking me onto a Valentine's train, but I was choosing to focus on the positive.

Mrs. Berns raised her penciled-in eyebrows. "Now you're cooking with Crisco. What is it?"

She leaned forward and we bumped foreheads. "Oof," we said in unison.

I did not let the collision or the cramped space deter me. I continued my search, digging around until I came up with the two white boxes. I yanked them out and handed her one. "Ta-da!"

She grabbed for the box like a child, opened it, and dumped out the contents. It fell into her lap with a tiny thud. "What the helicopter?"

"It's a reading light designed to look like an eighties boom box!" I crowed. "So if one of us wants to read and the other wants to sleep, we can."

I was initially too pleased with myself to note her expression. I'd received the reading lights free at a library conference and been looking for the perfect place to use them. What better time? We could have the nerdiest slumber party in history. I tapped hers. "See? You open this speaker, and the light comes on. You open this one, and there's a clamp so you can attach it to your chair or bed. You snap them shut, and voilà! You're back to a tiny boom box."

I returned my attention to her face too slowly to anticipate the arm pinch. It burned.

"Read? This is the Valentine's train." She tossed the gift back into my lap. "Unless you meant to say 'boob box,' I've got no use for those."

"I'll just stick it in your purse, then," I said, refusing to let my mood sour. "You never know when you might need it."

After tucking the box into her bag, I returned to the pamphlet describing the train's amenities and soon discovered that because we were bunking in a sleeper car, all our meals were included.

My eyes widened. The words came out as a whisper. "We get to eat in the dining car?"

Mrs. Berns rolled her eyes, an action she quickly abandoned as I discovered increasingly regular "train treasures" over the next hour. My loudest glee came when I discovered our itsy-bitsy bathroom had a tiny shower and free honey-scented soap. Mrs. Berns was on her third bottle of champagne by then. In all fairness, the bottles were a tenth of a regular one's size, and the woman could drink a fish under the table.

"Look!" I said after I returned to my chair, dropping the laminated information card and pointing out the window. "A deer!"

Judging by how fast cars passed us, the train was traveling around fifty miles an hour. Detroit Lakes had long vanished, and we were now in open country. Western Minnesota in February is mostly prairie, occasional tufts of golden-brown grass peeping through the snow dunes.

"Are you twelve years old?" she demanded. "There's deer all over the place back home. Do you want to draw me a picture of it, and I can stick it on the fridge?"

I snatched her champagne from her hand and took a swig before handing it back. "Mrs. Crabby Appleton, rotten to the core . . ."

She crossed her arms. "Excuse me for believing the advertising. I was told our cabin would be 'roomy,' and I get to be pissy about that lie for as long as it takes."

"Come on, grumble bunny. Let's go explore! That'll cheer you up, and you'll see that we get to use the whole train. It's not like we're going to be stuck here the whole time."

The irony was not lost on me that only an hour earlier, hiding out in our room the whole time and avoiding social interaction had been my exact plan and she was the one who'd been excited for this trip. Something about being on a train had stoked my feeling of adventure, while the smallness of the transportation seemed to have had the opposite effect on her.

"No." She pouted.

Someone knocked at our door. I leaned over and slid it open. It was a new porter, maybe the one who had been sick earlier. He wore the same uniform as the previous one, but he was older, maybe sixty. He handed me a card. "I took the liberty of making a dinner reservation for you two at seven thirty, immediately after we leave Fargo."

I squealed. It was all I could do not to hug him. Someone had made a reservation for me to eat a free meal on a train! Well, a meal Mrs. Berns had paid for, in any case. "Is the dining car just like it is in the old-fashioned Westerns?"

His lips twitched. "Fewer cowboys, ma'am, but I expect the food hasn't changed much."

I smiled back, glancing down at his name tag. "Thank you, Reed. By the way, I'm Mira, and this is Mrs. Berns."

He tipped his hat at both of us. "Nice to meet you, ladies. You can contact me with any problems, but I'm not assigned to your car. There's a nasty bug going around—nothing to worry about, but a lot of us staff are pulling different shifts. Might see you in the dining car. That's my regular. Otherwise, Sylvester is your porter. He handled boarding at the last stop, so you may have already met him."

51

Reed tipped his hat again and moved on to Ms. Wrenshall's room, number 3. I got out of my chair to watch the action. Ms. Wrenshall didn't answer. I glanced to my right, at Room 1. I hadn't seen anyone go in or out. I stepped into the hall and spotted the Do Not Disturb placard hung over their curtained window. I wondered why Ms. Wrenshall hadn't used hers. She'd said, after all, that the porter, presumably Sylvester, had been getting her up at all hours. Maybe she was just trying to make trouble.

Reed walked toward the rear of the train, probably passing out dinner reservations to all the sleeper cars. I turned back to Mrs. Berns to again beg her to explore with me and found her snoring softly.

"You should have just told me you needed a nap," I whispered, unfolding a blanket from the closet to drape over her. I grabbed the Do Not Disturb sign, closed the door behind me, and stuck the placard in its slot on the door before heading to the action.

Chapter 10

I'd counted sixteen cars before boarding the train. Two in the rear appeared industrial, and the five in front of these were sleeping cars with two levels, including Car 11, where Mrs. Berns and I were bunking. The coach seats started at Car 9, Jed was in Car 8, and according to the train layout map, Car 7 was the viewing train with a café in the lower deck, Cars 5 and 6 were coach cars, Car 4 was the dining car, and everything forward of that was employee quarters or the engine.

Moving from Car 10, the first sleeper car, to Car 9, the last coach car, was a wake-up call. I'd been too excited when I'd come in from the other direction, and everything had looked new and fun. Coming this way, the sleepers' quiet elegance was replaced by the raucous feel of people waiting for concert tickets. Most coach seats were full, and conversation droned steadily. Some people hollered across the tight aisles, and the crowd was surprisingly young, about half male and half female.

Walking on the train was difficult. It swayed steadily but would also jerk at odd times, tumbling you into the lap of a stranger if you didn't hang on.

Car 8 had a similar feel. I thought Jed would be right at home here, but he was nowhere to be seen. "Excuse me?" I asked the pretty brunette in the seat next to his. "My friend Jed was sitting here. Do you know where he went?"

She smiled at me and blinked. I waited politely for an answer before I realized she had earbuds in. I made the motion to remove them, thinking she'd be perfect for Jed. "My friend," I repeated, "was sitting here. Do you know where he went?"

"Jed?"

"Exactly."

"He's so nice! Um, I think he was going to play cards with some people somewhere. Maybe?"

I raised my eyebrows. "Thanks." *Maybe.*

Realizing that my kidneys had become champagne purses, I made my way to the lower-level restroom. Because of the space limitations, the steps leading down were steep and curved in on themselves at a ninety-degree angle, which meant that I couldn't see farther than four steps ahead of me. I reached the first landing halfway down the stairs and was about to turn to the right when the sounds of an argument zipped through the enclosed space.

". . . and again. I don't know why you do it." It was a man's voice, and the words were clipped.

"I do it because you ask me to do it. What do you think? That I aim to hurt myself?" A woman's voice, but not harsh. It was intense and focused, almost as if she were enjoying the heated discussion.

Was this the couple I'd noticed arguing outside the station? This pair sounded older than the two I'd spotted, but voices are not as good a tell as many people assume.

"I tried to use the bullet," the man said. "You wouldn't let me."

The hairs on the back of my neck bristled. I peered around. If I moved forward two inches on the landing, I'd be able to identify them. Then again, they'd be able to see me, and they were talking bullets.

"I'm chugged full of your complaining," the woman said. "Up to here with it."

I couldn't resist. I sneaked one eyeball to the edge of the landing and peered around, trying to expose as little flesh as possible. I spotted a flash of yellow. That wasn't satisfying, so I peeked even farther before I pulled back, my heart hammering.

The man had been literally right around the corner, his back to me. I could have leaned around the landing wall and touched him without moving more than five inches.

"Yeah, well, you're stuck with me, at least until we get the job done," he said. "Now, I gotta take a leak. I'll meet you at the car with all the windows. I'm getting claustrophobic arguing down here."

I spun around, planning to climb up and out of there before they spotted me, but I came face-to-face with the brunette who shared a row with Jed.

"Hey!" she said. "Bathroom's full?"

I nodded—I didn't want the bullet-wielding arguers below to be able to identify my voice—and raced past her, which was no easy feat given the tight quarters. She'd probably assume I was in such a hurry because I had gastrointestinal issues. I could live with that.

Back in Car 8, I considered taking an empty seat and pretending I belonged long enough to get a full eyeball on the couple who'd been arguing, but my heart was still beating faster than it should, and I knew that if they suspected someone had been eavesdropping, my face would give me away. Instead, I hurried to the viewing car.

The sun had recently set, but the car was still impressive. The entire roof and walls were made of glass. The world slid off the windows like ink. The chairs here were smaller and arranged to face out so every seat was a good view. Unfortunately, they were all taken. A bartender poured beers at a counter in the middle of the room. I was impressed by how steady he was, even though the train rocked side to side as it moved forward.

Watching the golden stream leave the can and glurg into the plastic cups reminded me that I still needed to pee. I made my way down to this car's lower level. There was a mini-café below, along with twelve booths and three bathrooms. One of the bathrooms was free, so I let myself in, studying the shower setup while I took care of business. It'd be weird to shower in this semipublic place, but if that was your only option, there were worse things.

I was washing my hands when the announcement came over the train loudspeaker. "We're approximately ten minutes from Fargo, North Dakota. If you're a smoker, this will be your time to indulge. The passenger exchange will last twenty minutes, all taking place in Cars Eight and Nine, so don't go far!"

I hurried out of the bathroom. I wanted to be in my room when the train stopped so I could people-watch again. When I reached the second level, I scanned around for Jed and didn't see him. He also wasn't back in his seat in Car 8, or anywhere to be found in Car 9. I walked more slowly through Sleeper Car 10 than I had on my previous two trips through it.

Right inside the door was a tray of cookies that hadn't been there before. They looked like they had raisins in them, but I grabbed one anyway, and then another for Mrs. Berns. The porter for this car had been smart enough to lock up or hide the champagne, but boxes of juice and a coffee tureen surrounded by cream and sugar were arranged behind the cookies. I'd grown up poor, so it was challenging for me to walk past free stuff without filling my pockets, but I consoled myself with the thought that these same freebies were probably available in my car.

Sleeper Car 10, according to the pamphlet, was full of roomettes—four on one side and four on the other. These roomettes were supposedly even smaller than our cabin, if such a thing could be believed, and because of their smaller size, the aisle ran straight through the middle of the car rather than angling to the right like it did in our car. I'd tried to peek in these roomettes earlier, but all eight of them had either a closed curtain or a closed door with the window shade drawn.

I was planning the best way to accidentally fall against one of the curtains so I could check out the spaces when the person in Roomette 4 saved me the trouble by stepping into the hall. He was maybe nineteen: old enough to grow a mustache but young enough for it to be sparse.

He saw me, and his eyes did that weird light-up thing they do when you recognize someone you haven't seen in a while. "Hi!"

My cheeks grew hot. I scoured my memory but couldn't find any file on him. He was plain-looking—white, brown hair, brown eyes, average nose, regular lips—and maybe six two, the spindly mustache his most arresting feature. "Hi?"

He held out his hand. "Name's Chad. Are you in this car?"

Relief swept over me, followed by annoyance. Why'd he give me the look if we didn't know each other? "I'm in this car at this moment."

He glanced around, unsure if I was joking or heading to my room. That was when I remembered that I wanted to peek inside his space.

"Actually, I'm a car over. Mind if I see your room? I'm curious what exactly a 'roomette' looks like."

He stepped aside and gave me the *be my guest* gesture.

I glanced inside. I couldn't make that whistle noise people use to express wonderment, so instead I made the sound I figured that whistle would make. *Phooo-eee.* "They sure named it right."

It was set up exactly like the room Mrs. Berns and I were sharing, minus any floor space, closets, or bathroom. In fact, it was like our room had been dropped into the Death Star trash compactor, every spare bit of juice squeezed out of it, leaving only the two pieces of furniture. Well, it was like that if you were a geek who loved *Star Wars*.

Otherwise, it was just a roomette.

He shrugged. "It's not much, but I call it home, at least until Portland. That where you're going?"

My head was stuck in his tiny space, so I didn't realize how close he'd been standing. His body spray smelled like sugar and ox testicles.

"That general direction." I flashed him a tight smile and made as wide a berth as the cramped space allowed before heading back to my cabin.

Chapter 11

The people-watching at the Fargo train station was more of the same, as far as I was concerned. Mrs. Berns and I surveyed the crowd from our second-story room, pulling a reverse zoo-creature act. Tiny snowflakes danced toward folks swathed in winter gear, hugging their goodbyes and lining up to board the train. The only remotely interesting character was a guy skimming the perimeters, smoking like his life depended on it, wearing an army-issue coat that reminded me of my dad's fatigues, which he'd sold at a garage sale twenty years earlier.

It wasn't the guy's jacket or the fact that he wasn't wearing a hat or mittens that held my attention, though those were noteworthy details. It was his expression, which landed somewhere dark between anger and excitement.

"Let's go eat."

I turned my attention toward Mrs. Berns. By the time I glanced back outside, the guy in fatigues was gone. "Our reservation isn't for another half an hour."

"It'll take us some time to get there, and who eats that late at night anyhow? I thought this was *Ameri*Train, not *FancyPantsEuro*Train. Those cookies you gave me echoed when they hit the bottom, that's how empty my stomach is."

I stared outside again. I might never know if Fatigues got on the train. "OK," I said. "I'm hungry, too."

And pretty excited to see the dining car. I had yet to make it that far in the train, but I'd seen enough reruns of *The Wild Wild West* growing up to know what to expect: curtained windows and plush couches in the anteroom; a lot of brocade and Victorian lamps; white-tablecloth tables lining the actual dining car; maybe a touch of impossibly sexy James West to keep things exciting, or—more in line with my luck—some second-string Artemus Gordon.

"It's not going to be like *The Wild Wild West*," Mrs. Berns said, closing our door after I stepped outside. "I promise you that."

My mouth swung open. "How'd you know that's what I was thinking?"

"Like I've told you before, you're easier to read than a billboard." She led the way. "Also, you just giggled and whispered 'James West' under your breath. Get a hold of yourself."

Good advice.

I followed her, both of us fighting to stay on our feet as the train careened and lurched out of Fargo. We were definitely moving faster now that we'd left all signs of civilization behind. I found myself unable to argue when she passed the roomettes and declared them so small that she wouldn't have had room to change her mind if we'd ended up there, stopped long enough to grab Jed in Car 8, proceeded through the viewing car (congested with a line snaking up from the cafeteria) and Coach Cars 6 and 5, and stopped at the end of the line at the dining car.

At least, Jed and I stayed at the end of the line. Mrs. Berns elbowed her way to the front, soon out of sight.

"It won't work," the man ahead of me turned to say. "They don't have any free tables. Even if you have a reservation, you have to wait until someone passes through here until there's room to go in there."

Not much to say to that. I asked Jed to fill me in on his day. He was telling me about the new card game he'd learned, an adult form of Go Fish called BS, and I was about to ask him to reveal the secret he couldn't tell me about back in Battle Lake, when Mrs. Berns returned, eyes triumphant.

"Our table is ready," she said.

The man in front of us swiveled, his mouth a perfect O. "How'd you do it?"

She pointed at a black plastic square that she'd taped to her wrist. "Diabetic. I have to eat regularly."

He nodded empathetically and made room for us to pass.

When we were away from that gentleman and threading our way through the tight crowd, I grabbed her wrist and held it up for scrutiny. "The boom box reading light!" Fastened as it was, it resembled a walkie-talkie watch or, if you didn't examine it too closely, a medical device. "Where'd you get the tape?"

"Old ladies are always prepared." She cackled. "And thanks for the reading light. Turns out you were right about me needing it."

Chapter 12

The dining car did not disappoint. It was crowded, with only four open seats. Each table was covered in a white linen cloth with a vase of fresh pink and yellow carnations near the window, perched between the salt, pepper, and sugar packets. White napkins held metal silverware. Outside, North Dakota passed by as it should: under the cover of night, its endless flat fields of white transformed into an exciting alien landscape through the magic of moonlight and shadow.

"Right this way."

The host appeared harried, and I didn't blame him. People from all sides asked him for more as we passed down the aisle—more butter, more wine, more dessert. The world would be a better place if everyone had to spend a week working in food service—two weeks if they were under the impression that 10 percent was a good tip or that waitresses thought it was charming when middle-aged men stopped them with a tray full of food and commanded them to smile. We were led to the single open table.

"A white tablecloth!" Jed glanced in dismay at his WHEN HELL FREEZES OVER, I'LL SNOWBOARD THERE, TOO crewneck. "I should have worn my nice T-shirt."

I patted his back and indicated the rest of the train. "No one else is dressed up. You're fine."

I sat in the far seat near the window. Jed sat next to me and Mrs. Berns across from us. I grabbed the plastic menus from underneath the sugar ramekin and passed them each one. Our choices were simple: steak, chicken, fish, pasta, or the nightly special.

"It's just like being back in the nursing home," Mrs. Berns grumbled. "If dessert is pudding, I'm outta here."

I pointed at the bottom of the menu. "Cream puffs, ice cream, or cheesecake."

"Lemme see that." She pushed the expand button on her boom box reading light. The light unfurled like an arm and automatically clicked on when it reached its full extent, illuminating her menu. "Well, I'll be. And a wine list, too. Guess we're staying."

"And this seat is for you."

All three of us looked up in surprise as the host extended his arm, indicating that the man behind him should sit next to Mrs. Berns. She darted her hand out to the seat, her reading light still extended.

"I don't eat with strangers," she said.

The host made a Droopy Dog face. "I'm sorry, but every seat must be used. That's how it works on the train."

"Well, lemme see him," Mrs. Berns said reluctantly, trying to peer around the host. "If he's cute, he can stay."

The man stepped out. He was maybe six feet tall, thick in the middle, his hair wet-looking and slicked back. He was wearing a thin gray suit, no tie, white dress shirt open at the collar. He smelled like a car salesman—specifically, stale cigarettes and waxy cologne.

My eyes dropped to his hands. You can tell a lot about a person by how they maintain themselves below the wrists. His fingernails were longish but clean, perfect white crescent moons at the end of strong, long fingers. No yellow cigarette stains on his pointer fingers. The only ring was gold, and on his pinkie.

I had one thought: *Cop.*

He extended the hand I was staring at. "Terry Downs."

"Nope," Mrs. Berns said, swatting him away. "You'll need to move on. 'Cute or scoot' is the rule here."

I felt bad for him with his hand out, so I shook it. "Mrs. Berns," I said, "I don't think we have a choice. Mr. Downs doesn't have anywhere else to sit."

Mrs. Berns blew a breath out with such force that her bangs flew away from her face. "Fine." She held her menu up so it formed a wall between her and the new arrival and talked pointedly to me. "What're you going to have?"

I glanced at Terry. He didn't seem to mind Mrs. Berns's behavior. Realizing I was caretaking the man when I'd only just met him, I made a conscious decision to let him fend for himself and shifted my full attention to my friends. "A salad, and maybe the fish?"

Mrs. Berns shook her head. "Fish?" She tapped her finger on the window. "You see any lakes out there?" Then she indicated the entire train car. "Do you see any ovens? Honey, don't order the fish. Our bedroom and our bathroom are the same room. Do you get what I'm saying?"

I did, but I really wanted the fish. She had a point, of course, one I hadn't thought of. Everything we were going to eat on this train had potentially been here since New York, and it would come microwaved. Pasta is always your best bet in such a situation. But something about someone telling me I couldn't have something made me want it a million times more. "I bet it'll be fine," I said quietly.

She held eye contact, her eyebrows raised in a *really?* I held my ground.

"I'm gonna get the peanut butter and jelly and some french fries," Jed said.

I glanced over. "I think that's the kids' menu."

He nodded happily. "I know! I almost didn't see it."

"Chicken for me," Mrs. Berns said, studying the menu. "It'll taste as good as chewing on my own leg, but at least I won't be painting the toilet brown all night."

"All right," I said, cutting her off before she got her steam up. Once she started talking about poop, she really committed. "So, Mr. Downs, did you get on in Fargo?"

He glanced at his watch, a thick gold affair so cheap-looking that it almost appeared bronze. "Yup."

"Where're you traveling to?"

He set his menu on the table and studied all three of us before speaking. Up close, he had a definite Nick Nolte vibe going on. "I'm traveling to—"

"Portland," Mrs. Berns finished for him.

He glanced at her sideways. "And how do you know that?"

She shrugged. "Lucky guess. Mira here and me, we're private investigators."

I groaned inwardly. This would not end well.

Terry gave her his full attention. "That so?"

"Yes, it is." She dug in her purse and pulled out the flyer for the PI conference and beamed her wrist lamp on it. "International gathering. Maybe you've heard of it?"

He chuckled, a deep, raspy sound that threatened to become a cough. "Heard of it? I'm going to it."

"You're a private investigator, too?" Jed asked, his voice awed. When I'd told him I was taking classes to get my PI licensure, he'd treated me like I'd just told him I was secretly Wonder Woman.

Terry reached into the inside pocket of his jacket as if to pull something out but stopped himself. "I am. Have been for ten years. My partner usually goes to the cons, but he had family issues this year, so I'm pinch-hitting. Hate to fly, so here I am."

"I hate to fly, too," I said.

"That's official, then," Mrs. Berns said. "Two dumbasses at one table. That's over quota."

He smiled at her. His teeth were surprisingly white. I sniffed again, discreetly—definitely cigarette smoke, and for sure coming from him.

He must have used whiteners and washed his hands frequently.

"You think it's stupid not to fly?" he asked.

Mrs. Berns clicked her wrist lamp back into place. "Yes. I also think most dogs have four legs, the sun rises in the east, and Dick Sargent was the best Darrin on *Bewitched*." She glanced up at the waiter approaching our table. "Looks like it's time to order."

"Reed!" I said, recognizing the temporary porter who'd made our dining reservation for us. "Long day for you?"

"Not too long," he said, smiling. "Car Eleven, is that right?"

"Not me," Terry said. "I'm coach class. All the cars were taken by the time I booked."

"I'm coach class, too," Jed said.

"All right," Reed said, pulling three slips of paper out of his apron pocket. "Three separate bills. Ladies, you order what you like. Everything but liquor comes with your room, and that includes desserts." He smiled at Mrs. Berns.

"I see what you're doing," she said, winking. "Trying to play to the weaknesses of an old lady and charm her into your bedroom."

My eyes widened. Reed played it cool and winked back. "You let me know if it's working, you hear?"

She grinned. "Will do."

The four of us ordered and were about to settle back into conversation when a ruckus toward the rear of the dining car caught our attention. I turned to see Ms. Wrenshall yelling at Reed. The other three people at her table—strangers to her, I presumed—appeared mortified.

"I did not order chocolate ice cream! I ordered vanilla, and a cream puff warmed up to go!" In her white furry dress coat and black pantsuit, I thought she looked a bit like a cream puff to go herself. And it might have been Mrs. Berns's reference to *Bewitched*, but I noticed Ms. Wrenshall also resembled Agnes Moorehead, the actress who'd played Endora on the show.

Reed was making placating gestures toward Ms. Wrenshall, but because he was using his inside voice, I couldn't make out what he was saying.

"She looks like trouble," Terry said matter-of-factly.

The three of us did not disagree.

Chapter 13

The lemon dill cod was not great, but because Mrs. Berns was watching me with her know-it-all face, I swallowed every last bite. Terry held his own in the conversation, maintaining a friendly/evasive style of chatter. I didn't mind, and even Mrs. Berns seemed to warm up to him toward the end. She and I were on our second helping of free ice cream, the cutest little cups of Häagen-Dazs with a wooden spoon magically included as part of the lid, when he excused himself.

"You're not going to the Valentine's dance?" Mrs. Berns asked as he pushed in his chair.

He shook his head. "I'm no Fred Astaire under the best of circumstances. I don't think I should try dancing on a train."

I watched him walk away, the ice cream expanding in my throat. "I'm *also* not a Fred Astaire," I said. "What's this Valentine's hoedown of which you speak?"

Mrs. Berns refilled my glass of merlot from the half bottle we'd ordered. We'd both commented that we should have simply brought the free champagne from our car. Next time.

"Not a 'hoedown,' though that'd be a hoot. Just a Valentine's dance held in Car 6. Jed, you coming?"

He stretched long, like a cat. "I say nay. It's been a long day, and I'm ready to hit the hay." His eyes lit up. "Did you hear that? I rhymed! Maybe I should learn to rap."

"Maybe," I said, accepting his good night hug. "Sleep tight. You know where our room is if you need anything."

I dropped a generous tip for Reed on the table—the least I could do, considering Mrs. Berns was currently paying for everything else—and waited impatiently for her to finish her ice cream.

"For someone who didn't want to go to a dance, you sure are antsy about getting there."

I pointed behind her. "Do you see that long line still waiting to eat? I want to give them a chance."

"Fine, but from where I'm sitting, it sure looks like you want to get your dance on." She stood, wiggling her hips suggestively. "Hey, speaking of a *hoedown*, you know what another weird word is?" Before I could speak, she answered her own question. "'Boy-howdy.' That's something a woman should never say."

The train lurched as I stood. I grabbed my chair for balance. That's when I realized I was more than a little tipsy. My cutback on alcohol the last year was making me a definite lightweight.

"You're absolutely right," I said, following her down the narrow aisle. She was swaying as much as I was, and it wasn't all the train's fault. "You wanna hear something else weird? Why is swearing so bad? It's just words. It's like, you can't wear your bra and underwear outside, but call it a bikini, and it's just fine."

She put her hand out and grabbed on to a bald man's head for support. "You're right!"

I nodded even though she couldn't see me. "I know."

We continued to pinball our way down the aisle, past the line of hungry-looking people still waiting for their spots, and all the way to Car 6, one ahead of the viewing car. Mrs. Berns entered first. It was full of coach seats, almost all of them taken, some of them holding sleeping passengers.

"Where's the party?" she asked, a little bit too loudly.

"Down one level," a woman in a nearby aisle seat said, placing her finger in the page of the book she was reading. "Can't you hear the music?"

I couldn't hear it exactly, but I could feel it. A thumping bass faintly massaged our feet.

"You wanna go party with us?" Mrs. Berns asked the woman. She was maybe in her midfifties, hair pulled back in a messy bun, an AmeriTrain-issued blanket pulled over her lap.

The woman held up her book. I recognized the cover of a bestseller that had been on the waiting list at the library since its release three months earlier.

"No thanks. I've got a good read. Besides, I'm not really a mingling sort of person."

I was really beginning to like train people. They were a sensible lot on the whole. And then there was Mrs. Berns. She grabbed my hand and pulled me toward the stairs.

And that's where we descended into the seventh level of hell.

Chapter 14

The bottom level of Car 6 must have been used for storage on regular routes. On the Valentine Train, however, it was home to swirling disco balls, heart cutouts, karaoke, a setup bar, and sweaty bodies trying either to dance or to stand upright. It was hard to tell the difference on a moving train.

Mrs. Berns didn't hesitate. She strode to the center of the car, clearing a path like Moses through the Red Sea, and proceeded to boogie down. The dancers surrounding her, average age twenty-four, made room.

Someone hollered into my ear, "Would you like to dance?"

I was on the top step, having not yet found the courage (or motivation, really) to enter the dance floor. I'd been too distracted to notice Chad of the roomette and body spray approach me. I thought that if he were a knight, that'd be his name. Chad of the Roomette. I giggled.

"People don't usually laugh when I ask them to dance," he said, hands in pockets, yelling over the music. He smiled shyly. "Oh wait, they do."

And there he went, playing the only card that would have worked on me: guilt. I stepped onto the floor. "Just one dance," I said, moving close so I wouldn't have to yell. I held up my pointer finger to underscore my seriousness. "And it's just a dance. I have a boyfriend."

"Oh." His face fell.

"Seriously?" I asked. "How old are you? Nineteen? Twenty?"

"Twenty-one, I swear!"

"Yeah, well, I'm twenty-nine. If you want a cougar, she's the queen." I pointed toward Mrs. Berns, who was twerking against a very happy-looking twentysomething.

"No cougar, just some dancing." He held out his hand.

I let him lead me onto the floor. The next karaoke singer chose "It's Raining Men," which, from any perspective, is a crap-poor song to dance to with a kid who is crushing on you while your belly is beginning to talk to you about that fish you ordered while you're on a train en route to your boyfriend in Portland. (You could argue that no song works under these circumstances, to which I'd counteroffer "Dream On," "Don't Speak," and "Let It Be.")

I tried hard, I really did. I kept a solid four inches between us, used my best *I'm old enough to be your teacher* face, and wiggled gamely, hands in the air because it was too packed to put them anywhere else. I was actually beginning to enjoy myself a bit—dancing is good for the soul—when the train took a deeper-than-usual lurch, sending the karaoke singer and machine into the far wall and someone into my back. Other than the sudden silence caused by the music stopping, this would have been no big deal, except whoever fell into me did so at such an angle that I fell forward.

And into Chad.

This also wouldn't have been terrible except that he was simultaneously unsettled by the force. Hands windmilling in the air, he shot backward as I shot forward, nothing to grab on to with my arms, the first point of contact my face.

And his crotch.

There are some things in this life you can recover from—accidentally forgetting to wear pants on the day you have to give your big speech, sneeze-farting on a first date, maybe even asking a man with a prosthetic arm if he's armed—but crotch-diving into a strange man inside a bizarre pocket of silence when a train car full of people are staring at you is a bell you cannot unring.

He helped me up, the karaoke singer caught her balance, and the machine was righted. The music resumed, but it was too late. The damage was done.

"I think I need to go," I said. My nose felt red and inflamed, and I probably had the imprint of his jeans snap burned into my forehead like a third eye. People were clearly talking about us, laughing behind their hands and tipping their heads in our general shamed direction.

To his credit, Chad was so uncomfortable that he couldn't make eye contact. "It's fine," he said. "I fell, too."

Really? Into someone else's pork and beans?

"It's not that," I lied. I could smell his body spray and realized it was not coming off him, but rather was now the scent of my face. "I'm just all danced out."

Ack. I was a better liar than that, but I wanted nothing more than to return to my cabin, close the sliding door, and scrub my face in the tiny bathroom.

Mrs. Berns appeared behind me. "Time to go, sunshine."

Thank god. I was too relieved to even ask her why she wanted to leave so early. Amateur move on my part.

"By the way, next time you need to blow . . . your nose, you could just ask for a tissue." Her cackles carried her all the way up the stairs. "Or, if you give head—" She paused here just long enough for the hot red blush to creep to my hairline, then coughed a little. "I meant to say that if you give me a heads-*up*, I'll just lend you a hankie."

She was laughing so hard she struggled to reach the top landing. I pursed my lips and asked the obvious. "I take it you saw me fall into him?"

"You surprise me." Tears were coming down her cheeks from laughing so hard. I knew those other two jokes had just been warmups. I braced myself for the king zinger. "You come off as so uptight, like you don't even want to dance. Next thing I know, you're playing pin the face on the donkey. Don't get me wrong, I applaud your get-up-and-go, it's just that . . ."

Wait for it. Wait for it.

"Most of us peel the banana before we eat it."

That was it. She was lost in a sea of hilarity. It took until we reached the viewing car before she had herself under control. Since all the other cars were sleepers, it made sense that people would congregate here for after-hours fun.

"It's as full as a tick in here," a woman nearby grumbled.

I glanced over at her and nodded in agreement. The car was standing-room only, and there was barely that. When the train rocked, as it was wont to do, we all lurched together like a big sardine wave.

"Outta my way," Mrs. Berns hollered over the mass of people standing between us and the other end of the car. It was no use. Her voice melded with the chatter, and we were left inching through the breath and scents of a motley group.

We'd gone all of four inches when the color green caught my eye. I stood on my tippy-toes to see around or over most of the warm bodies; my gaze landed on a man wearing army fatigues, the same fellow who'd been suspiciously watchful of others at the Fargo train station. (Of course, I'd also been watching him, but I *knew* me, so that made it OK.)

Fatigues was maybe six people away and to my right, and he made me even more uncomfortable up close. He wasn't talking to anyone, just leaning against the glass and holding a plastic cup of what looked like beer next to his cheek. It was the look in his eyes that sent my radar beeping. They were dark and deep-set, with a chilling, happy light in them—the creepy joy you see in the face of a kid who thinks it's funny to set off firecrackers in a live frog's mouth or squeeze a cat into a microwave.

I found myself leaning in his direction, searching for some identifying feature—a last name on the front of the uniform, a unique necklace or ring on the hand holding the beer—when he glanced up, locking eyes with me. My neck grew instantly cold. His expression didn't change. If anything, it intensified, and a smile began to form on his thin lips.

"Move," I grunted to Mrs. Berns.

"You sure you wouldn't rather have me fly? Or possibly lay an egg? Because either of those would be easier at this point." She turned, probably to swat me, and saw my face. "What's wrong? You sick?"

Now that she mentioned it, my tummy gurgles were getting . . . oilier. Dang fish. But that wasn't the reason for my current discomfort.

The train lurched again, and just like that, my eye contact with Fatigues was broken. "There's a creepy guy over by the window," I whispered, as if he might hear my voice above the thrum of thirty different conversations.

"Yeah, there's a bunch of 'em." Mrs. Berns twirled her finger overhead. "It's the Valentine Train."

"This one is extra ishy." I gave her a nudge at the same time two people in front of her miraculously found room to squeeze to the side, and we moved forward nearly twelve inches.

"Noelle!" I yelled.

"What?" Mrs. Berns tried to follow my gaze, but she was too short. It wouldn't have mattered because my story would have made little sense. Ahead, standing in line at the snack counter, was the woman who'd bumped into me at the Detroit Lakes train station, the girl with the Velveteen Rabbit perched on her hip. Both of them appeared like they'd just been released from the gulag, their faces drawn, eyes drooping. The little girl had tear tracks down her cheeks.

We moved forward another fourteen inches as the mom made it to the counter.

"Do you have warm milk?" Her voice was soft, but I was close enough now to hear her request.

The server behind the counter shook his head. "Afraid not, but I can sell you the milk, and you can bring it downstairs and heat it in the public microwave."

She nodded gratefully.

The server must have noticed the same pitiful expression I'd observed, because he offered her a plastic glass of water while he rummaged in the mini-fridge behind him for milk. She accepted the water, barely sipped from it, and slid him a five-dollar bill when he handed her the small carton.

She didn't wait for the change.

"Ma'am?" he called after her. "Ma'am, the milk was only a dollar."

But she was better at slipping through the crowd than Mrs. Berns and I were, even with a child on her hip. She disappeared.

That's when the weirdest thing happened. Reed, my temporary porter and waiter, appeared from behind the server who'd just sold the milk.

He grabbed the water glass that the woman had taken a sip out of—leaving the other dirty glasses alongside it—and disappeared from sight.

Chapter 15

I mulled over the weirdness of what had just happened all the way to the other end of the viewing car, which took approximately seven minutes to reach. I stood near the door for three more minutes as Mrs. Berns signed us up on the Valentine Train activities board that had appeared since we'd left for dinner. My stomach's wobbles grew more acrobatic as I noted what she was enlisting me for—a makeover, a Hunt for Love event, a music mixer, a painting class, an aerobics class, a scavenger hunt, and a geology lesson in the viewing car as we passed through the Rocky Mountains.

"Everything is more fun on a train!" she said.

I nodded. She was turning my words against me. But I knew that attending these events with her was a small price to pay for a train ride that would bring me to Johnny, even if only for a few days.

"Hey," I asked, changing the subject as we stood for a moment in the quiet bubble that separates cars, a tiny shifting room encased in a rubber accordion. I liked to pretend that it was a foyer on *Star Trek*'s *Enterprise*. Don't judge. "Over dinner, you guessed that Terry was traveling to Portland. How'd you know?"

The door in front of us slid open with a pneumatic hiss, and she lowered her voice out of respect to the quieter feel of this car. "Lucky guess. It's the final stop on the train, and who gets off in Montana or Idaho?"

"Hmm."

We passed Jed. Like the rest of the inhabitants, he was asleep, a fuzzy blanket pulled tight to his neck. Mrs. Berns softly kissed his cheek before heading back. I smiled, grateful to have such wonderful people in my life, even if both of them sometimes got on my nerves.

The remaining cars were also quiet, packed full of people sprawled in various stages of sleep, reading, playing on mobile devices, or engaging in soft conversations. Even so, it was a relief to reach our sleeper car—no mass of carbon dioxide–producing bodies, no laps to fall into as the train unexpectedly rocked left or right, no bright lighting.

"It's nice to live large," Mrs. Bern said, echoing my thoughts.

I nodded. "Do you think it's weird that our doors don't have locks on the outside? Like, you can't lock your room unless you're in it."

She slid open our door. Our space appeared just as we'd left it. "I suppose they don't want to deal with keys, what with people getting on and off every stop and forgetting them. Besides, who's going to commit a crime on a train? They'd be stuck. It's like peeing in your own bed."

The hiss of the car-connecting door caught my attention. I glanced over, and my heart jumped. It was Noelle, or the girl I'd come to think of as her. Just like that, I was brought back to that big silver car and my friend's wide, terrified eyes before the door closed and that man drove off with her. A cold sweat broke out on my forehead, and I tried to steady myself so I didn't come across as a creeper. This girl was not Noelle, even if I'd connected the two in my mind and subsequently developed an affinity for her.

"Hey," I said to her mom, who had her hands on Noelle's shoulders. If possible, the woman looked even more tired than she had back in the viewing car. "You guys get your warm milk?"

What little color she had drained from her face. I wasn't doing a bang-up job of not being weird.

"Sorry. I was in the viewing car when you guys ordered it," I added.

The little girl held up her milk carton, a tired grin on her face. Her hair was snarly, as if she'd been sleeping earlier.

I smiled back and held out my hand. "My name's Mira."

The girl tucked her rabbit under the arm holding the milk and offered me her left hand as I held out my right. I ended up giving her a strange, upside-down shake so our hands fit, and both of us giggled.

"How do you like the train?" I asked her mother.

The girl answered me instead. "Good," she said shyly.

I smiled down at her. "Me too. Are you guys in one of the sleepers?"

She pointed to the door she was standing in front of. "We're right here!"

I pointed to my own. "We're neighbors. You guys going to Portland, too?"

The girl nodded. "We're from New York. That's where I live."

She stepped forward and hugged my waist. It was unexpected, and one of the sweetest things I'd ever experienced. My heart warmed, and I was leaning forward to put an arm around her when their cabin door slid open.

A man loomed in the opening, his hair black and curly, his eyes scared. He was slender, wiry, around my age.

"Aimee?" he asked the little girl, his alarmed glance shooting down the hall. He relaxed slightly when he spotted Aimee's mom behind her.

"Hi," I said, extending my hand even though Aimee still clung to my waist with a child's lack of self-consciousness. He took my palm. A wedding ring glinted on his ring finger. His hand was surprisingly soft. A quick shake, and he released me.

He reached forward and gently pried Aimee off me. "Sorry if she's bothering you. She's friendly. She shouldn't be out this late"—here he flashed the woman a pained expression—"but she couldn't fall asleep, and her mom thought some exercise and warm milk would help."

"I hope it does."

He nodded, gently directed Aimee into the cabin, then stepped aside so her mom could enter. He gave me one last look before sliding the door closed and locking it from the inside. Aimee pulled aside the curtain over the door's window to peek out and wave before the cloth was forcibly pushed back and she disappeared from view.

The door of Cabin 3 slid open. It was a busy night on the bridge of the *Enterprise*.

"Hello, Ms. Wrenshall," I said even before she poked her head out.

I could almost feel the pause, and then only her head appeared. "I heard a noise out here."

In our cabin, out of view, Mrs. Berns rolled her eyes before disappearing into our tiny bathroom.

"Sorry," I said to Ms. Wrenshall. "It was me talking. I'll be quieter."

"I certainly hope so. I mean it. I hope you're not going to be loud."

I thought I caught a faint whiff of tobacco. If she was smoking in her cabin, she was going to get in troooouuuble. "I think we're all going to bed."

"So you won't be loud?"

I'd been patient and generous up to this point. However, she was pushing it too far by making me assure her using her exact words: *we won't be loud*. I wouldn't play that game. In fact, it was a hill I was willing to die on. "Pretty sure we're going to bed."

She scrunched up her face. "So . . . loud. You won't be that?"

"I'm a quiet sleeper."

She stepped a little farther into the hall. "You're saying that you won't be loud, then?"

I could play this all night. There should have been awards for this. They'd be called The Pettys, and I'd win them. "I sleep deeply."

She scowled. "Not loudly?"

"I bet I'll sleep even *more* intensely on a train. It's like a big rocking baby bed."

"You won't be—"

"Oh, for Chrissakes!" Mrs. Berns yelled from inside our bathroom. "We won't be loud!"

(Note to self: bathrooms on trains are poorly soundproofed.)

Ms. Wrenshall's lips pursed before she scuttled back into her room, slamming the door behind her. I did the same, minus the slam. Mrs. Berns finished up in the bathroom, and when she came out, she surprised me by tossing our luggage to the floor and choosing the top bunk.

"Less stuff will fall on me if the train crashes," she said.

Made sense to me.

I finished my evening ablutions and crawled into bed. True to my prediction, I fell asleep immediately. It'd been a long day. Forget that— it had been a long *year*. My subconscious reveled in the rhythm of the train, the muffled *clackety-clack* of the rails underneath us, the metallic shiver as the cars shifted. It was like traveling deep in the belly of a dragon, only safer. I would have happily slept through the night, and thought I had until I was awoken suddenly.

"Huh?"

Darkness. Random flashes of light outside. The digital clock read 2:34 a.m.

I blinked, shapes coming into focus. *I'm in a train car.*

Once I had myself placed, I mentally backtracked to figure out what woke me. I sat up, the top of my head grazing Mrs. Berns's bunk. She was snoring softly. Everything else was quiet except for the *rumble rumble click, rumble rumble click* of the train sliding through the night.

But there it came again, making me jump. A noise like a door being slammed, but not quite that. It was both tighter and more hollow. The sound turned my blood icy.

A gunshot?

It still was February, after all, even if we were on a train.

I was past due to uncover a corpse.

Chapter 16

My heartbeat was so loud that it sounded like someone was pounding on my head. I tried to steady my breathing so I could hear everywhere at once. My eyes went to the door of our cabin. Had we locked it?

When the next hollow bang rang out, I rolled out of bed and lay flat on the floor, my heart galloping. We were under attack from all sides, and I couldn't catch my breath. How could I get Mrs. Berns to safety without drawing attention to us? How close were the gunshots? Were they coming nearer?

The noise repeated four more times, mimicking the backfiring of a car, before I realized it must have been some function of the train— some normal sound that I hadn't noticed when I was falling asleep, or maybe some maintenance that was only performed at night. I forced my breathing to calm, feeling like a fool.

Stumbling across a corpse a month every month for nearly a year made a person jump at shadows, it turned out. I crawled back onto my bed and reached for the curtain, pausing as I thought of that *Twilight Zone* episode where William Shatner spots an apelike creature outside his airplane window.

I pushed through the fear and slid it open, observing nothing but the snow-dusted Dakotas slipping past under the brightness of a million stars. Or maybe we were on the moon, so vast was the sense of an empty, wide world. In either case, the train was on its tracks. We were not in danger. I concentrated on slowing my heartbeat.

My emotions finally under control, I realized I needed to use the bathroom, and urgently. Maybe that was what'd ultimately woken me? The lemon dill cod, tapping Morse code signals on the inside of my stomach? *You shouldn't have eaten me. Stop. I'm crawling back up your throat to discuss exactly why not. Stop. I don't think you're going to like this conversation. Stop.*

I was almost relieved. My corpse-finding affliction wasn't what had gotten me up. Eating train fish had, and I had just stretched my neurosis across that. It was a fine point, but when you don't have a lot, you tend to cling.

Out of respect to Mrs. Berns and our small space, I chose to use the Car 11 public bathroom rather than our private one. My jammies were decent, and who cared what my hair looked like? I stepped out of the room, almost running into Reed.

"Sorry!" I said. Dang social conditioning.

He stepped aside, ducking his face so I couldn't read his expression. "You're up late."

A sound down the hall and to the right pulled my attention. Was that a person stepping into the shadows? I hesitated, but my curiosity got the better of me, and I started to walk in that direction before Reed grabbed my wrist. "Can I help you with something?"

My head was full of cobwebs. I'd gone from an imaginary threatening situation to one that felt genuinely uncomfortable. "Were you standing outside my door this whole time?"

He finally looked me head-on. His face appeared tense and tired, and then, like water running out of a cracked jar, the tension melted away and he relaxed. "Naw, I'm happy to report that I have better things to do, though not much." He smiled ruefully. "Ms. Wrenshall called for a porter, and here I am. Can I get you something while I'm here?"

"No." I was now zero for two on reacting appropriately to stuff. I needed to dial down the paranoia, ASAP.

"What're you doing up at this hour, anyhow?" he asked.

The fish burbled in my stomach, as if to get his attention. *Help me! I want to get out of here. It's so lonely.* I placed my hand over my stomach to muffle the pleas and tried to think of a suitable lie. I certainly couldn't reveal that I had the bad poops coming on and didn't want to inflict them on my roommate. Unfortunately, my liar likes to sleep in.

"I was just going to stretch my legs." *In front of me, while I sit on the toilet.*

Reed had the decency to let that go. "All right. Well, if you need anything, just flip on your light." He pointed into my room, at a green light glowing softly in our wall. "That'll call a porter—probably me, the way tonight's going."

"Will do."

"I'm heading this way." He pointed toward the rear of the train.

"Me this way," I said, pointing the opposite direction. I stepped around him and took the short steps to the bathroom, just then noticing I was barefoot. I did not have the luxury of time in which to address this, and so I entered anyway. It was small and neat, with the sort of lighting you'd expect in a Panamanian jail, which suited my situation just fine. I locked the door, double-checked the lock, and got down to business.

I knew I was going to be a while, so I settled into my thoughts. The pros so far of train travel: it was magical. It really was. A big silver dragon takes you on an adventure across the country. People feed you, they offer entertainment of sorts, you can be alone or in a group at the snap of a finger, and nighttime is like the world's biggest slumber party. Plus, you can do absolutely nothing and still be going somewhere, so it's like evolution for lazy people.

Cons: the lemon dill cod was to the bad poops like gasoline was to fire. Another point: the staff was at turns helpful and peculiar. Also, specific to this train, there was:

1. The oddly sensitive Ms. Wrenshall next door.
2. The exhausted-looking Aimee and crew on the other side of us (though I'd put Aimee herself in the pro column).

3. The as-yet anonymous couple who'd been arguing about bullets earlier, using strange phrases like "chugged full" and "aim to."
4. Me giving a face job to Chad at the dance. (I blushed all over again at the memory.)
5. And the army fatigues guy who looked ready to unleash something wicked on all of us.

It was an odd potpourri, but so was life, right? Maybe it felt a little stranger because we were a de facto community, all forced together, but I bet these people were no weirder than the average supermarket crowd.

In any case, I was going to make the best of it and focus on Johnny at the end of the trip, and on the fact that I was getting away from Battle Lake and (please, oh please) away from the dead bodies.

I finished my business, washed my hands for the full alphabet, quietly apologized to the other people of Car 11 for fouling their atmosphere, and sneaked back to my room. It was cozy. It was safe. I fell gratefully into my bed like you can only when you've been completely emptied out, and I tumbled into the deepest sleep I'd had in months.

I bet I would have slept until noon the next day if not for the blood-freezing scream.

Chapter 17

In the next instant, the train gave a loud heave and came to a stop with such force that I was tossed out of bed. Mrs. Berns fell on top of me with a *woof*.

"See?" she said groggily, stretching. "You sleep in the bottom bunk and stuff falls on you when we crash."

She'd knocked the wind out of me, so I couldn't respond. When my breath returned, still wheezing, I squirmed out from under her and helped her to her feet. I made sure she was OK before I pulled aside the curtains.

We were at a dead stop. It was early morning, the sun rising in a canvas of tangerines and lavenders. The geography was similar to North Dakota but with less snow—endless prairies covered in a fur of brown grass and only patches of crusty-looking ice.

The train coughed to life and lurched forward again, tossing me back into Mrs. Berns. It made a chugging, unhealthy sound, coasting slowly for a few more minutes before it pulled into a station.

The brick building was similar to the one in Detroit Lakes, except I saw GLENDIVE spelled out on its front.

"Montana," Mrs. Berns said from beside me. "Wonder why the crappy first stop before the station?"

"I wonder why the *scream*." My heart was still thudding. "Did you hear it? It came right before the train stopped."

"Scream?"

Had I been imagining scary stuff again? I thought about peeking into the hall to find out if anybody else had heard anything. Ms. Wrenshall saved me the trouble. She yanked open our door, her face a clown mask of terror.

"Did you hear?" Her voice was a rasp of its former self. "There's been a murder."

Chapter 18

Mrs. Berns sighed and slid her arm around me. "Sounds about right."

I fell back into my bed. I hadn't escaped my curse. The murders had followed me. My brain raced down every dark alley before I came to my senses. This wasn't about me. "Who was it?"

Ms. Wrenshall was not a woman who washed her makeup off before going to bed. That's what gave her the clownish look more than anything—that, and her fear. She pointed next door.

My heart stopped and I jumped to my feet. "Aimee? The little girl?"

Ms. Wrenshall shook her head. I pushed her aside, but a man roughly the size of a boxcar blocked the aisle. He wore a blue suit and a conductor's hat. His face was grim.

He held out his hands so I couldn't slip past him, then pointed behind me. "We're going to have to ask you to stay in your cabin. The police are on their way."

"Please," I begged. I couldn't lose her twice. "Was it the little girl? Was it Aimee?"

"I'm afraid I'm not at liberty to say."

"Please."

Something in my voice touched him, and his face softened. "Naw, it wasn't the little girl. It was her mother."

My legs weakened. It was better news, but it was hardly good news. "Oh no. Where's Aimee? And her dad?"

The conductor's face tightened back up. "That's what we're trying to find out. Now please, you can help by staying out of the way."

Ms. Wrenshall walked backward into her room, and Mrs. Berns pulled me into ours, closing and locking the door behind us. She sat me on my bunk.

"I know what you're going to say," I told her, suddenly very tired. "You're going to tell me it's not my fault that someone was murdered on this train, that it's just a coincidence I was right next door. You're going to tell me I'm a good person, and the fact that bad things happen near me doesn't change that. Am I right?"

She swatted me upside the head. "Nope. You're dead wrong. Which, by the way, would be a fantastic nickname for you. 'Dead Wrong.' Because you always find corpses, and you're usually wrong. But I digress. I was going to tell you that I don't believe in fault or fate. I believe in making the best of any situation you're in, and let the why of it be figured out above." She pointed upward.

"On the roof of the train?"

She smacked me again. "By the Flying Spaghetti Monster. My point is that it's not our job to get caught up in stuff we can't fix. Our job is to take our lessons where they're delivered. So, you and dead bodies have a thing going. You could say that's bad."

I raised my eyebrows. She held her swatting hand up as a warning. I dropped my eyebrows.

"Or you could say that it gives you the opportunity to help people, which you happen to be very good at. Just like I could say I'm old, or I could say I'm experienced. Ms. Wrenshall next door could say she's neurotic, or she could say she's eccentric. We all have our quirks, and it's our job to build on our strengths rather than dwell on our weaknesses. So get over that quivering bottom lip and those tears that are thinking of falling, and do it now." She planted her hands on her hips. "You've got a murder to solve, and that little girl is going to need you to crack it quick-like."

Chapter 19

Mrs. Berns was right, though I hated to admit it. I was going to spend zero more time feeling sorry for myself and would do whatever I could to help Aimee. Unfortunately, the conductor wasn't letting anyone near Aimee's room.

So I did what I could: I unlocked and cracked our door, and I listened.

The EMTs arrived twenty minutes after the train stopped at the station. They made quick work of bundling up the body. I heard one of them clearly say, "No visible cause of death." Some of my stress lifted. Maybe it hadn't been murder. Maybe Aimee's mom had died of a heart attack or some other invisible disease. She was young for that, but it wasn't unheard of. But then, where had Aimee and her dad gone? That was weird.

I poked my head out when I heard the EMTs leaving the room, but there wasn't much to see. The tight angles of the hallway meant they couldn't use their gurney, so they had Aimee's mom's corpse in a black body bag, held between them. The conductor glared at me, so I ducked back into our room, but not before noting that Ms. Wrenshall was also peeking out of her doorway.

It wasn't until three hours later that we were brought breakfast, and another hour after that the Glendive chief of police showed up. He was not a Gary Wohnt, and for that I was grateful. He was around six feet tall, late fifties, built like Santa Claus with a hound-dog face. His blue eyes were kind. I'd spotted him coming through the crack in the door and so had time to shoot to my seat and pretend I was reading across from Mrs. Berns when he knocked at our door.

"Come in."

He smiled at both of us, holding out a hand. "Bob Harris. I'm head of the police force here in Glendive."

His voice was deep and gravelly, perfect for a radio announcer. I liked him instantly. "Mira James. This is Mrs. Berns. Have you found Aimee and her dad?"

His lip twitched. "You don't waste time. Did you know the family?"

"Just from the train ride," I said. "We got on in Detroit Lakes, back in Minnesota. Aimee said they're from New York, so I assume that's where they got on."

"That's right," he said, glancing down at his notes.

Mrs. Berns coughed. "Was she murdered?"

I kicked her, but it was too late.

"Too soon to tell. Do you know this gentleman?" He held out a mug shot. The guy was lean and hungry-looking, with pockmarked skin and a sneer.

Mrs. Berns shook her head. I mirrored the gesture.

"Do you think he's involved in whatever happened to Aimee's mom?" I asked.

Harris's lips tightened. "Not directly. His body was found at the Fargo train station, near some abandoned cars. Two gunshots to the head, point blank."

That information tried to sink in but was not having luck. "Wait, there've been *two* murders connected to this train?"

By way of answering, Chief Harris glanced back at his notepad. "You're on your way to the PI conference in Portland, aren't you, Ms. James?"

My eyes widened. I'd misjudged him. He might have looked like a kindly small-town sheriff, but he'd done his homework. I wondered how often he was underestimated. Probably made his job quite a bit easier. "I am. I'm not a licensed PI, though."

He kept staring at his notes. I wanted to snatch them out of his hand. Did they say that I was a dead-body magnet, possibly that I should receive a little extra scrutiny if a corpse showed up in my vicinity? Or maybe it was a blank sheet of paper, and good ol' Bob was just trying to get me to confess to killing the woman next door. *Curse words.* Silence was my archenemy. I felt compelled to fill it. "There's another PI on this train, a licensed one. His name's Terry Downs."

Chief Harris raised his eyes. He didn't appear particularly excited by that information. "You don't say. What else can you tell me?"

Not much. We settled back into silence. I lasted all of twenty seconds. "Aimee reminded me of someone."

He cocked an eyebrow. "Who?"

I sighed. I'd gotten myself in too deep. There was nowhere out but forward. "A girl who was abducted when I was five. Her name was Noelle."

Mrs. Berns stiffened next to me. I'd never told her about Noelle. What would've been the purpose?

"Do you think there's any connection?" Chief Harris asked.

I didn't, except for my failure: I had let the abductor take Noelle, and now no one could find Aimee. I swallowed past the tightness in my throat. "No. But I'm worried for Aimee. Can you tell me if she's been located?"

He stared at me for an unblinking eon, and I recognized the steel behind the kindness of his blue eyes. He would do what he could to solve this. "She has not. Neither has her father. According to Ms. Wrenshall next door, you two were the last ones to see Aimee and her dad. What time was that?"

I told him about the brief interaction outside their door last night, and everything else I could remember, which wasn't much. Mrs. Berns had little to add. After it was clear we had no more to offer, Chief

Harris thanked us for our time and was about to step out when one last question seemed to occur to him, almost as if it were an afterthought.

"Before I go, can I ask? Did you hear a scream last night?"

I nodded. "You mean this morning. Right before the train stopped just outside of Glendive."

"No," he said, his expression odd, "at two thirty-four this morning. Ms. Wrenshall said it woke her up, and she looked out into the hall. She saw you talking to a porter just outside the room where the dead body was discovered."

Chapter 20

Wrenshall was a yellow-livered tattletale.

I tried to explain myself, even stooping to share the bad-poops aspect of it, but I stumbled over my words. It sounded suspicious, even to my own ears, and I was on my side. Chief Bob Harris listened without expression, writing furiously. I was beginning to hate that notepad. Once my story spilled out, he left, promising to return if he needed more information.

After he closed the door behind himself, Mrs. Berns began shaking her head.

"What?" I asked.

"I've heard *confessions* that sounded less guilty. Why'd you get so nervous all of a sudden?"

I threw up my hands. "Were you not sitting through all of that? Ms. Wrenshall fingered me as being outside Aimee's door around the same time as a scream, and the next day, Aimee's mom's found murdered? I look like a suspect!"

"Well, you sure do now." She squinted. "You also look like you're unnaturally poop-focused." She waited a beat, then leaned forward and dropped her voice. "Your good qualities are not always immediately apparent, you know what I mean?"

My heart sank because I did. I knew exactly what she meant. I was potentially in deep on this latest murder and disappearance, and I was trapped like a peanut in a can while suspicions swirled around me.

"You want to talk about that girl getting abducted when you were young?" Mrs. Berns asked.

The switch in focus almost gave me whiplash. "Not much to tell. We were playing, and a man tried to get us into his car." I swiped at my eyes and kept my gaze on my hands. "Noelle was in front of me, or I would've gone first and been the one who was stolen."

She didn't respond. I finally looked up and saw tears on her face that matched mine. She didn't hug or lecture me, just met me where I was at, and I loved her for it.

The train wasn't going anywhere and neither were we, so we settled into reading. I was periodically distracted by commotion outside our window—train staff being taken out by the police and led back in, passengers being brought out to smoke under guard, men in suits inspecting the train, peering into every crack. It was tense.

No one entered or left our end of the train for about an hour, which was why the next movement on the platform caught my eye. I glanced up. Mrs. Berns was asleep across from me, *Cosmo* open across her chest. Staring back outside, I couldn't identify what had drawn my attention from my book. It was going on late afternoon now, and shadows were falling across the platform.

Then I spotted it—two people, scurrying from the brush at the side of the track toward the train. Both figures were slight, but one could have been a child. Aimee? I jumped up, pressing my face to the glass, but the people were too far away. If they hopped on the train, they must have boarded at the caboose.

I fell back into my seat, heart hammering. That had definitely looked like Aimee and her dad, but my eyes and ears had played so many tricks on me the past twelve-plus hours. It could have been any two people—a couple who had slipped off for a rendezvous, workers who'd sneaked to town and wanted to reboard before the police came back, local teenagers come to check out why the train was stopped for so long.

But what if it *was* Aimee and her dad?

If I told Chief Harris, it might make me look even more involved. Plus, Aimee might be in trouble. I could make it worse by narcing her out. I'd just decided that my best bet was to keep my mouth shut until I got more information when a knock fell on our cabin door.

I jumped in my chair. Mrs. Berns snuffled awake.

"Yes?" I said, my hands clammy.

The door slid open. Ms. Wrenshall slipped in. She wore a new face of makeup and looked far more composed than she had that morning.

"They're gone," she whispered.

"Who?" I asked, my mouth downturned. I was still cheesed at her for telling on me. I knew that wasn't fair, but I was low on care.

"The Glenlivet police."

"Glendive," I corrected her. "And I'm sure they're around somewhere."

"No, I just saw them drive off. All of them. The parking lot is on the other side of the train, and I was out in the hallway, peering through those windows."

Mrs. Berns leaned forward. "Out in the hallway, eh? When you were distinctly told to wait in your room? Say, I think I saw you slink next door in the middle of the night last night, too."

Ms. Wrenshall's eyes widened. "That isn't true!"

Mrs. Berns shrugged. "Probably not, but it'd make me feel good to tattle, like you did on Mira."

Here's one way to identify a best friend: they'll act petty in your stead so you can take the high road. "Now, Mrs. Berns, that's not entirely fair. Ms. Wrenshall had to tell the truth when she was asked. But I wonder what else she saw last night?" I turned my attention to the woman in question, clasping my hands. "Do tell."

Her eyes glittered. She'd guessed this game. "So I tell you everything I saw to keep you from lying about my whereabouts last night?"

"Bingo!" Mrs. Berns said, smiling. "You're a lot smarter than you look."

Ms. Wrenshall grimaced. "I'll tell you what I told the police. I heard a scream at two thirty-four this morning. It was such an unusual time that I remembered it: two, three, four. Anyhow, I'd been staring at the clock because my insomnia wouldn't let me sleep. I lay in my bunk, waiting for another scream, when I heard voices in the hall. I peeked through and saw you and that Black porter talking. He went toward the back of the train, and you went toward the cabin where the murder happened."

I choked on my own spit. "You told the police that?"

"It was the truth."

"I had to poop!"

Mrs. Berns made a *tsk*ing sound. "Remember what we talked about? You really should broaden your conversational topics or people will avoid you."

I was about to explode when I had a thought. "Wait," I said to Ms. Wrenshall. "You didn't call for the porter last night?"

She pursed her lips. "Why bother? They never come after-hours."

But last night, when I'd nearly run into Reed outside my door, he'd told me she'd called for him.

Which made one of them a big, hairy liar.

Chapter 21

Ms. Wrenshall definitely wasn't lying about the police leaving the scene. I couldn't spot any of them outside, and the parking lot on the other side of the train was empty of official vehicles. With the police gone for the moment and both my neck and Aimee's on the line, no way was I staying put in my cabin, police orders be damned. I herded Ms. Wrenshall into her cabin and convinced Mrs. Berns that we couldn't *both* leave our room. One of us needed to stay back and lie and/or eavesdrop if the police returned. She relented only after I promised she'd get to "run reconnaissance" next time.

Police tape crisscrossed Cabin 1. I had no intention of violating the space and possibly messing up an investigation, so I just peeked inside. The room appeared not only clean but empty. The only evidence that someone had been rooming there was in the mussed-up bed. Otherwise, there was not a stitch of luggage, clothing, food wrappers, or reading materials. The room presented as if Aimee's dad had known they'd need to make a quick getaway and had packed up beforehand.

I guessed he was the number-one suspect. Husbands always were when a wife was murdered. If she was murdered, that was. The jury was still out on that one. But if she hadn't been deliberately killed, why would Aimee and her dad have fled? And was it coincidence that a man had been murdered in Fargo, shortly before Aimee's mom had died?

Strange days, indeed.

After I'd gotten as much as I could from a visual scan of the room, I headed toward the rear of the train, where I thought I'd seen the two people board. Cars 12, 13, and 14 were similar to my own—a welcome kiosk of coffee and snacks at the head of each near the public bathroom, then arrays of rooms to one side of the aisle, all their doors and curtains shut. It was almost like walking through a ghost train, except I could hear hushed talking behind the doors.

The foyer between each car felt like an unsafe elevator as I waited for the door behind me to close and the one in front to open. Something about being in the rubber between trains now made me feel vulnerable.

Beyond Car 14 was storage. I was worried I wouldn't be able to access it, but the door slid open with ease. I spotted hundreds of suitcases, snowboards, and some odd-shaped packages. The walls seemed closer than in the rest of the cars, and once my eyes adjusted, I could make out what looked like cupboards behind the luggage racks. I peeked around and found nothing suspicious. The lower level was identical to the upper, both in layout and in the lack of anything out of place. I was about to return to the floor above when I heard a scraping sound near the rear. I whipped around.

"Aimee?" My short hairs were on alert, each one vibrating, but there was no answer. Suddenly, I felt seriously afraid. I ran up the stairs, glancing behind me the whole way. It took every ounce of my willpower not to scurry back to my own room yelling "Mom!" Instead, I forced myself to walk toward the last car on the train: the caboose.

I opened the door at the far end of the storage car.

I stepped into the bladder between.

I pushed on the panel that would let me into the caboose.

Nothing.

I pushed again, but it wasn't opening. The foyer was dark, but I felt around with my hands until I located it: a recession for some type of key. This car was off-limits to passengers. Part disappointed and part relieved, I made my way back to my own cabin.

Police chief Bob Harris was waiting when I arrived.

Chapter 22

My stomach dropped audibly. Hoping that Chief Harris subscribed to the "If I can't see you, you can't see me" school of thought, I kept my eyes locked on my feet and brushed past him and into my room. Because I was looking down, I didn't see Mrs. Berns until it was too late. I knocked her to the ground, where I first noticed that she was shirtless. I grabbed a blanket from the nearby chair to cover what was an admittedly nicer bra than any I owned.

"Stop it—I got this," she hissed to me as I helped her up, pushing me to the side.

I watched with a cross between horror and admiration as she continued what was certainly a seduction to distract the police chief from my absence.

"So, Chief Bob, as I was explaining before Mira so rudely interrupted us, I find that yoga greatly increases my flexibility and stamina." She smiled slyly before dropping into what was supposed to be Downward-Facing Dog but came across more as Canine in Heat. I had to look away. Bob Harris had the decency to do the same.

"And as *I* was explaining," he said, glancing down the hall uncomfortably, "I am afraid I don't have time for yoga, and I'm incredibly sorry to have interrupted your practice just as you were, ahem, removing your shirt."

I almost felt sorry for him. He was trying to do his job. "Can we help you with something?"

He trained his gaze on me, careful not to let it land anywhere near Mrs. Berns, who was Cat/Cowing with all the single-mindedness of Jenna Jameson on set. "You can start by telling me where you were just now."

Mrs. Berns, realizing her audience had moved on, stood and pulled on her shirt. "She was looking for a place to poop because she clogged our toilet here."

I blushed, but it might have been from pride at how quickly she concocted that lie by sewing together last night's truth with this moment's falsehood.

"It's true," I said, playing the blush for all it was worth. "My tummy's still upset. I went to Car Twelve to use their bathroom."

"Why not use this car's public restroom, like you did last night?"

I held my hands, palms up. "Trying to spread the wealth."

He seemed to be struggling for words, then finally gave up and ran his hand through his thinning hair. "I stopped by to let you know that we're lifting the lockdown. Everyone is free to move about the train, but you can't disembark for the time being."

"Woo-hoo!" Mrs. Berns yelled. "I was going stir crazy."

"Have you found anything?" I asked.

"Have you?" he replied, reminding me that he was not a man to underestimate.

I lifted a shoulder. "Just that the toilet paper in Car Twelve is no softer than in Car Eleven."

He nodded thoughtfully. "The train will be staying put for a while. It goes without saying that the scene of the death is off-limits. I'll have someone posted outside the door. There will also be police officers posted around the train to make sure no one comes or goes."

"Thank you," I said, because a response seemed warranted.

He risked a glance at Mrs. Berns, then back at me. "You two are quite a pair."

You have no idea.

Chief Harris left, presumably to share the news with the other sleeper cars. Mrs. Berns informed me that she'd removed her shirt immediately after I'd headed out because her girls were her "best weapons in the fight against getting busted." Enlightened on that front, I led the way to the snack car to collect food and information.

Car 10 had the same subdued feel as the other sleeper cars I'd just visited. The atmosphere in Car 9, however, was chaos. A pair of thirtysomething men argued with what I was guessing was a plainclothes officer stationed at the exit. Kids were either crying or running up and down the aisles, and a makeshift food war meant that Froot Loops were being tossed from one side of the car to the other. Mrs. Berns and I kept our heads down as we threaded our way through.

"They're going to have to let these people out soon," I muttered.

Mrs. Berns nodded her agreement and led the way to Coach Car 8, which had yet another feel, likely due to the hazy, sweet smell of pot and the makeshift music coming from some of the snowboarders. One strummed on an acoustic guitar, another played harmonica, and Jed beat his chair tray like a bongo. The rest of the train car was either swaying to the music, whispering in small groups, or napping.

"Now this is more like it," Mrs. Berns crowed. She raised her voice to be heard above the music. "Who's got the good stuff?"

Jed stopped playing his tray-bongo to wave at us. "Mira! Mrs. Berns! I'm so glad you two are OK. Wanna make music with us?"

"You betcha," Mrs. Berns said. "As soon as I sample your weed."

I nudged her. "Nuh-uh. No wacky tobacky for you. We've got work to do."

"Just a toke?" She tossed me pleading eyes. "Helps me to focus."

"Helps you to think the word 'titter' is the most hilarious thing ever invented before you fall into a deep coma, is more like it," I said. "Remember New Year's Eve?"

She got a faraway look in her eyes before she started giggling. *"Titter,"* she said.

I pushed her forward. "Exactly. Let's keep moving. Jed, can you keep your ear to the ground for us? Let us know if you hear anything about why the train is stopped?"

It'd occurred to me that maybe not everyone knew there'd been a possible homicide onboard, and certainly most people didn't know that there had been a fatal shooting at the Fargo train station.

"Sure, man. And can you pick me up some salted peanuts and a Coke while you're in the café car?"

I told him I would, and we continued on. The viewing car was packed, as usual, but the mood was calm overall, maybe because the people here were close to food. Still, it was a wonder the officers outside the windows weren't making them nervous. I tapped an older man on the shoulder, a white-haired guy right inside the door who was reading in one of the cup chairs.

"Excuse me, do you know why the train is stopped?"

Mrs. Berns turned, her expression at first confused and then keen. She picked up right away that I was testing to see what everyone had been told. "Yeah, no one is telling us anything back in the sleepers."

He put his finger in the book to hold his page. "Something mechanical. I hear it's making some people on the train antsy, but I'd rather they take the time to fix it than go off the rails, wouldn't you?"

"Definitely." I tipped my head toward the window. "But why are the police out there, if it's just mechanical?"

He pulled a cell phone out of his pocket. I thought I really should invest in one of those, but who would I call? My friends were either with me or could reach me on a landline.

"I can tell you that firsthand," he said, "or close to it. I boarded back at Fargo. Two dangerous convicts escaped from the prison there, and they think they might be on this train. Damn phone's been ringing off the hook with family telling me."

Chapter 23

Well, that was a new spread on our crap toast.

We thanked the man for the information and made our way to the lower half of the car to the snacks. A line of people snaked up the stairs, so we queued up at the end. I leaned in close so no one could hear me and whispered into Mrs. Berns's ear. "What do you make of all that?"

"That we should have flown," she replied, not bothering to lower her voice.

"No, about the escaped convicts."

She sighed and finally lowered her voice. "That we're locking our door from now on. And that the death next door is taking on a distinctly more murderous tinge."

The line inched forward, and we found ourselves on the first step leading down, giving me a false sense of privacy, though I kept my mouth close to Mrs. Berns's ear. "I think I saw them."

"What?"

I made the mistake of talking a little bit louder. "Aimee and her dad. I thought I saw them sneak onto the train. That's part of the reason I left."

A woman spoke behind me, her voice shrill. "You saw the little girl?"

I swiveled, my heart plummeting. Ms. Wrenshall stood there, sucking a pint of milk through a straw. "I meant back in Detroit Lakes," I stammered.

"What's this?" Terry Downs, our PI dinner companion from the previous night, appeared behind her shoulder.

"Mira thinks she saw the daughter and husband of the murdered woman reboard the train."

Trying to convince someone that the truth is a lie is a tricky move, one I call the Reverse Fib. It should not be attempted by amateurs, but if you find yourself cornered, here is the key rule: the Reverse Fib must itself be at least 50 percent truth because the person you are RFing will already have caught a whiff of honesty; to lead them away from the original truth, you need to mimic that scent.

"That's not true! I saw them get on back at Detroit Lakes, and I was wondering if they were lying about being from New York."

Neither Terry nor Ms. Wrenshall looked like they were buying it.

"Have I talked to either of you about yoga?" Mrs. Berns asked, beginning to pull up her shirt. I grabbed her hands, my mind scurrying for a more appropriate way to throw them off the trail, when the crackle of the viewing car PA system saved me.

"Ladies and gentlemen, I have an announcement. We have a very special guest boarding."

Conversations in the viewing car hushed immediately. Ms. Wrenshall and Terry stood aside, giving Mrs. Berns and me room to step back onto the top floor. Everyone stared expectantly toward the speakers mounted in the corners of the cabin, as if the someone special were going to walk out of one of them. Instead, he strolled through the door nearest the dining car.

I recognized him immediately.

Chapter 24

I am not a big TV watcher. It isn't elitism; I just have terrible reception out at the double-wide. However, one channel came in consistently, and that was RCN, which was devoted to reality television. As a die-hard people-watcher, I have no issue with reality TV other than the scripted feel of it.

That said, a show that I'd caught once or twice had rubbed me wrong. It was called *Attenborough PI*, and featured Doghn (pronounced "Don," which says all you need to know) Attenborough, an "actual private investigator with twenty-three years of experience running his own agencies in three different countries, escaping danger, thwarting criminals, and saving lives and reputations."

He'd been propelled into the national spotlight by solving some high-profile case I couldn't remember the details of, and he'd rolled the exposure into a TV show. He came across as an arrogant, precious man, and I was looking at him right now, in the flesh.

He appeared smaller in person than on TV, no taller than five five, with a head so big it looked like he was standing near me even though he was ten feet away. His predominant characteristics were a mustache curled up at the tips and a cherubic pink nose.

"Hello!" He held his hand in the air to quiet the excited murmuring. I hadn't been able to place his accent when I'd watched his TV show, and it was no clearer in person. It seemed like a Mississippi twang wearing a British coat. "Doghn Attenborough. Pleased to meet you all. I hear you've had a little trouble." He chuckled dryly. "Well, don't worry, I'm here to help."

Several people on the train clearly recognized him. Mrs. Berns was not one of them. "Who's the puffy little rooster?" she asked me, not using her inside voice.

Doghn's smile slipped, but he glided through the packed car to where she and I stood with Terry and Ms. Wrenshall. He opened the blazer of his three-piece suit, retrieved a silver case, and flicked out a business card in a signature move that I'd seen him perform on his show.

"Doghn Attenborough, actual private investigator with twenty-three years—"

Mrs. Berns scratched at his card.

"What are you doing?" he asked.

"It looks like a couple extra letters fell onto your first name, Don," she said, "and I was trying to see if they came off. It'll be mighty expensive to reprint these if not. Maybe some Wite-Out?"

He sniffed. "That is the correct spelling of my name."

This close, he smelled like Aramis, which my high school gym teacher used to wear. I associated the odor with swishy pants, whistles, and incompetence. "You said you're here to help?" I asked.

I didn't add to the question because I wanted to hear exactly what he thought the trouble was. The possible murder of Aimee's mom? The fact that Aimee and her dad were missing? The gunshot victim back at the Fargo train station? The escaped convicts who might or might not be on the train? The mechanical problem that likely didn't exist?

He snatched his card back from Mrs. Berns and returned it to the silver case. I wondered if that was the first time he'd ever had to do that. "The missing persons case, obviously."

"Who's missing?" I prompted him.

"A father and daughter."

The rest of the train inhabitants had returned to their conversations, though some appeared to be surreptitiously eavesdropping on Doghn.

"And who called you to help?" I asked. Seriously. The guy lived in Michigan, as far as I knew. Why would the police ask him to come all the way to Montana to help with what looked like a tragic but not particularly unusual missing-persons-possible-homicide case? And how had he arrived on such short notice?

"I'm the PI. I'll ask the questions here," he said, stroking the tips (swear to god) of his delicate mustache.

Mrs. Berns harrumphed. "Mira here is a private investigator, too, and so is Terry," she said, stabbing her thumb at the man who'd been quietly absorbing all this. "I'm in training. We're all headed to the PI conference in Portland, so I'm sorry to inform you that you're not the belle of this ball."

"Is that so?" Doghn glanced at me with renewed interest before letting his eyes flit to Terry. "Well, we must work together! The more the merrier. Let us first go to the scene of the crime. Porter, deliver my bags to my room!"

Reed materialized behind Doghn, a valise under each arm. He appeared disgruntled at best. We all followed with varying levels of enthusiasm.

For my part, I couldn't wait to hear the story of how Doghn had reached this train and how much he knew. I was also itching to find out what the law would think about him being here to "help," how he'd found a room on what was supposedly a booked-solid Valentine Train, and most importantly, if he could locate Aimee.

I hoped with every inch of me that he could.

Chapter 25

Following Doghn was a bit like following a parade float. He gathered people as he passed, showering them with attention, signing autographs. I noticed two women scribble furiously when they saw him approaching and slip him notes as he passed. Celebrity is the oddest thing—a twisted version of the human need to believe in something bigger than ourselves.

I giggled at the thought. Doghn was a munchkin among men. He was famous, though, and many people clearly idolized him.

"Mira! Mrs. Berns!" Jed called out, spotting us coming toward him. "Did you get my peanuts and pop?"

Doghn was in front of me. He gave Jed a passing glance, distracting him from his original question.

"Hey, dude," Jed said. "Didn't I see you board back in Fargo? How's the train treating you?"

Doghn stopped. "What?"

"I thought I saw you get on back in Fargo, only you didn't have that bitchin' face fur back then. Right?"

The look Doghn gave him was withering. He parsed out his words as if English were not Jed's first language. "Son, I did not board this train in Fargo. I boarded here, just now. And I assure you that this 'face fur' is not removable. If you'll excuse me?"

Jed's face fell. I was going to comfort him, but Mrs. Berns took care of it. "The guy's an asshole, kid." She ignored Doghn's glare. "Also, we forgot your Coke and peanuts, but here's five bucks. See you at dinner?"

"Sure thing," Jed said, taking the money. He squeezed behind Terry and made his way to the viewing and café car. The rest of our posse continued back toward the sleepers, Doghn signing more autographs and collecting more notes as he went.

The travel through Car 10 went much quicker, as no one could see Doghn unless their door was open, which seemed to disappoint him.

"Where is my room?" he called behind him.

Reed, who brought up the rear, told him to continue to Car 14.

I paused, causing Mrs. Berns to run into me, Ms. Wrenshall into her, and Terry into her. "Hey, Reed, I thought all the sleeper cars were taken?"

"Car Fourteen has a room reserved for the conductor. It's been assigned to Mr. Attenborough for the duration of the trip."

Must be nice to be famous. "Where's the conductor sleeping?"

"Car Three, with the rest of the staff."

I returned my attention to Doghn leading the pack. He'd just stepped into the foyer separating two cars. I jumped in so I was next to him. The foyers were much easier to navigate without the train moving, and I wanted to keep an eye on the guy. He pushed the button opening the next car, and both he and I navigated the hallway's sharp angle in front of the welcome kiosk.

Police chief Bob Harris was waiting for us.

I stayed back, letting Doghn barrel into that fight on his own.

"Doghn Attenborough," he said, extending his hand. "I'm guessing from your haircut and bearing that you're in charge of this investigation?"

One point for Doghn.

That's when I remembered the case he'd become famous for. It had gone cold when he was brought on board. A business owner had been in Detroit for a conference. Hotel cameras caught her going into the elevator, presumably to her room, around two a.m. The cameras never caught her leaving. A utility man discovered her in a ditch twenty-four hours later: she'd been brutally beaten and left for dead. She remained in a coma for weeks. When she awoke, she couldn't remember anything about the attack.

Police were able to trace her steps for the entire evening preceding her attack, including a tryst she had with the night manager before entering the elevator. The night manager was a suspect for a short while, as was a conference employee. Each agreed to a DNA test, but their DNA did not match what had been found beneath her fingernails. The police had reached a dead end.

Enter Doghn Attenborough, private investigator.

He was, according to the story I'd read, a modestly successful local PI at the time. The hotel chain where the woman had stayed hired him to look into the case. Apparently, she was suing the hotel for breach of safety.

Doghn reviewed all the records. The hotel had cameras at every exit. The woman had not left by any of them. Her room had been on the hotel's third floor. Every window on that floor and above had a built-in security feature that ensured it could not open wider than three inches.

Even so, to be thorough, the police searched the ground below her window, as well as the property around the entire hotel. There was no sign of a struggle. It was a mystery. Doghn conducted his own investigation of the room, hotel, and grounds, but by the time he was brought in, the room had been cleaned hundreds of times, and two winters had come and gone, changing the landscape around the hotel. He found nothing.

Then he began watching the hotel security tapes of that evening.

He viewed them dozens of times, he claimed, until he caught it: the victim going into the elevator at 2:12 a.m. She waved at someone, later identified as the night manager. She was alone on the elevator when the doors closed. Only a handful of people rode the elevator throughout the night, and then many more the next day. By the time the utility worker discovered the unconscious woman, Doghn counted more than a hundred people riding the hotel elevator, and only one was suspicious.

He was a big guy, linebacker big. That wasn't a crime, and neither was the fact that he carried a huge suitcase as he exited the elevator at 5:34 a.m. The problem was in how he picked up the suitcase, almost as if it had something heavy in it—maybe 119 pounds, awkwardly folded.

Like a body.

The man, Rolf Nilsen, was a traveling salesman originally from Ohio. His DNA matched the samples found on the woman as well as DNA connected with seven other assault cold cases across the country. It was an impressive bit of sleuthing, and I respected that. It was Doghn's personality that I wasn't a fan of, at least not yet.

"Bob Harris, Glendive Police." He offered his hand to Doghn. "I'm holding down the fort for the time being. Can I help you?"

"I'd like a look into that room." Doghn pointed over Chief Harris's shoulder at Aimee's empty cabin, still festooned with police tape.

"I bet you would," Chief Harris said, smiling kindly. I wondered if Doghn was going to fall for it. "But this is an active investigation. No one's going in or out unless they're official. Sorry."

Doghn stroked the tips of his mustache and then glanced furtively into the room. "Thanks for your time, *Bob*," he said, before addressing the rest of us. "The law has spoken. Any good PI respects that. I'll see you all at dinner?"

I watched him walk away, Reed and luggage in tow. *Well, that was anticlimactic.* Ms. Wrenshall murmured something about being tired and disappeared into her room. Terry said he needed to get back to the snack car. Mrs. Berns echoed that thought.

Chickenshits.

I tried to follow them, but Chief Harris gently grabbed my arm. "Got a minute?"

To be arrested? "Sure. What's on your mind?"

Could he hear my pulse? Of the many unsavory aspects of being a corpse magnet, arousing police suspicions was one of my least favorite.

He led me into my cabin and closed the door behind us. My blood instantly thickened. This was not good.

"Would you like to sit down?"

Could he see my knees shaking? "Sure." I indicated the chair across from me. "You?"

"No thanks."

Curse words. He'd walked me right into this one. With him standing and me sitting, he possessed all the power in the room. He pulled out his notebook and flipped it open.

"What do you think of Mr. Attenborough?"

I tried to hide my surprise. I'd thought he was going to ask me if I wanted the fish, chicken, or veggie option in prison. "A little theatrical for my taste, but I think he's competent."

Chief Harris nodded. "Me too."

I leaned forward. "What's he doing here?"

"As near as I can tell, he was driving to the same conference as you when he caught wind of the train kerfuffle via the police band radio. I'm guessing he's here for the publicity, and that AmeriTrain would be financially grateful if he could turn this around quickly for them."

"Makes sense." My hamster wheels were spinning. Chief Harris was trying to quid pro quo me, which meant he hadn't yet found anything. It was a good plan, except he didn't know that I had my own agenda. "You guys find Aimee yet?"

He glanced out the window. Two police officers stood on the platform, relaxed, chatting. "Nope. Not her dad, either. You?"

"Nope. Do you know what killed Aimee's mom?"

"Nope." He had the graciousness to smile. If he didn't before, he now knew that I knew the game we were playing. I tried not to like him too much. I had a feeling that would be dangerous, as his only skin in this game was solving this case. He didn't care whether I fell on the friend or foe side of the score sheet.

"Any lead on the body back in Fargo?" I asked.

By way of answer, he reached inside his coat pocket and yanked out a photo. "You recognize this guy?"

My throat tightened. It was that creeper Fatigues, the one who'd slunk on the perimeters at the Fargo train station and hairy eyeballed me in the viewing car.

"I saw him outside at the Fargo station and then on board last night."

"Good eye. His name is Chester Pimmel. He escaped prison two days ago, along with a man named Steve Nunn. Chester is a bad seed, rotating through juvie and jail since he was twelve. His most recent conviction sent him to the federal pen. Voluntary manslaughter. He assaulted a woman outside a bar, and when her boyfriend found out and came after him, Chester killed him. Said what he was doing with the woman was consensual and that he was just defending himself from the other man and it got out of hand." I wanted to cover my ears, but Chief Harris continued.

"Steve Nunn is a follower. History of petty crimes, then he kills someone driving drunk and ends up behind bars for twenty years."

I swallowed past the lump in my throat. "They're both on the train?"

"No. Steve is the body found at the Fargo train station, his face pierced with lead. We discovered Chester in one of the train's lower-level bathrooms. He's being held for questioning in Steve Nunn's murder as well as the death of Sofia Ramos."

"Aimee's mom?"

"The woman who died next door," he cautioned. "So far, we only have her name, not her relations to any of the other passengers. I was hoping you could help in that area."

I shook my head. "I really don't know anything I haven't already told you. I understand how it must look from where you're sitting—standing—but I just had a couple brief conversations with the girl, Aimee. I never saw her before the station at Detroit Lakes, or after I ran into her just before bedtime last night." Unless I'd seen her reboard with her dad a few hours ago, but I was keeping that card tight to my chest for the time being.

Chief Harris watched me so intently that I felt my talker begin to kick in. I tossed a question into the chute in the hopes of distracting him. "Is that why you let us all move around the train? Because you think you caught the killer?"

He kept staring at me, well past the point of uncomfortable. I felt all sorts of confessions burbling up—sometimes I picked my nose when I was driving, but only at the nostril edges, and I didn't like corn because once, when I was a kid, I'd seen a pile of animal scat that was almost entirely whole pieces of corn held together by some fur and loose turd, and ever since then, I couldn't look at corn kernels without thinking, *Poopcorn*. When Johnny slept over I sometimes got up early and sneaked out of bed to brush my teeth and hair, apply lip gloss and a dab of perfume behind each ear, and slip back in so he'd think I was half-unicorn, and—

"What are you thinking?"

I snapped back into focus and glanced at Harris. He appeared truly puzzled. I opened my mouth, and then I closed it. "You don't want to know."

He almost looked like he believed me. "The odds are good that Mr. Nunn was murdered by Mr. Pimmel. We still don't know the cause of Ms. Ramos's death. Given that, and the serious snowstorm that's heading up from the south, we're not only letting you move about the train, we're letting the train continue on its route."

"Really?"

He shrugged. "Sometimes capitalism trumps justice." He made a huffing noise. "Who am I kidding? It always trumps justice. AmeriTrain brings business to this part of the state. The DA doesn't want to 'draw out an extensive investigation' when it seems clear to him who killed whom and why. We're treating Ms. Ramos's death as due to natural causes. If we're wrong, we have information on every passenger here."

Made sense, but it still surprised me that they were going to let their crime scene roll away.

Chief Harris seemed to read my mind. "What choice do we have?" He handed me a card, this one much plainer than Doghn's. "Call if you see or hear anything, all right? The conductor said he had a phone you can use, or you can talk to one of the plainclothes who will be at every stop this train visits."

I didn't know whether to be flattered or suspicious. Was he banking on me confessing or cracking the case? Either way, I didn't think I'd need Glendive, Montana, police chief Bob Harris's card.

I couldn't have been more wrong.

Chapter 26

Chief Harris left my door open when he departed. I heard him knock on Ms. Wrenshall's cabin and give her a courtesy update much briefer than mine before he left our car, reappearing on the platform, where he approached the two officers. Their posture immediately straightened. He was a man who commanded respect, despite his initial aw-shucks, small-town demeanor.

Or maybe because of that, and maybe because he got the job done.

His working theory was off on this one, though. I felt it in my bones, and I guessed he did, too. Something stinky had happened to Sofia Ramos. There was no reason for Aimee and her dad to disappear otherwise. And it seemed unlikely that the convict's murder was connected other than coincidence. Most killers had their MO, and violent men who murdered using guns didn't turn around and kill quietly, without leaving a mark. If Sofia had been murdered, I was confident that Chester Pimmel hadn't done it.

"Knock knock."

I jumped, my head swiveling to the open door. Chad, my "dance" partner last night, stood in the doorway.

"Yes?" I didn't mean for my voice to be so sharp. Shame did that to me. Looking at the kid, I couldn't help but remember the *squish-crack* his privates made when I face-planted into them.

"Have you heard? The train'll be moving again within the hour."

"Yup." I didn't want to encourage this friendship. He seemed like a perfectly nice person, but I had too much on my plate already.

"Hey, I was going to ask you . . ."

He didn't say anything more, just stood there with his face open. Man, did it make me crabby when a person asked a question that wasn't really a question. *Grow a pair.* I stared him down.

"Well," he said finally, glancing at his feet, "I was wondering if I could join you for supper."

Mrs. Berns appeared behind Chad and pushed underneath his arm to enter our room. "Least you could do is say yes, Mira, after you molested him last night. Usually, it's kosher to buy dinner *before* you explore a man's crotch, but whatever floats your boat. Oh, and Doghn will be eating with us, too. He told Reed, and Reed told me. We're on for six thirty."

This dinner was going from bad to worse. Eating with Doghn? Then I had a realization. "We can't. Where will Jed sit?"

Mrs. Berns began rustling through her gigantic purse. "On his ass. He said the dining car is too expensive, but I think he's got the hots for that cutie he met in Car Eight. He stocked up on sandwiches for the both of them and told me they're going to have a picnic in a private place he found on the train. Said we're more than welcome to join him, but I know a man making a play when I see one. So, Face Magnet," she said, turning to Chad, "you can join us at six thirty. Don't expect any more action, though. Mira is a love-'em-and-leave-'em type."

"Thank you!" Young Chad had the good sense to disappear before I could retract or otherwise modify Mrs. Berns's offer.

I pointed a glare at her. "Did you ever think that I didn't want to eat with that kid?"

"Did you ever think that whining makes your arms red?"

I glanced at my arm, bare below my T-shirt. "Does not."

She pinched me, quick, hard enough to leave a mark. "Does too. See? Here's my life philosophy: the devil you know is always better than the devil you don't. More specifically, if we have to share a table, I'd rather it be with anyone but Ms. Wrenshall. I don't like that biddy. So strap in and prepare to be entertained. That's the least we can expect of our dinner guests, right?"

I supposed. I redirected my creaky attitude, vowing to suspend my judgment of Doghn and Chad and make the best of it. And who knew? I could pick up some investigation tips from Doghn. He might be annoying, but he was also superb at his job.

Mrs. Berns and I took turns in the bathroom getting ready. She showered first, yelling through the door that it was like hosing yourself off with a straw and that maybe the space capsule was roomier and she was worried her sides weren't going to get clean because there wasn't enough room to turn around. I read my book through her remarks and squeezed in when she was done. She hadn't been exaggerating. The bathroom was set up like an RV's—it contained a regular-size toilet and sink and, separated by a thin wall, a shower approximately the size of a drinking glass.

The showerhead was detachable so you could clean your shady spots. If I'd dropped my soap, though, I would have needed to step out of the shower in order to bend over and reach it. You know how I know this? I was just beginning to soap up when the train lurched forward. I was thrown against the shower wall, bruising my shoulder, and would have fallen to the floor if there'd been room. As it was, I found myself wedged at an odd angle, face pressed to the glass.

"You OK?" Mrs. Berns hollered.

"Fine," I called, only it came out "fnnn." I de-wedged myself, opened the shower door so I could turn around and fetch the soap, and cracked the bathroom door. The muffled sound of cheering filtered in.

"Guess people are happy we're in motion again."

Mrs. Berns peered up from where she'd been doing crosswords. "You fell when the train started moving, didn't you?"

I put my hand to my forehead. "Maybe." I pointed out the window, using my other hand to hold the bathroom door in front of my body. "It'll be nice to get a change of scenery."

She didn't even bother looking out the window.

"No, it won't," she said, going back to her crossword. "It's bad juju to leave before we find out what happened to that poor woman next door. I suspect things will get worse from here on out."

Chapter 27

"It's all in the details."

Apparently, Chad was a great fan of *Attenborough PI* and couldn't get enough of Doghn and so had been asking him questions nonstop. I didn't mind. It saved me having to make small talk.

"But how'd you know the body was in the suitcase?" Chad asked.

Doghn smirked. "It was the way he squared his knees before he grabbed it, like he knew it was going to be heavy. Then that little jerk just before he got it off the ground. I'm telling you, you pay close attention and the world opens up to you."

Chad was so starstruck that he hadn't even cut into his steak.

Doghn, however, had no such compunctions. He jabbed his fork at Chad's sirloin. "Are you going to finish that?" He was on his second entrée and had already ordered dessert. The guy liked his food.

"Maybe you should try the lemon dill cod," Mrs. Berns suggested. "Mira enjoyed it last evening. Said she'd never forget it."

I kicked her under the table. She and I had stuck with bread and salad tonight. Both were delicious, surprisingly. I wondered if the train staff had loaded in fresh supplies back in Glendive.

"So," I interrupted, curious what version he would tell, "how'd you come to hear about the missing persons case on this train?"

Doghn patted his mouth with his cloth napkin tucked in his collar before letting it drop against his chest. "Luck and a police radio. I was driving to the same conference as you in Portland when I heard the call come in."

"Driving?" Mrs. Berns asked. "I thought you said you live in Michigan."

He breathed through his nose. "Only a fool would trust their life to an airplane."

Dang it. There's nothing worse than finding out a weirdo has the same neuroses as you. Makes you look unbalanced.

"Where's your car?" I asked.

"By now, back at the rental station. AmeriTrain agreed to return it for me and supply me train accommodations in exchange for my services."

"And for keeping this case off your TV show?" Mrs. Berns asked.

Doghn allowed her a small smile. "The AmeriTrain corporate offices and I came to the mutual agreement that it would be best if this case was solved quickly and quietly."

"If you're going to go missing, the best place to do it is on a train full of PIs, I bet," Chad said. "That little girl and her dad won't be gone for long."

I wondered how much Chad knew about Sofia Ramos's death, or Steve Nunn's murder back in Fargo, for that matter. It'd be a stressful train ride for any civilian who discovered the truth. Doghn either wasn't worried about how much everyone else knew or didn't care. "If they're even on the train anymore, which I suspect they aren't," he said. "Before we arrived at dinner, I received word from my connections that the prisoner who escaped has confessed to shooting his accomplice back at the Fargo train station. He claims no such responsibility for the death of the woman in Car Eleven. I suspect she died of a heart attack, and that her male companion was involved in some sort of illegal activity that wouldn't stand up to scrutiny. He and the child could be crossing into Canada by now."

My eyes shot to Chad. Would all this talk about death throw him off his meal? No such luck.

"Two dead bodies! People are whispering about that stuff on the train, but I didn't know whether to believe them. How cool!"

Mrs. Berns elbowed me and pointed her fork at him. "This is a quality you should look for in a man. He doesn't mind corpses."

"When I was in high school," Chad said, continuing as if he hadn't heard her, "we had some satanic killers in town. At least that's what the newspapers said they were. Four killings in a year, all local teenagers, all their bodies found in the middle of a pentagram."

I didn't like the hungry look in his eyes. "Did they catch the killer?"

He glanced down at his steak before looking back up at me. "No." His face was expressionless.

I hid my shiver.

"You can have my steak," Chad said, sliding it over to Doghn. The train lurched, and a splash of blood from the rare meat spilled onto the table.

"Uh-oh!" Doghn cried. "Don't waste the juices!"

And just like that, I lost my appetite. I signaled to the waitress and asked for as many desserts as I was allowed, planning to bring them to Jed, and stood to excuse myself.

"Not without me, you aren't," Mrs. Berns said, throwing her napkin over her salad. "We've got activities planned for tonight. Remember? The beauty parlor, then a painting class. This is still the Valentine Train, after all. Let's roll!"

I sighed so deeply that my breath reached my toes. I felt guilty about my earlier whining, though, so I kept my peace about these planned activities. "Let me run this dessert to Jed, and I'll meet you for the makeovers. What car?"

"Six. They're labeling it the Love Car. Bottom level, same place as the dance last night. You remember the dance, right?" She smiled. I could see how much effort she was expending not to make a joke at the expense of Chad and me. I appreciated it.

"Meet you there in twenty." I left ahead of her, wriggling my way through the cars. People were surprisingly subdued, eating their home-brought meals, settling into their chairs, engrossed in their technology, books, or companions. It was nice, but I wondered what it'd be like if they all knew they'd been traveling with a murderer. Then again, who ever knows that? Murderers might be walking among us at any time. Our job is to focus on the good.

Jed wasn't in his seat when I got there, so I placed the cream puff, cheesecake, and flourless torte on his seat along with a note telling him where it had come from, though I imagined not knowing wouldn't slow him down. I then headed back toward Car 6 and Mrs. Berns but was slowed by a long line that'd appeared in the viewing car in the five minutes since I'd passed through.

"What's the deal?" I asked the person in front of me.

"Free ice cream. An apology for putting us so far behind schedule."

Given the traffic jam, I figured I might as well use the bathroom and wash up before continuing to my makeover. I descended to the lower level, where the restroom was located, but found another line holding me back. "More ice cream down here?"

The woman in front of me turned and smiled. "Yep. I don't know if it's worth the ten hours of my life AmeriTrain took back at Glendive, but it's better than nothing, right?"

True words. I nodded, and she returned her attention to her friend. They were debating whether there'd be more choices than chocolate and vanilla, and I was deciding if it'd be a better use of my time to stay in this line and get a bathroom *and* some free ice cream or to try navigating through the top-floor line when I heard a familiar angry voice coming down the stairs.

"I aim to use the bullet in my own good time." I knew it must be the couple I'd heard arguing the day before. The Fargo shooter had already been caught and confessed, if what Doghn had said was true, but still. I wanted to lay eyes on this couple, with their strange wording and constant aggression.

I pushed my way back to the main level and stood on my tippy-toes. Lots of heads and shoulders. I strained to hear, hoping to catch more of their conversation and maybe figure out their dialect, but there was nothing. I was surrounded by men and women of all ages and sizes, as well as children. Unless the two spoke again, I'd have no way to pick them out of the throng. Problem was, everyone was talking, making for a constant hum. I must have caught the previous snatch of conversation as the couple walked right past the top of the stairs.

Frustrated, I snaked my way through the crowd, keeping my ears on high alert. I heard nothing suspicious, but I kept up the vigilance all the way to the lower level of Car 6, where I found Mrs. Berns just getting out of the makeshift beauty chair. I gasped.

"Do you like it?" she asked, fluffing her hair.

The new curls were nice, for sure. What I found alarming was one of her eyebrows. While one was just fine, the other looked like it'd been erased and then penciled in by a scared five-year-old. "What happened?"

The train gave one of its vigorous heaves. By now, everyone on the train was acclimated to the unsteadiness of the ride, and we all grabbed the nearest surface out of habit.

"Isn't it great?" Mrs. Berns indicated the jerky train. "It's like beauty roulette down here. You never know if you're going to walk away looking like you got a facial or beat up. That's why I only got one eyebrow done. I didn't want to have all the fun in a single night."

She smiled at the stylist and handed her a five-dollar bill. "My friend Mira is next." She turned back to me. "What's your poison? Eyelash dyeing? Adding bangs? A manicure?"

The train swayed vigorously, throwing Mrs. Berns into me. I had a flash of permanent freckles à la misplaced dye, the bang cut I'd given myself at age four, and fingernail polish all over my clothes. "I'll pass for today. But thank you."

The stylist shrugged. Mrs. Berns and I got out of the way so the next brave soul could take the chair.

"How's Jed doing?" she asked.

I started toward the stairs, Mrs. Berns in tow. "Fine, probably. He wasn't in his seat, so I left the dessert. He's either getting high or getting a girlfriend, which are two of his favorite things."

"I love that kid."

"Me too." I really did. Jed was one of the last innocents. A kinder heart I'd never met. I vowed to spend more time with him on this trip. Back in Battle Lake, we didn't get nearly enough chances to hang out. Here, there were no excuses, and it belatedly occurred to me that I hadn't even heard his secret yet.

The painting class was scheduled to take place in the viewing car, though I figured there was no way they'd have room for us what with the ice cream giveaway crowd. However, when we arrived, it turned out that anyone who hadn't signed up for painting had been kicked out for the next hour. Mrs. Berns and I eased into two seats near the rear of the car, as far away from Chad and Ms. Wrenshall as we could get. We accepted our aprons and settled in for instructions on acrylic painting.

It was pretty straightforward stuff. The thirty or so of us each received a canvas with a pencil sketch of a field of poppies on it. We were also handed a paper plate covered in dollops of red, yellow, green, white, and black paints. The sharp smell took me all the way back to elementary school art class.

The instructor led us through the painting process step by step, demonstrating how to mix colors and apply strokes. We each had a plastic cup in our cup holder that contained water and a variety of brushes. We were allowed to paint in ten-minute increments before more instructions on the next step. Paint the stems; wait. Paint the petals; wait.

During the waiting periods, when I didn't have anything to do, I became acutely aware that Ms. Wrenshall was flirting with Chad. They seemed as though they'd never met before because both had that awkward body language—one glancing at the other when they thought they weren't looking, and then blushing and glancing away when they did.

I could catch only bits of their conversation, but Chad seemed uncomfortable with whatever they were talking about. I pulled my attention away from them and turned it outward, to the inky pregnancy of the impending storm that Chief Harris had mentioned. Even inside the car, the air had the electric smell of weather on its way. You grow up in Minnesota, you know what it feels like when a big one is about to hit. The sensation gets under your skin, and you want to run both away from it and toward it at the same time.

After twenty minutes, I got tired of the waiting and storm watching and went ahead and did my own thing with the poppies. Mixing the colors was my favorite part. A drop of yellow added to the red made the most vibrant blood-orange color. Swirling and dabbing, I was able to give my flowers texture. If I held my brush lightly while painting the stems, they ended up looking more fibrous. Even the train's side-to-side motion supported my vision, giving my strokes a natural inconsistency.

I was completely engrossed in the painting, and it was the best feeling. All the stress of the trip melted away. I forgot that Chad and Ms. Wrenshall were in the room. I even forgot Mrs. Berns was right next to me. The whole world fell away as I dropped into the zone.

When my painting was complete—a glorious canvas of boisterous flowers and lush greenery—I dropped my paintbrush into my water glass and glanced around. Most people weren't even three-fourths finished with their paintings, though everyone wore similar intent expressions—except for Ms. Wrenshall, who was too busy looking at Chad's painting to work on her own.

"I'm going to use the bathroom downstairs," I whispered to Mrs. Berns. I gazed at her painting for the first time since I'd fallen into the zone. Heat crawled up my cheeks. "What the cuss?"

Rather than poppies, she'd covered her canvas with naked cherubs. At least, that's what I thought they were. They might have been pink piglets, though they were definitely all male.

Mrs. Berns raised her intact eyebrow. "It's art. I can do what I want."

Distancing myself from her, I slipped out of my seat and pinballed my way to the stairs. The instructor flashed me a polite but distracted smile. I smiled back. Everyone else stayed focused on their artwork. Even Ms. Wrenshall was back at work. I was wondering if she was a professional cougar, and if Mrs. Berns had sensed it and that's why she disliked her, when I hit the next step down.

And spotted Aimee.

Chapter 28

Her back was to me, but I was sure it was her. "Aimee!"

The little girl ran toward the other end of the car. She had to weave around people talking, playing cards, and standing in line for the snack counter. I thought I had her cornered, because most cars could be crossed on only the second level; however, when I reached the rear, I discovered nothing but bathrooms and a luggage rack. I was digging through the luggage, sure I'd find her, when I noticed the blood on my hand.

I screamed and fell backward, hitting my head on the bathroom door.

The people nearest helped me up. An older bearded guy asked if I was OK.

"Blood!" I pointed at my hand.

His eyes widened, but then he leaned in. "You sure? It looks like paint." Unconvinced, I smelled it. Sure enough, it was a streak of acrylic. Good grief.

"Did you see a little girl run back here?" I asked.

He glanced at his friend, a woman wearing a Sturgis T-shirt. I recognized his look. It said, *She's been sniffing some fumes.*

"Honey," the woman said to me, "there's no kids back here. See? It's a dead end. Just luggage and bathrooms. Did you lose your daughter?"

Pulse thudding, I pulled loose from them and yanked open all three of the bathroom doors. They were all empty. My stomach gurgled greasily. Had I hallucinated Aimee twice? I mumbled my apologies and sidled away from the strangers' worried glances. I returned to the overhead floor, which was just as I'd left it, with the instructor appearing bored and the students bent over their paintings.

I slid into my seat.

"You look like you saw a ghost," Mrs. Berns remarked. "The bad poops come back?"

I shook my head. "I thought I saw Aimee."

She put down her brush. "Did you?"

I felt a headache forming. "I don't think it's possible. No one else saw her. Plus, the only way in or out of that car is through the stairs, and there's no way she slipped past me."

"Or me. Nobody has come up those stairs since you went down." She harrumphed. "All the weirdness of this trip is getting to me. We should head to bed early."

I glanced out the windows. It was dark, but even so, I could tell that the flat lands of eastern Montana were giving way to the foothills of the Rockies, with the mountains beyond. Dramatic shapes rose in the near distance, making me feel both protected and minuscule. I guessed we were just about at our top advertised speed of 150 miles per hour now, trying to make up for lost time.

I wondered why there were no stars, but then I remembered the impending storm. The wind already screamed at the cracks of the train, possibly giving warning, and if I trained my eyes outside, I could see that a heavy snow fell in the distance. I suppressed a shudder. Something felt very wrong, and it wasn't just my phantom Aimee sighting. I was about to take up Mrs. Berns on her suggestion to head back to the sleeper car when the door nearest us burst open.

Doghn Attenborough spilled through, his countenance grim. "It was murder," he announced.

The already-quiet viewing car grew as still as a graveyard.

"What?" I asked.

He swiveled his attention to me, though he didn't lower his voice. "The woman found dead in the cabin adjacent to yours. She was poisoned."

A hissing whisper replaced the silence as people shared shock with their friends. Overhead, heavy, disorienting snow began to pelt the skylights.

"And that's not all." He held one hand in the air ominously.

I could tell these were theatrics, that he was used to playing for a camera, but I still felt myself leaning forward. The wind continued to shriek, hurling the sudden snow like bullets against the glass.

"The escaped prisoner didn't kill her. The poison she took was administered to her before he boarded. That means we have a killer on this train."

A woman screamed. Some of the painters leaped to their feet, upsetting their paintbrush-filled water glasses. They rushed toward the doors—to what, I didn't know.

I stood and tried to raise my voice above the chaos. "Everyone, listen! Stop! Don't spread this panic across the train!"

The people closest to me slowed. I found I had the attention of most everyone in the car and no idea what to say.

"You're sure it's poison?" I asked Doghn, keeping my voice loud, so as to include all the passengers.

Doghn nodded. "I had the coroner's report read to me over the phone."

"Her husband could have murdered her," I said.

This was a chancy gambit. I didn't know if anyone would be reassured by that fact. What I did know was that nothing good would come of hundreds of frightened people trapped in a moving vehicle.

"And since he hasn't been seen since Glendive, he could have gotten off there," I continued. "Which means that we're all safe."

Doghn shook his head. "If he wanted to murder her, why board a train with his family?"

Our captive audience turned toward me like tennis fans at a match.

"That's a good question." I scoured my brain. "How about this? What if the killer is not the husband but someone who boarded earlier and then got off at Fargo? They might be two states away by now."

Doghn squinted at me. "I've gone through the passenger logs and had AmeriTrain cross-reference them for me. No one got off at Fargo. This is a destination train. People are riding it for the long haul. The only missing people are the husband and child of the murdered woman, and as I said, neither are likely suspects because of the timing of the murder. No, we have a killer among us."

Mrs. Berns had been right to call this guy an asshole. He cared more about being the center of attention than he did the repercussions of playing this scene out in front of civilians. I had one last chance to wrest control.

Or I would have, if the train hadn't screeched to another abrupt stop at that exact moment, sending bodies colliding and incomplete paintings and plates of acrylic paint across the room. I was just able to grab Mrs. Berns's wrist to keep her from being catapulted into the fray.

"What was that?" Ms. Wrenshall shrieked. "Why have we stopped?"

As if on cue, the lights flickered and then went out. A blood-chugging scream rang out from one of the cars, and then there was silence.

Overhead, snow fell audibly, like dirt on a casket.

We were stuck.

Chapter 29

The silence lasted the length of a heartbeat.

The lights flickered back on.

Chaos erupted.

Passengers gushed up from the lower level like ants leaving a flooded nest. Others shoved and crawled to reach the exits, fighting against people coming in from each end. Parents called for children, men for women, women for men. Little kids (and some not-so-little ones) cried. I pulled Mrs. Berns toward the window in the hopes of waiting out the pandemonium.

Doghn squeezed in next to us. I wanted to elbow him, but in fairness, this wasn't totally his fault. A stopped train and the momentary loss of power had as much to do with the panic as his ill-planned words. Still, I couldn't let him off scot-free.

"You didn't have to tell the whole car about the murder," I hissed.

He reached into his jacket pocket and pulled out a candy bar, which he ate as he watched two people fight over a bottle of water. "You might be right," he said thoughtfully.

I caught a flash of blue, AmeriTrain's colors, toward the car's fore section. I followed the color until Reed appeared in front of us. "People as silly as a soup sandwich," he said. "You three OK?"

We all nodded.

"You know where Terry Downs is?" he asked.

"Haven't seen him," I said. "He wasn't at dinner, and I didn't spot him when I went to Car Eight to bring dessert to a friend afterward, either." It occurred to me that I didn't know which car held Terry's assigned seat.

"Then I've still got some work to do." Reed pointed at Doghn and me. "The conductor wants to see you two in his office, front of the train, other side of the dining car. He wants Mr. Downs, too, so tell the conductor I'll be back as soon as I locate him."

"How're we supposed to get through all this?" Mrs. Berns pointed at the clot of passengers.

"*You're* not," Reed said. "I'll escort you back to your car while I look for Mr. Downs. This train may seem like a straight line, but there's some ins and outs you learn if you work here long enough. You two will have to figure it out on your own," he said, referring to Doghn and me. "I recommend you stick to the sides. It gets easier the farther forward you go."

Reed grabbed Mrs. Berns's hand and started threading the crowd.

I clutched his uniform before he got too far away.

"Why're we stopped?"

"Too much snow ahead, gotta wait for the special snowplows. Trains like this one aren't much for going backward. We're snowed in until we hear otherwise."

Chapter 30

Doghn turned out to be a skilled crowd navigator. He knew just when to duck, spin, push, and step aside. He was a contradiction, that one, equal parts genius and buffoon. I'd have to keep an eye on him—an unsavory thought at best.

The dining car was the most challenging to navigate since that was where many of the people were striving to get to. Something about snowstorms and intermittent electricity brings out the food hoarder in all of us. The staff was doing a good job trying to calm the crowd and assure them that there'd be enough supplies to last us until spring, but people still pushed and moaned like cattle. I was thankful most of the food was stored at a lower level, one that none of us knew how to access.

Car 3 was on the dining car's other side, and it was a revelation. First of all, the only people in it were staff, so it was peaceful compared to the rest of the train. Second, it was a honeycomb of bunks: little tubes for people to sleep in and store a couple changes of clothes, some personal items, and not much more. The bunks were stacked six high and twenty long, with a bathroom at each end of the car. They all had names on the front, almost like mailboxes, only the sci-fi human-body-storing kind. I made note of Reed's bunk at shoulder level and followed Doghn forward, navigating around the staff, who were making bets on how long until help came.

I wanted to listen to that conversation, but not as badly as I wanted to see what the conductor was after. If he asked for me, Doghn, and

Terry, odds were good that he wanted us to investigate, but what exactly? And at what point should I tell him that I wasn't so much a licensed private investigator as I was a person who was always in the wrong place at the wrong time?

Car 2 was set up like Car 3, except there were half as many bunks to allow room for two offices. One was marked CONDUCTOR, and the other seemed devoted to storage. Through the forward door, I could make out the engine that powered the train—or at least, that was meant to power the train. I returned my attention to the conductor's office. The same burly man I'd met outside my door after Sofia Ramos's body was discovered spoke on a SAT phone, looking approximately fifty years older than he had when I'd last seen him.

He held up his hand to Doghn and me, signaling to give him a moment. We stood on the other side of the sliding door. More waiting. It was going to be the end of me.

"I think you're a wiener," I said to Doghn, by way of conversation.

Turned out stress made me super honest.

Doghn's eyes glittered. "I think you're not licensed."

"You can think what you want," I countered, "but Chief Bob Harris was pretty free with the information back in Glendive, so if we're being called here to help in finding the killer who may or may not be loose on this train, I'm a valuable asset."

I was likely more *ass* than *et* in a professional investigation, but damned if I was going to be left out. I didn't want the glory; I wanted to find Aimee, and I craved absolutely every lick of information there was to be known about a killer roaming this train. I was trapped here, too, after all.

The wind shrieked against the side of the train, rattling the metal, pushing hard enough to sway the behemoth. How long would we be able to stay here? Food wouldn't be an issue, since we had at least enough to last until Portland, and we could obtain water from the snow outside. What about heat and light, though? How long did snowstorms in the Rockies last? I was a Minnesota gal, born and raised, so I wasn't

135

afraid of a blizzard. It was being trapped in a snowstorm with a killer who gave me Donner Party–level willies. I had a vision of a group of us following the train tracks west through the storm in search of help.

When the conductor finally slid his door open, I let the question spill: "How long can we survive on this train without moving?"

He ran his hand over his face. The stubble on his unshaven cheeks rasped in response. "Ten days, easy."

"And how long will this storm keep us here?"

"Hard to say. The system is squatting over us for the next two days. Corporate might send someone to clear the tracks before it passes. They might not. It's expensive and doesn't always work."

Two days. Dang. That was a long time to be trapped with hundreds of unsettled strangers and one executioner.

"Can you come in?" The conductor stepped aside. "I'd like to wait until the third PI arrives to get started. In the meanwhile, coffee or tea?"

He knew that Doghn, Terry, and I were PIs, or at least were headed to the PI convention. Of course he knew about Doghn, but for the first time, I wondered how he knew about Terry and me. I'd told Chief Harris. Had he said something to the conductor? I supposed it wasn't outside the realm of reason.

Doghn and I stepped into his office. It was large, by train standards, with the outside wall lined with locked cupboards, the front-facing wall strung with dials and wires and various flashing lights, a desk covered with maps and paper, and two extra chairs.

Doghn and I each took one. I noted that the confined space smelled like a recently opened jar of man—a sort of sour, sweaty skin smell laced with old coffee and cheap cologne. There wasn't a window to open, so it wasn't the conductor's fault. Still, a bit of air freshener wouldn't have killed anyone.

Doghn took the proffered coffee while I thought back to the last time I'd slept. I was amazed to realize all that had happened in the course of a single day. Sofia Ramos's body had been discovered around five o'clock this morning—I made a mental note to find out who had discovered it—and the train had stopped moving about two hours after we left Glendive.

Since, an escaped prisoner had been located, and according to Doghn, the coroner had had time to ascertain that Sofia had been poisoned. That seemed like a quick turnaround on toxicity tests, but I supposed a case like this moved to the front of the line, as we were all potential victims—a.k.a. sitting ducks—if she actually had been murdered. The prisoner had since also confessed, we'd eaten dinner, Mrs. Berns had gotten part of a makeover, I'd painted a field of poppies, and I thought I'd spotted Aimee twice.

Quite a day. No wonder I was exhausted.

Still, coffee was the last thing I needed. It would just give me the jitters, and sleep was going to be a tenuous prospect as it was. I listened to Doghn and the conductor make small talk, mostly about Doghn's show, until Terry arrived.

"Sorry it took me so long," he said. "Pandemonium back there. I'm afraid I left your porter behind to try to instill order."

The conductor rubbed his face again. He leaned back, snatched an intercom mouthpiece off the wall, and clicked a button. "This is your conductor, James Christmas."

What a great name! I liked the guy a whole lot more suddenly. Who doesn't like Christmas?

"I understand that this is a stressful situation; however, it doesn't have to be. This storm will blow over in twenty-four hours." He eyeballed me and Doghn. We didn't contradict him. "We have food and water to last us for ten days, and fuel to last us for twice that. The next stop isn't far away. We're in good shape. Once the snow clears, we'll be on our way.

"As a good-faith gesture, AmeriTrain has authorized me to supply free food and beverages for all passengers. Our porters will be going through each car and taking names. We'll turn the viewing car into a second dining car, and you'll all be assigned twice a day to come to one or the other for a meal. The only way I can make this work is with your cooperation, so please return to your seats so we can gather the necessary information. All train staff, report to my office."

The lines on Christmas's face seemed to deepen as he made the announcement. I suspected he did not have permission from AmeriTrain to give away their food and beverages, but it was a wise move on his part.

"Well done," Terry said. "That oughta calm everyone down for the time being."

The first staff members started lining up outside the conductor's door. He issued a terse "be with you in five" and slid the door shut. Terry stood behind Doghn and me, and the conductor sat himself at his desk.

"Here's the beans. We're stuck. I don't know for how long. It's my understanding that all three of you know a woman was found dead on the train this morning. Her name was Sofia Ramos, and we just learned that she was poisoned. The police do not have a motive or a suspect, and they believe the killer may be on this train. They're aware of our situation, but they can no longer reach us because of the weather. I have been authorized to share information with you three. If you can solve the case, great. All I care about is that no one else dies on my train while we're stuck here. Does that work for you?"

We all nodded.

"So Sofia Ramos was most definitely murdered?" I asked, my heart hurting.

The conductor squared on me. "Yes. Nerium."

"What?" Terry asked.

I quietly echoed his question.

Doghn interrupted. "Oleander," he said. "It's a common shrub, poisonous when ingested, slow-acting."

I thought back to the previous night. "I didn't hear much commotion next door. Wouldn't she have been throwing up if she'd been poisoned?"

"Depends," Doghn said. "Oleander can mimic a heart attack, though the dose has to be specific to the body weight of the person who ingests it. It takes sixteen to twenty-four hours after ingestion to begin working."

"That means that whoever gave it to Sofia was an expert," I said. *Exactly like Doghn seems to be.* "They would have had to give it to her before Fargo and at such a precise dose that she'd die in the night without drawing attention to herself."

"Her husband?" Terry asked.

I turned on him. He looked rested and well fed. "Maybe. That's always the first suspect. But Doghn made a good point: Why wait until she was on the train to kill her?"

Terry shrugged. "So people would ask that question?"

Doghn interrupted. "What do we know about Ms. Ramos and her family?"

"Very little." James Christmas shuffled through the paper on his desk and came up with a single sheet, which he skimmed. "She was a housekeeper in New York and was traveling to Portland. We haven't been able to find anything on the man and child who shared a room with her, though we're assuming they were her husband and child, as they all have the same last name—Emilio Ramos and Aimee Ramos."

"Illegal immigrants?" Doghn asked.

"You mean undocumented," Christmas said, and I liked him more for it. People were not illegal. He set the paper back down. "That would explain why they ran when she died, but it also makes it more likely that Emilio is not the killer."

I grimaced. "Then who? And why?"

"That's what the three of you need to find out."

Chapter 31

Turned out Doghn had very specific ideas on how to conduct the investigation. He thought we should interview the most likely suspects. That meant the people who boarded at Penn Station with the Ramoses, passengers in the same car, and the staff, since they had the most access to the Ramoses' food and cabin.

The more he unfurled his plan, the more excited he became, twirling the ends of his mustache like helicopter blades, his eyes flashing. I wondered (and not for the first time since Chief Harris had suggested it) if all this was a publicity stunt for Doghn. He'd need to violate whatever privacy agreement he and AmeriTrain had decided on, but I bet that'd hurt them more than him in the long run.

All told, though, his plan made sense.

Except for one thing.

"I don't want to be part of the interviews," I said.

All three men seemed startled. The conductor asked why.

"One of us should be searching the train's nooks and crannies, in case Emilio and Aimee are still on here, hiding somewhere." That was, surprisingly, the truth. I wanted to find Aimee more than I wanted to find out who had killed her mother. One was a scared little girl; the other was past helping.

Doghn's eyes narrowed. He seemed mad he hadn't thought of that himself. "What if we hear something during questioning that could help to locate the Ramos survivors?"

Good point. "I'll have one of my trained assistants sitting in on the interviews. They'll be able to decide what I need to know and serve as a line of communication between me and the three of you." I'd deliberately kept the sentence gender-neutral, as I had yet to decide whether Jed or Mrs. Berns would do less harm.

Interestingly, both Terry and Doghn appeared to be scrambling for reasons to deny me free rein on the train. In the end, they couldn't come up with any. James Christmas gave them a copy of the passenger logs, including boarding dates and locations. He handed me two universal keys, one to open every door and the other to open every storage unit on the train. He also handed me a set of walkie-talkies.

Who got the better end of that deal?

I agreed to send my "assistant" back here to the office, where the interviews would be conducted, within the hour. Christmas went into the hallway to instruct his staff on setting up interviews for the chosen passengers. Reed was their first subject.

I hurried to find Jed and Mrs. Berns. Happily, the conductor's bribe had mellowed most of the people, and I made my way to Coach Car 8 with limited interference. I found Jed asleep in his chair, smelling of marijuana, his mouth open, drool leaking from the corner, clutching his teddy bear. I'd seen Mr. Cuddles at his place back in Battle Lake, but figured it was a bit of childhood memorabilia, not an active companion. This was not how I wanted to be represented on my train investigation.

I hurried on to Sleeper Car 11 but found our cabin empty. A note said Mrs. Berns was back at the Love Car. Retracing my steps to Car 6, I descended to the lower level, which was where I found the beauty parlor still set up, though it was almost ten at night. Mrs. Berns was in the chair, her expression gleeful, the left half of her hair significantly shorter—and less even—than the right.

"Mrs. Berns!"

"Horrible, right? I can't tell you how fast my heart is beating. I feel alive!"

Corn nuts. Assistant candidate number two was not looking promising, either.

"You sure you don't want to sit in the chair?" she asked. "There's nothing like it."

I turned to walk back up the stairs. *Drooling stoner wins by a hair—literally.*

"Mira! Where're you going? Don't you want to stick around for the late-night scavenger hunt? It was supposed to be held tomorrow, but they moved it to tonight to lighten things up around here."

On second thought, maybe Mrs. Berns *could* help. I made my way back to her and handed her one of the walkie-talkies. "The conductor has me, Doghn, and Terry trying to find out"—I lowered my voice so as not to cause alarm, in case there was anyone left who *didn't* know there'd been a murder on the train—"what happened in the adjoining cabin. I'm going to give you this. Let me know if you see anything while you're on the hunt."

It was a risk giving her the walkie-talkie, and not just because Jed wouldn't be able to contact me right away if he heard something valuable during the interviews. More worrisome was Mrs. Berns's tendency to treat walkie-talkies like traveling karaoke mics. I was willing to take the chance, though, because if she spotted Aimee while she was on whatever cockamamie nighttime scavenger hunt the train had planned, I wanted to know ASAP. Nothing Jed learned sitting in on the interviews would be that time sensitive.

Mrs. Berns was only too happy to accept the talkie. We calibrated our frequency knobs, and I left her queuing up for the scavenger hunt. By the time I returned to Jed, the only thing on him that'd moved was his drool.

"Jed." I shook his shoulder. "Wake up."

"I don't want to go to school."

"It's Mira, Jed. I need your help."

One eye opened, and then the other. He wiped his chin. "Hey, dude. Was I sleeping?"

"And then some. Sorry to wake you. Can you help me?"

"For sure." He sat his chair up and rubbed his face. He glanced to his right. "This is my girlfriend, Eliza. I'll have you meet her when she wakes up, 'kay? She's beaucoup awesome. Whaddya need help with?"

The guy even *woke up* kind. I filled him in on the situation in a few short sentences.

"But I'm not a detective," he protested.

"Don't worry," I said. I pointed at his SMOT POKER T-shirt. "Did you pack a button-down?"

He nodded.

"Grab it, and put it on over your T-shirt. Then just keep your mouth closed and ears open during the interviews. You're listening for anything that will help me find Aimee or figure out who killed her mom. Watch for suspicious behavior, but especially watch Terry and Doghn. If they seem particularly interested in someone, you should be, too."

"Terry?" Jed scratched his scalp. "That guy we had dinner with the first night? He makes me feel weird."

It was unusual for Jed not to like a person, but Terry had instantly made me think *cop*, and he'd probably done the same for Jed. In the animal kingdom, cops are the lions, and pot smokers are the easily distracted gazelles. "It'll be fine. Please? We need to help this little girl."

"Oh, for sure." He stood, reached for his duffel, and pulled out a wrinkled but logo-free oxford. "We got to find her. You can trust me."

I was sure of it. I gave him directions to the conductor's office. I was deciding where to start my own search when Mrs. Berns pushed past. She was with Chad and two other people I didn't recognize.

"Mrs. Berns!"

She didn't answer me, so I scrambled to the front of her group and grabbed her arm. "Hey, why're you ignoring me?"

She stopped, rolled her eyes, and handed me a slip of paper. At the top, it said, SCAVENGER HUNT DIRECTIONS. They were simple:

1. You will be assigned a group of four. Your group will elect a leader and come up with a name.
2. Your group cannot talk to one another except in the diaphragms between cars. Keep your voices down even in these spaces. If you are caught speaking outside of the foyers, your entire group will be disqualified.
3. Each group will locate six objects. Yours has been assigned to collect these six: the front page of a South Dakota newspaper, a photo of your entire team inside the Car 14 lower-level bathroom, a Granny Smith apple, an empty water bottle, a pen with the AmeriTrain logo on it, and a tiara with a red heart in the center.
4. None of the objects will be hidden on fellow passengers or otherwise in locations where you would have to disturb people or enter locked spaces to retrieve them.
5. The first team to return with all six objects will win a free dinner or free makeover session for each person in the group, your choice.
6. In the case of a tie, the staff in charge of the scavenger hunt will make the ruling call.
7. Have fun!

I pointed at the foyer. Mrs. Berns followed me. I gestured for the rest of her group to wait on the other side of the door.

"Can I join your team?" I asked.

"Nope. You're deadweight."

"What do you mean? You're the one who talked me into becoming a private eye."

"That's completely different. You're looking for a girl. That'll distract you from finding the objects. I want to win this thing!"

I studied her crazy eyebrows and lopsided hair. I suspected she was addicted to the adrenaline rush of the train's makeovers. There was no helping her. "OK, I won't be part of your team. But I might be tagging along."

"It's a free train." She signaled to her group. They joined us in the shifting accordion. "The plan hasn't changed," she told them. "We get the bathroom photo first. Chad, you've got your camera ready?"

He held it up. Looked like Mrs. Berns had been elected leader of her group.

"Excellent. Then we split up afterward and reconvene in the viewing car front diaphragm every ten minutes or after we've found our assigned object, whichever comes first. Goooo, Loungin' Scroungers!"

Not a great team name, but I was otherwise impressed with Mrs. Berns's leadership skills. I decided to follow them to the restroom because I was heading that way anyhow, having decided to start at the back of the train and work my way forward. I still didn't know what I was looking for, but I would follow Doghn's big duh advice about keeping my eyes open.

The Loungin' Scroungers were doing a good job keeping quiet, though I suspected nobody else cared. The train certainly didn't have staff to spare to babysit them, though whoever had thought of the scavenger hunt had been smart to build in quietness as one of the requirements. It meant nonparticipants would not be disturbed.

The Scroungers zipped their lips, lowered their heads, and made their way to the rear of the train. I followed them, eyes peeled, alert for any sign of Aimee or her dad. I still thought they might be on board, despite Doghn's suggestion otherwise.

For the most part the passengers seemed settled in for the night, and the majority of them had their shades closed, as if they didn't want to be reminded of the shrieking snow pelting the windows, trapping us in place. When we reached Car 14, the last sleeper on the train, I was slightly amused to discover that the first bathroom to the left was a single stall rather than handicapped accessible. The Loungin' Scroungers had to squeeze into there as if it were a clown car or a phone booth, only gross.

I pretended to have trouble focusing Chad's camera, then I acted as if I wanted to get the shot just right. It was great watching them try to move in the small space. I was giggling up until I caught Mrs. Berns's glare.

"Fine. Say cheese!"

I pressed the digital camera's button. There was a click, and the hallway and bathroom were illuminated. In the glare of the flash, I saw it:

Help, written on the side of the bathroom wall.

It could have been there for years or minutes. It looked like it had been scribbled with red lipstick. The flash disappeared. I blinked. The Scroungers began filing out.

That's when, in the edge of my vision and the dimness of the lighting, back toward more luggage racks, I spotted her. "Noelle!"

Chapter 32

I handed off the camera and raced to the rear of the car. There was nobody there, just the last cabin, and beyond that, a small space for luggage and shadows. I tapped against the wall above and behind the luggage and discovered it was actually a cupboard. It sounded hollow. My heart sank until I remembered.

I had keys!

I dug in my pocket and was thrilled that the first key I chose opened the cupboard. Inside were bathroom supplies. No little girl.

"Noelle?" Mrs. Berns asked, coming up behind me. She wiped her arms, as if to rid herself of stray hairs. She carried a distinct urinal cake smell.

"I meant Aimee." Honestly, though, I wasn't sure. The stress of the train ride was getting to me. "I thought I saw her."

"Dead end back here." Mrs. Berns kicked the wall.

I didn't like the way she was looking at me, as if I were made out of glass. "Yeah. Dead end."

The adrenaline rush of thinking I'd spotted Aimee was ebbing, leaving me with a nauseated feeling. I wanted nothing more than to lie down. I needed to clear the cobwebs. "Hey, I think I'm going to head back to the cabin after I check in with Jed. I'm beat. If I don't get some rest, I'm gonna see ghosts." *More* ghosts, in any case.

"All right. Call me on the walkie-talkie if you see the front page of a South Dakota newspaper, a green apple, a water bottle, a pen with the AmeriTrain logo on it, or a tiara, 'kay?"

I nodded, too tired to answer, and dragged my feet toward the stairs. It was twenty-four years of regret and hopelessness resurfacing, leaving me feeling five years old and powerless all over again. Chad stepped forward as if he wanted to say something, but he kept his mouth closed.

For that, I was grateful.

At the top of the stairs, I took a sharp right, intending to head forward on the train. A quick check-in with Jed and the other PIs, and then I was putting myself on bed rest. I was more trouble than help in this state. I was just outside the door of Room 4 in Car 14 when I heard a conversation that chilled my bones.

"That's not the right bullet! You're never going to git 'er if you keep picking the wrong one."

Chapter 33

It was the woman that I'd twice heard arguing with a man in the stairwell. It was the same voice, the same mysterious twang, the same topic. Visions of Aimee in harm's way exploded in my brain. I slid open the door and charged in, my heart in my mouth, my eyes scouring the room, searching for any trace of the girl. What I discovered instead was a couple on the bed, both as naked as the day they were born, an array of marital aids laid out beside them.

"Oh. No." I wasn't sure if it was an apology or a command. I was too busy trying to keep my eyes from burning up in my sockets and my stomach from dropping to the floor.

Interestingly (and by "interesting," I mean "horrifying"), neither of them covered themselves up or seemed particularly alarmed at my inopportune arrival.

They were both in their mid to late sixties. I was sure I'd passed them on the train before, but they were unremarkable, the man around five eight (I thought—he was lying on his stomach), with a middle-aged paunch and more hair on his back than his head. The woman had one of those faces that rested in the scowling position and gray-blonde hair feathered in a seventies style.

"Hi, honey," the woman said. "Are you our third?"

The hoot exploding behind me broke the horror paralysis.

"More discoveries like this, and finding dead bodies might look like a treat," Mrs. Berns howled from my shoulder. "Excuse my friend," she said to the couple, who now looked confused. "She sleepwalks."

Mrs. Berns yanked me back and put her hand on the door. Before sliding it shut behind her, she had a quick conversation with the couple about the merits of a particularly hefty-looking purple unit near the edge of the bed.

"I need to wash my eyes," I moaned.

She pushed me down the aisle, her Loungers following like baby ducks. "Since when do you randomly open other people's bedroom doors? And why didn't you invite me? That's a game I could get on board with."

"I heard them talking about bullets. What with the murders, and the missing people . . ." I trailed off. A memory of one of Kennie Rogers's least successful home businesses, the refurbished marital aid company, came into my head. The Bullet was the name of the smallest device in her inventory.

Dang. It.

"I see you connecting the dots, partner. I also see you needing some sleep. You sure you want to check on Jed before you crash?"

I wasn't, but I figured I wouldn't be able to close my eyes without getting the latest update, at least for Aimee's sake. "Give me your walkie-talkie."

"No."

I held out my hand. "I need to hand it off to Jed. That way, he can update me on what they find out in the questioning and I can get some rest."

"No."

"I promise I'll give it back to you as soon as we find Aimee." I didn't think that promise was mine to make. "Also, you can help me with the investigation first thing tomorrow. Deal?"

Mrs. Berns grumbled but lifted her sweater and unclipped the walkie-talkie from her waistband. "You know what they call people who give presents and then take them away, don't you?"

"What?"

"Dinks. Now quiet with the talking. Us Loungers are supposed to be silent. You don't want us to lose this whole scavenger hunt, do you?"

I did not.

It took me fifteen minutes to return to Car 2, my quickest end-to-end trip yet. Most everyone I'd passed was asleep, giving the train a ghostly feel, especially with the whistling scream of the wind slicing at the outer walls. Hearing it chilled me despite the close, hot air.

When I reached the conductor's office, I glanced through the window before entering. Jed, Terry, and Doghn had their backs to me and were sitting across from Sylvester, the porter who'd been rude to me way back when we were in Detroit Lakes a million years ago. Jed sat in the middle and copied every gesture either PI made. If Doghn put his hand to his face, Jed did the same. If Terry nodded, Jed shook his head twice as vigorously. If either of them wrote something down, Jed scribbled, probably nonsense words and hearts.

Man, I loved that guy.

I knocked on the window. Sylvester glanced up, and the three men facing him turned around. I signaled to Jed. He excused himself and met me in the hall, sliding the door closed behind him.

"How's it going?" I asked.

"Fine." He seemed relieved to see me, but then his face slid a little. "You look tired, Mira. Or sick. A little gray, actually. You OK?"

"It's been a long day, you know?" I nodded toward the door, where Terry and Doghn had stopped to watch us. I wondered if either was a lip reader. I moved Jed so he was facing me, his back to them, blocking their view. "Did you find out anything?"

"Naw. I still don't like that Terry guy, though. Gives me the heebie-jeebies. I think he's a cop."

I pictured the monster bag of weed Jed likely had stashed somewhere on this train. "He probably used to be. Most PIs have a law enforcement background. He's got bigger fish to fry now, though. Anyone see anything strange? Confess to anything?"

He pointed his thumb back at the office. "The porter says weird stuff is disappearing from the train. Salt and pepper shakers, forks, packets of butter, bread rolls. He said they keep that stuff under close watch to make sure it stays stocked, but that they keep coming up short."

"Do Terry and Doghn think it's anything?"

"Terry said it's probably people worried the train isn't going to move before we run out of food. Doghn has been quiet. He just keeps stroking his 'stache and asking about who got on and off back in New York."

"And you didn't hear anything interesting from the other people who were interviewed?"

"Sylvester is only the second. Reed, the guy who got us dinner reservations the first night? He was the first."

I perked up. "How did he seem? Suspicious? Evasive?"

"Like an open book." Jed stroked an imaginary mustache. "This investigative stuff is hard. I don't like to think of people lying."

"I'm sorry." I was. He hadn't signed on for this, no matter how exhausted I was. "Look, I can take over. You go back and catch some sleep."

"Dude, sorry, but you're the one who needs the shut-eye. You look like someone packed your face bags in the dark, and in a hurry." He glanced at his feet as if it hurt him to share the news with me. "Sorry, Mira, but it's true. You go on back. They said they're going to only interview one, maybe two more people tonight. I can handle it."

I considered arguing, but I knew he was right. I hugged him and backtracked toward my sleeper car. The wind continued to shriek outside. I had a vision of what we must look like from the sky, a black steel snake trapped at the base of the Rockies amid endless white, slowly getting buried by snow, slowly disappearing from the world.

My throat began to close, and all the exhaled carbon dioxide expanded in my nose, making it difficult to swallow. My heartbeat started to pick up, though I willed it to slow, commanding my growing anxiety to recede. There was nowhere for me to run. I had to make peace with being trapped on this train with a killer, and with sweet little Aimee being out there unprotected.

Chapter 34

I cobbled together five or six fitful hours of sleep, momentarily waking, disoriented, when Mrs. Berns tiptoed into the room. While she climbed into bed, I checked that the walkie-talkie was on before falling back asleep, only to be startled awake by a clanging outside that quickly subsided. I lay in bed, missing Johnny, thinking of my mom, wondering why I kept falling down this dead-body rabbit hole.

When 5:12 a.m. rolled around, I couldn't lie still any longer. I opened the shade. It was dark as a grave outside. My heart tripped a beat. Were we really buried by snow? It could happen, and then how would we be found? The search and rescue team would have to follow the tracks from our last known location. Our air might not last that long. I tried to loosen my T-shirt collar as I stuck my face against the cool glass. Giving my eyes a moment to adjust, I could make out the snow line almost level with the bottom of the train. I sucked in a deep breath. We weren't buried; the sun just wasn't up yet.

A flash of flame sparked outside and to my right. I craned my neck and could just make out Ms. Wrenshall, more in the shelter of the train than out of it. She was smoking, and she was talking to someone. That person was also smoking. I couldn't make out any features, but I could see the orange glow of his or her cigarette ember moving out of sync with Ms. Wrenshall's. What would the smokers do when their cigarettes ran out?

"Happy Valentine's Day!"

The exuberance of the voice startled me, and I banged my face against the glass trying to escape it. "Thanks."

Mrs. Berns was in the bunk above me, her face hanging upside down over the edge, curlers elevating her hacked hair. In the night-light's green glow, her butchered eyebrow appeared particularly regretful.

"And happy Valentine's to you, too." I meant it. She was a bright spot in this situation, even though she was the reason I was on this train, next door to where a murder had happened, trapped in the Rockies, worried sick about a little girl I didn't even know.

"I can see what you're thinking," she said, still upside down. "That maybe this train ride wasn't the best use of your time." Her head disappeared, soon replaced by her feet as she slid off her bunk.

"And that's one way of looking at it," she continued, "but here's another: at least you're luring the murder away from Battle Lake. Too much has already happened to those nice people since you moved to town."

I wrinkled my nose. "This is supposed to be a pep talk?"

She shrugged. "I've always found the truth a better companion than bullshit."

She'd slept in one of those long T-shirts designed to make you look like you had a skinny bikini body. I raised my eyebrows.

She glanced down. "This shirt is *not* bullshit. It's good fun. There's a difference. BS is if I tell you that everything is going to be OK, or that I'm sure it has nothing to do with you that you find dead bodies, or that Iowa is just as good as Minnesota. If I start lying to you like that, then who're you going to believe? No, it's better I'm always honest with you."

She had a point. "So you can't put a bright spin on this?"

"Sure I can." She grinned. "It's Valentine's Day. We're not dead. What more do you want?"

I rubbed my eyes. "Coffee."

Unsure what the breakfast protocol was on a stalled train, I tugged on clean clothes and ran a brush over my teeth and a different one through my hair. Mrs. Berns elected to stay behind to shower. When I stepped into the hall, it was as quiet as a funeral. I tiptoed toward the exit to see if Ms. Wrenshall was still there. I could smell the lingering cigarette smoke over the chill of marauding winter air, but the entry was empty. I slid open the door anyhow, wondering at the conductor's wisdom in unlocking them while we were stopped.

The winter bite kissed my face. It was less cold than I'd expected, and smelled a little like melons. Minnesota winter wind can be knife-like, but this mountain air was milder, despite having carried a boatload of snow out here.

Judging by the footprints right outside the door, we'd gotten ten-plus inches of snow overnight, and it was still falling. A half dozen or so cigarette butts littered the ground. Previous ones could have been snowed on. I suspected there were little smoking outposts like this at every exit along the train. In fact, four cars up, another spark of flame caught my eye, bright as a laser in the dawn shadows. I couldn't make out if it was a man or woman in the dim predawn light.

I reentered the car and hoofed it toward the dining room. Some people were stirring, but for the most part, the passengers remained under a blanket of sleep. Jed was in his chair, fully reclined, Eliza curled in his arms. I made a mental note to ask him about her. She seemed like a nice-enough sort. I untangled his blanket from around his legs and pulled it to cover both of them up to the neck. They barely stirred.

The viewing car had a little more action, maybe a dozen people in the chairs, conversing in hushed tones. It was mostly pairs, though I saw one group of four that gave off a distinct "how do we break out of here" vibe, glancing at me suspiciously as I made my way through. We might have had food and fuel to hold us until the storm passed, but I doubted we had the patience.

No coffee was available in the viewing car, so I continued toward the dining car. The forward cars were a bit livelier than the aft, with people awake and reading and kids running up and down the aisles. I had to swerve to stay out of the path of a seven-or-so-year-old girl being chased by a boy at least two years older. They both had red hair and freckles, probably brother and sister. I felt sorry for their parents. How hard would it be to entertain kids on a train? Maybe we could organize a snowman contest later.

The redheads' reckless game crossed cars, and they zoomed around me in Car 5, tripping me. I landed on my knees near the dining car's door, catching a peek of what was happening on the other side as I fell: Reed, in a heated argument with Sylvester.

I rose to my feet and pushed the door open without thinking. The air smelled of fresh-brewed coffee and testosterone. Both men immediately stepped apart.

"Everything OK here?" It was a ridiculous question. Both men were flushed, and Reed's hands were fisting. He looked ready to swing.

"Fine," Sylvester said, his eyes wide with fear or adrenaline. He brushed past me, knocking my shoulder on the way.

Reed watched him go, his eyes boring holes in the guy's back.

"What was that about?"

Reed flicked his glance at me, visibly composing himself. "Sorry. We had a disagreement about how to best distribute the food." He held my gaze too deliberately, signaling to me that he was lying. So be it.

"Have any coffee brewing?" I asked.

"Sure. We were about to start setting up continental breakfast in the viewing car. You can help me bring it out."

Here's something unflattering about me: I love to spontaneously help, but I hate to be told to help. It takes away any sort of karma points because you don't even have a chance to say yes. Helping when you're commanded to becomes work without pay, and it makes me grumpy. I couldn't think of an excuse to get out of breakfast duty, though, so I took the bread basket he handed me.

"Is it true that food is disappearing?" I asked.

He glanced over from the coffee he'd been pouring into a large tureen. "Where'd you hear that?"

"The interviews last night."

He returned his attention to what he was doing. "Yeah, it's true. Only it's not food so much as utensils—forks, knives, salt and pepper shakers—though someone is getting into the cream puffs, too."

"A selective thief."

He nodded. "I'd call him peculiar." He hoisted the big silver coffeepot. His arm muscles flexed through his sleeves. It occurred to me that this guy was awfully fit for a porter.

"You guys work out a lot on the train?"

"You're looking at it." He set the tureen on a nearby table and tipped his head toward the door. "Open it for me?"

I led the way through the cars. Like the pied piper, Reed picked up followers as we went, the scent of fresh-brewed coffee drawing them in. I hoped they didn't mind stale pastries on the side.

By the time we reached the viewing car, we had a line of twenty-some people queuing up for refreshment. I grabbed a rich cup for myself and then left them to it, intending to head to the conductor's office in the hopes that he would have information to share. I was halfway out of Car 7 before I had a thought. I returned to Reed's side. He had his work face on, cheery and compliant as he handed out coffee.

"Do you know which car Terry Downs is sleeping in?" I asked. "He's one of the PIs."

Reed didn't break his smile. "You just passed through it. Coach Car Five."

The car immediately on the other side of the dining car. "I didn't see him in there."

Reed shrugged. *I'm not the boss of him,* the gesture said.

"If he's seated in Car Five, where would his luggage be?"

Reed tipped his hat. "Car Five, ma'am. Down below."

I'd need to figure out how he did that—said the most polite thing while conveying the impression that he thought I was as stupid as hair for asking. That was a skill I wouldn't mind adding to my arsenal. "Thank you."

I pushed through the coffee-clamoring throng and into Car 6, checking every seat to make sure Terry hadn't migrated. He hadn't. He also was nowhere to be found in the top level of Car 5. I supposed he could be in the lower-level bathroom, or out smoking—he had smelled like cigarette smoke on our first meeting, hadn't he? I slipped downstairs, to the lower level. It contained bathrooms and luggage. I didn't know what I expected to find, but my heart had begun thumping pleasantly. I hate murder. I hate terror. But I *love* snooping.

Not only do you find cool stuff, but you also feel like you're *doing* something. I realized that that's what the problem was: I was being too passive, letting other people investigate, sitting on the sidelines and worrying about Aimee. It was time to *do* something instead, and what better place to start than by investigating the investigators? Top-down approach, that's what I always say. I chugged my coffee and tossed the cup in a trash can.

I estimated there were more than a hundred pieces of luggage in the bottom of Car 5. I decided to go at them systematically, starting with the pieces closest to the landing and working back from there. Not a single identification tag went unread. People occasionally came down to use the showers or restrooms, but they paid me little notice. I was simply a passenger looking for her bag in the sea of suitcases.

I was on the second-to-last rack, breaking out a nice sweat from having to flip all the heavy suitcases around to get at the AmeriTrain name tags on each, when I found it: Terry Downs's bag.

The canvas duffel was more suited to the gym than a cross-country trip. It was packed tight and lock-free. Glancing furtively behind me, I tucked it under my arm and made for the bathroom, stopping at the last moment to slide a random red suitcase from the racks. If Terry caught me going through his stuff, I wanted a cover. Apparently, it was going to be "I like to go through other people's stuff." While not great, that's infinitely better than "I wanted to go through *your* stuff because I wanted to see if you are who you appear to be."

I slid the door and lock closed behind me, snapped down the toilet seat, and unzipped the bag. And there it was on top, for all the world to see.

Chapter 35

My eyes identified it first, but my nose was a close second as the rich smell of sticky green ganja curled up my nostrils and asked me to play. I tugged out the gallon-size zippered plastic bag full of orange-dusted bud. The funny thing was, I recognized the bag. Identifying a generic ziplock was not as hard as you'd think, at least when there was a note scribbled on the side in my handwriting: *Jed: choc. chip cookies. Enjoy.*

I'd given him the fresh-baked treats as a thanks for shoveling the library sidewalk for me, unasked, after our last snowstorm. And he'd apparently eaten the cookies, rinsed out the bag, and stuffed it with green.

For the love of Betsy. I needed to buy him a fresh box of storage bags. More importantly, I needed to decide what this meant. Was Terry *really* a cop, and if so, why was he pretending to be a PI? And why had he taken Jed's weed? Had he come here for something unrelated, possibly a drug sting, and simply stumbled onto the murder and missing persons case?

I scrounged through the rest of the bag, searched for clues. Besides Jed's weed, the duffel contained two pairs of blue jeans, size 33, folded neatly; four shirts ironed and sealed in vacuum travel bags; four pairs of clean (I hoped) underwear and the equivalent pair-balls of socks; deodorant, a toothbrush with a travel-size mint toothpaste, and a comb;

and a carton of generic cigarettes. Those might come in handy if the train went prison riot on us.

I stuffed the loot back in exactly as I'd found it, minus the weed. Let Terry wonder where it'd gone. I rezipped the duffel so I could easily search the one outer pocket. There I discovered a cinnamon gum wrapper and a ticket stub to see a newly released comedy at a Chicago theater. Nothing else.

Not helpful. I was considering my options when a pounding on the door made me clench my butt cheeks hard enough to clap. "Occupied!"

"Yeah, I know," said a female voice. "So are the other two. You gonna be long?"

"Who else is out there?"

Pause. "Just me."

I tossed the duffel strap over my shoulder, grabbed the red suitcase, whispered a prayer that the woman on the other side of the door wasn't its owner, and dashed into the open.

"Just cleaning up," I said, tossing her a smile. She appeared more bored than startled.

I shoved the red suitcase and then the duffel back where I'd found them and made my way up the stairs, a huge bag of weed tucked in my shirt and my thoughts racing. Who was Terry Downs? And how good were Jed's pot smoker instincts that he'd immediately gotten a bad vibe from the guy? I smoothed my hair and tried to do the same for my face as I cleared the landing on the second level. If anyone was watching, I needed to look like a calm woman who'd just gone down to use her morning toiletries. If someone were paying real close attention, they'd notice I appeared no cleaner coming up than I had going down, but it was a free train, right?

Doghn's cabin was next on my list. Odds were good that he was still in it. If that was the case, and I accidentally woke him up, I'd just say I was wondering what time the interviews were starting today.

The redheaded kids were now in the viewing car, gnawing on day-old bread like feral bear cubs, their mother ignoring them to mess with her phone. Watching them eat, I was blindsided by a memory of Noelle. We'd been huge fans of the *Little House on the Prairie* TV show that summer. We'd fight over who got to be Mary, who, while not the star, was the prettiest. Noelle always won because, she'd argue, my hair was darker and I had freckles. TV-Mary was a cream-faced blonde. Plus, Noelle had said, we were best friends forever and always, and best friends didn't fight.

I was cool with that.

Pillowcase bonnets over our heads, we'd wrap rolls in a handkerchief, tie it around a stick, and pretend we were walking cross-country. We'd traverse only Koronis Park, but if you did it right, that could take hours. On this particular day, our mission was to reach the slides without Chuckie, a.k.a. Nellie Oleson, spotting us. He seemed to have a sixth sense for the days we didn't want to see him, and so as soon as he saw us crossing the park wearing our moms' aprons and our pillowcase bonnets, he charged at us from his house, stealing our bread and telling us we were as stupid as poop.

"You know what's really stupid?" Noelle asked. (She said it "thtoopid.")

"What?" smirking Chuckie Greaves asked, chewing on our precious bread, our carrying stick broken at his feet.

"You. We put girl juice in that bread. Now you're really going to turn into Nellie Oleson!"

We high-fived each other, feeling too empowered even to laugh as Chuckie ran home crying.

Girl juice. I could have used some now.

I pulled myself out of the memory and back into the moment. Reed was no longer serving coffee. He'd been replaced by a porter I didn't recognize who'd also had the good grace to bring out sweet rolls and butter. I nabbed one for Mrs. Berns and another for myself and made my way back.

Jed and Eliza were still asleep, and Terry Downs was nowhere to be seen. Mrs. Berns was gone from our room. Since I had stuck to the train's top floor, she could easily have been on any lower level. I left her roll with a brief note saying I'd meet her for lunch at noon if I didn't see her before then, and I stashed the monster bag of weed under my mattress. Forget the princess and the pea; this was the PI and the pot.

I munched on my pastry as I headed toward the rear of the train. It was a little dry, a little greasy, but it filled the hole in my belly just fine. Ms. Wrenshall's door was closed, but light leaked out past the curtains and through the crack at the bottom. On a whim, I knocked.

"Come in."

I slid open the door. Her room looked like a Tasmanian devil had napped in it. Dirty clothes hung off the second bunk and lay strewn across the floor, toiletries were stacked everywhere, and the garbage overflowed with tissues. Ms. Wrenshall was seated in front of the window, the chair opposite her stacked with newspapers.

"Wow," I said.

"The porters don't clean." She ran her hand over her uncombed hair, revealing a face where all the makeup appeared to have been applied one inch below the feature it was supposed to enhance. "What am I supposed to do?"

"Yeah. Um, they're serving rolls and coffee, if you're interested. Not sure how long they'll last."

"Thank you."

She returned to gazing out the window. The sun was now rising, so more of the landscape was visible, but not much. It was a winter moonscape out there, as unsettling as a face without features, and the storm was beginning to pick up again. There was something so sad about her in that moment.

"You OK?"

She gave me the first genuine smile I'd seen from her, though it was a shade of one. "I don't like being still. Things catch up to you when you stop moving."

Oddly, I knew what she meant. "Hold on." I stepped back into my room, grabbed the roll I'd gotten for Mrs. Berns, ripped off the chewed end of mine, and made what was left as presentable as I could. I returned to Ms. Wrenshall and offered both.

"Thank you," she said.

"Yeah. Do you want to have lunch with Mrs. Berns and me?"

"Maybe." But she was digging into the rolls, not really listening to me.

I made a mental note to check on her, or have someone else check on her, regularly. This woman was not doing well.

I yanked her door shut behind me and hoofed it to Doghn's. Car 12 was quiet, but Cars 13 and 14 had a festive air, with all the doors open and people talking in the hallway. They had their coffee machine going and cookies out. They must have figured out where the hospitality food for the sleeper cars was stored. Good on them. They seemed more than willing to share, but I demurred, continuing to Car 15.

Unlike the previous two cars, all the doors in this one were closed. I could hear the merriment from Car 14 leaking through the cracks. It sounded far off, like listening to a party your parents are having while you're in your room upstairs, grounded.

I knocked on Doghn's door. No answer. It wasn't yet 7:30 a.m. He could have been asleep. In fact, odds were good that he was, because I'd walked the train from Car 4 backward and hadn't come across him or Terry. Wait a minute! Did that mean they were up in the conductor's office, investigating without me? I definitely wanted any updates they could offer. I needed to hurry. I'd just do a quick peek in here and then head out.

I slid Doghn's door open. His room was dark, the shades pulled shut. I slipped in, letting my eyes adjust. My heart thumped because I still wasn't sure if he was in the room. Could I pull a Ginger from *Gilligan's Island* if he turned out to be in bed? *I came to seduce you, my buffoonish little friend.*

I steadied my breathing. I didn't want to be too realistic if I had to call on my backup plan. I didn't think I heard anyone in the room besides me, but I stood still as a stone for another thirty seconds to be sure. When I was certain I was the only pulse there, I flicked on the light.

There was a body in the bed.

A big, unbreathing body.

Chapter 36

"Holy hair on fire!"

I scrabbled for the door, but I was shaking too badly. I couldn't get a grip on the handle. The walls felt slick with oil, everything colluding to keep me trapped in the room with the huge . . . wait a minute.

Doghn wasn't that big. He also didn't have three heads.

I stepped toward the bed, my legs rubbery, and whipped the blanket back, trying to touch it as briefly and as far from my body as possible. There was no waxy, staring corpse underneath. It was only three baby dolls at the top, a pile of clothes in the middle, and a stash of salt and pepper shakers where the feet would be.

What the nutcracker?

I leaned in for a better look. The dolls were cherubic and plastic, about the size of a newborn, two wearing dresses and the third in a sailor outfit. The girls appeared relatively new, but the boy doll appeared to be well loved.

The clothes below the dolls were folded, and far too numerous and diverse to belong to one person. The pile contained, at a glance: pantyhose, women's underwear, dresses, jeans in five different sizes, T-shirts, and kids' pajamas.

Below the clothes were at least two dozen salt and pepper shakers, most the stubby kind found in the sleeper cars but a couple the long, elegant glass shakers the dining car stocked. Below the shakers was a pile of wickedly sharp steak knives, their silver blades glinting in the dim light.

Doghn was a magpie. A thieving, glossy bird, stealing weird bits from here and there.

The realization created a painful thudding in my stomach. Was he also a murderer? That was quite a leap, but weirdness can sometimes be a gateway quality. He hadn't boarded until Glendive—or had he? I scrambled back in time to remember what Jed had said when he first encountered Doghn back in eastern Montana. What was it? Had Jed thought he'd seen Doghn in Fargo?

Unlikely. With his mustache, height, and C-level fame, Doghn would have had a hard time blending in. Still, I made a note to ask Jed as soon as I saw him, which would also be when I'd return his hefty and highly illegal bag of weed to him.

"Spying on the spy?"

I swiveled like a surprised cat—straight up, 180-degree turn, straight down.

Doghn stood in the doorway, his cheeks flushed, beady eyes sparking fire.

Chapter 37

"There you are!" When in doubt, state the obvious. It confuses people. "I've been looking everywhere for you. Didn't you hear?"

His eyes narrowed, but some of the flush left his cheeks. "Hear what?"

"You didn't hear a thing?" I was fishing for a hint of what direction to steer this lie. *Help a lady out already.* Snaking one hand behind me, I surreptitiously tugged the blanket back over the pile of booty.

Doghn scowled but seemed reluctant to step into his own space. I filed that away. "You mean about the train not moving until tomorrow?" he said.

Dang. That was a bad-news sundae topped with hot crap sauce. It also would not account for my being in his room. "No. Why can't we move until then?"

He waved his hands vaguely. "Storm has started up again. It won't pass until tonight, and it'll take the snow cutter another day to reach us."

"Oh. Well, that makes my news even more urgent. I was told that the conductor wants to see us in his office. That's why I came looking for you." This was a risky lie, as it was very possible Doghn had just met with the conductor. It was the only excuse that made sense for me to be in his room, however.

Doghn stroked the end of his mustache and raised an eyebrow. "So you came into my bedroom to tell me?"

I didn't like the glint in his eye. "You didn't answer when I knocked. I was worried."

"Well. We should certainly go visit the conductor if he wishes to see us. After you?"

Doghn stepped to the side, a conniving tilt to his features. He knew I'd seen what was under the blanket. We now had an unspoken agreement that we wouldn't talk about it, and that I owed him one for getting busted invading his privacy.

I hated owing people. I'd need to even the score.

I slapped the light switch, stepped into the hall, slid the door closed behind me, and started walking toward the front of the train, hyperconscious that Doghn was staring at my back this very moment, angry, and that if I couldn't figure out a way to reach the conductor alone before Doghn and I did together, I'd have some more 'splainin' to do.

I tried scooting ahead, but Doghn stuck to me like white on rice. I was slapping the opening panel to my car when I smelled it: the sweet, sweet aroma of marijuana burning.

My stomach dropped. Mrs. Berns must have located the stash.

Indeed, when I slid open the door to our room, I found her and Jed sitting in the recliners and staring out the window as if the newly energized snowstorm were the best TV show they'd ever watched.

"Ahem."

They both turned at my cough. Jed's face lit up. Mrs. Berns scowled when she caught sight of Doghn over my shoulder.

I waved away some smoke and pointed at the chairs. "I see you two made my bed."

Jed nodded happily. "Just Mrs. Berns made it, but she found something I'd been missing. Thanks, Mira!"

"We'll talk about it later. In the meanwhile," I said, making my eyes big to indicate that they needed to follow my lead, "Doghn and I are going to find the conductor because he told you he's looking for us, right?"

"Dude, I just got up," Jed said, pointing at this face. "You got something in your eye?"

I desperately turned to Mrs. Berns. "Jed seems to have smoked too much and doesn't remember telling me the conductor needed us, which is why I was back in Doghn's car looking for him."

"That sounds like Jed." She pointed toward my face. "You sure you don't have something in your eye? You keep making them big and then small."

I sighed loudly. "There's cookies back in Car Fourteen. Catch you two later."

Doghn and I barely hopped out of the way as the pair bumbled past us and raced toward the rear of the train. I made a quick scan of the room to make sure there was nothing illegal left in sight and closed the door behind me.

"Pot smokers," I said to Doghn. "Can't remember much."

He still appeared suspicious, but I cared less. I had my cover. If the conductor seemed confused when I told him we'd heard he needed us, I could blame it on the weed my friends had ingested.

"You guys find anything else out during the interviews last night?" I asked as we started walking again. I knew they hadn't. Jed would certainly have woken me otherwise.

"Nothing." Doghn stopped to arrange his bow tie before we stepped into the coach cars.

"Hey," I said, a thought occurring to me. "Where were you just now when I came looking for you?"

Doghn pushed past me, adjusting the pens in his suit pocket, presumably so he was ready to sign autographs if called on. "Searching the train for clues."

I jogged to keep up with him. Alas, most of the car was too busy passing the time to pay either of us much attention. "What'd you find?"

"Nothing."

I persisted. "Don't suppose you know where Terry is?"

"Don't suppose I do."

A hand lunged out from one of the chairs, stopping Doghn. He turned, his expression happy, and then it fell.

I followed the muscled arm to the face that belonged to it. The guy was four hundred pounds if he was an ounce, and as hairy as a hermit. His T-shirt said You Can't Fix Stupid.

"You know who's in charge?" the man asked. His voice was gruff.

Doghn peeled the guy's fingers off his arm. "The conductor. We're on our way to see him."

"When you do, let him know we'd like some news back here, 'kay? We're not prisoners. We deserve to know what's going on."

"Certainly." Doghn started to walk away.

"Wait!" I said. I glanced around the train. On closer inspection, what I had thought was fatigue was something else entirely. Pinched eyes, drawn mouths, some faces fearful, some angry. These were unhappy people. "Doghn, didn't you say the train is moving tomorrow?"

That got most everyone's attention. Whispers ran like wind up and down the car. Doghn became fidgety. "Yes, after the storm passes."

I turned one hand palm up. "And . . ."

"And the storm is supposed to pass later tonight."

The hairy hermit pointed out the window. "It looks here to stay to me."

It sure enough did. Now that the sun was up, I could see the snow swirling as thick as a milkshake out there.

"I talked to my wife just now," a man toward the front of the car said, his voice raised, "and she said the storm is supposed to pass by tonight, too."

"Then they gotta cut us out," the hairy hermit hollered back.

"I know that, dumbass," the man in front said, his face screwing in anger. "I was just saying when the storm was going to pass."

The big guy started to stand. I put a hand on his shoulder. I'd spent enough time in bars to know this was not going to end well without major distraction.

"So we know the storm stops this afternoon," I said, pitching my voice so everyone could hear it, "and that the snow cutters are on their way. We should be moving by tomorrow morning at the latest. In the meanwhile, you all have scheduled times to eat, right?"

At first, no one wanted to agree with me. Then, with grumbles, people began to hold up their reservation cards.

"Perfect," I said. "Eat a lot because there's plenty. And we'll ask the conductor to make hourly announcements. OK?"

I got a few nods, but more importantly, people's faces didn't seem so tight. "I'll let you know what I find," I said to the big man directly. "Promise."

He shrugged. "Not a lot I can do if you don't." He settled back into his seat and closed his eyes. Doghn hurried away and didn't say another word until we were in the foyer separating the cars.

"*That's* why I didn't want to say anything about the storm," he told me, his voice pissy.

"They needed hope."

"And what if the storm doesn't stop as scheduled? Or if the snow cutter can't get through until Monday?"

I leaned past him and pushed the panel that would open the door. "Then they deserve to know that, too."

"You're going to have a mutiny."

I didn't have an answer for him. The more coach seats I walked past, though, the more I wondered if he was right. There was a distinct odor of unrest in the air. It wasn't until we reached Car 5 that the dark mood shifted. It probably had something to do with the bartender serving bloody marys.

Except, he wasn't in uniform.

He was Morris, the oyster to Mrs. Berns's slot machine who'd tried to pick her up back in Detroit Lakes. He must have gotten into the liquor stores in the viewing car, and he was opening up for business bright and early.

Curse words.

Doghn was right. We didn't only have a killer to contend with; we also had a few hundred stir-crazy passengers.

Forget Valentine Train.

This was turning into *Murder on the Orient Express* meets *Lord of the Flies*.

Chapter 38

When we reached the employee car, I made an excuse about needing to run back to the dining car for some water. It was too late anyway to intercept the conductor and come up with an excuse for why I'd been in Doghn's room. Given that, I might as well jump fully into the investigation. The sooner the murder was solved and Aimee was found, the sooner I could be done with Doghn.

And I very much wanted to be done with Doghn.

I also wanted to search Reed's bunk. Terry was a pot stealer at best, but more likely an undercover cop, maybe even DEA. Doghn was a weird little hoarder and possibly a murderer. But what was Reed, besides in the wrong place at the wrong time, and with frequency? I wanted to like the guy. He was funny and helpful and smart. He'd also been in the hallway the night Sofia Ramos was murdered and Aimee and her dad disappeared, and he had something weird going on with Sylvester. He definitely had the access to murder someone. I wanted to find out if he also had a motive.

Doghn continued through the staff car and toward the conductor's office, and I pretended to turn toward the dining car but flipped back around as soon as I heard the door close behind me. If anyone was in this car, they were asleep or having some serious quiet time. It was impossible to tell which tubes were empty, however, as the door to every honeycomb bunk was closed. I stepped to Reed's. It was chest level, second from the bottom, fourth from the left. REED RYAN read the slip of paper, with a New York address scribbled under the name.

I didn't knock. If he wasn't in there, I might wake up someone who was sleeping. If he was in there, I was screwed either way.

The door opened out, which surprised me. It was not any bigger than a cookie sheet, and for a chilling moment, I became aware how much these cubbies resembled body drawers in a morgue. It was an efficient use of space, whether the body was alive or dead, but it was still creepy as all get-out.

I peeked in, a cool wash of relief accompanying the realization that it was empty. The second thing I noticed was how neat the bunk was. An ambient light bathed everything in a green glow. The bed was made to military standard. A shelf ran the length of it, but it was empty. The three cupboards lining the right side were closed. This meant I'd need to crawl in to see what they contained.

Glancing around first, I hoisted my foot onto the handle of the bunk below, cleverly designed for exactly that purpose. I was about to lift myself off the ground when the door to my left slid open and Reed walked in. Of course. I had the luck of the Irish when it came into breaking into people's stuff.

Reed was a cool cucumber. Rather than speak, he stopped, watching me. His face was expressionless. Mine felt very "hand in the cookie jar." I tried to unscrew that expression and replace it with "relaxed," but it snapped back to "guilty" every time.

"There you are," I said. Remember: when in doubt, state the obvious. "I was looking for you."

He continued his silence, his brown eyes steady. His calmness was unnerving.

"I was wondering when the train was going to move again," I asked.

He crossed his arms. "Tomorrow. For sure."

I was impressed by his self-control. He wasn't wasting any words asking me why I was invading his privacy. I closed the door to his bunk, grateful he hadn't caught me bumper-end out like Pooh in the hunny jar.

"Excellent." I squared up to face him. I wanted him to stop looking at me like that, as if he'd just made an important and unpleasant discovery about me. "If that's true, I think you all should open up the stores rather than have them wait for scheduled times. Get people well fed and happy. There's some mutiny brewing in those cars."

I nodded toward the other end of the train, but he didn't follow my gaze. Rather, he inspected me from foot to head, as if seeing me for the first time. It was a clinical stare, the examination of a surgeon wondering what body part to slice into first. My stomach was splashed with sour, and it suddenly felt very, very urgent that I find Aimee. If she was on this train, and this train was about to move, she was in extreme danger. The air was thick with bad things afoot.

"Did you hear me?" I puffed myself up, feeling my blood begin to boil.

All extreme emotions, even fear, led to anger for me. It's a good reaction in the wild, less useful when dealing with humans. "People are getting upset out there," I added. "A passenger in the viewing car broke into the liquor. If the staff at least pretends you're on their side, you can hold off a riot until we move again."

He nodded slowly. It didn't seem to be a reaction to my words. Rather, he had made up his mind about something. "We're on it. In fact, I was just coming to speak to the conductor for approval to set up a buffet in each car. Limited beverages, unlimited food."

"Perfect. Good. Glad to hear it. And glad I found you." It took all my willpower to turn, exposing my back to him, and march toward the conductor's office.

As I strode forward, I heard a ticking sound, ever so gentle, completely relentless, counting down on Aimee's life.

Chapter 39

Terry was already in the conductor's office when we arrived. I felt a flash of jealousy—what information had he and Doghn gathered without me?—before remembering that we were all on the same team.

Or, at least, we probably were. I was certain one of the men currently in the conductor's office knew more than he was letting on.

Reed quickly received permission from the conductor to share all the wares with the passengers. James Christmas appeared even more tired than he had the day before. His face was so gray it was almost green, and the lines around his mouth pointed downward. This had to be the worst train trip of his life, if not the worst in the history of AmeriTrain. Two train-adjacent murders, one of them on board, and a full-on storm stop in the Rockies.

"Valentine Train" would soon enter popular culture to mean "the worst ever." As in, "Dude, I heard your house burned to the ground the same day your car broke down."

"Yeah, I'm having a Valentine Train of a week."

Actually, the term might come to describe my life: "Watch out for Mira James. She's got Valentine Train luck."

I found myself suddenly craving a Nut Goodie, my go-to soul soother. It's a Minnesota candy, and appearances suggested a juvenile who thought fart jokes were funny (they are) had designed it. Basically, it's maple nougat sprinkled with peanuts and dipped in chocolate, shape be damned. I preferred them frozen, and I had a method for eating them. First, I'd nibble the chocolate and peanut ridge until I reached the nougaty part; then I'd chisel off chunks and suck on them, letting the chocolate turn warm and melt, revealing salty peanuts and then, finally, the nougat itself, which was as fresh and rich as homemade maple candy.

"Mira."

I came to, awakening from my sugar fantasy to find the men staring at me. I smoothed down my shirt, surreptitiously checking for any lady boners. Nope, I was good.

"Yes?"

Terry looked more amused than annoyed. "We asked you if you wanted to sit in on today's interviews or have your, ahem, colleague join us again."

"You're still going to go through with them?" I asked, refocusing on the moment. "If the train is going to move soon, shouldn't we just wait until the next stop and let the police handle this?"

"I'm in touch with the Coeur d'Alene police," Doghn said, twirling his mustache. "They will be waiting for us when we arrive. In the meanwhile, there is no harm in continuing the interview process. Who knows what we may find that could aid them?"

Or what we could miss because we were trapped in the conductor's office while the murderer walked around free. Unless he was himself in this room right now. I suppressed a shudder. I still wanted to search more of the train, but I needed to get a better handle on Terry and Doghn. Neither was who he appeared to be.

"Sure, I'll sit in," I said. "But I have to check in with my assistants to let them know where I'm at."

Terry pointed at my waist. "What about the walkie-talkie?"

Excellent question. I turned it on, filling the room with crackling. "Hello? Jed? Mrs. Berns?" No answer. I tried a couple more stations, and nothing. I couldn't blame either of them—I'd turned my own off—but still, it made me look pretty stupid.

"How about we meet back here in thirty," Terry suggested. "I have an errand to run myself."

That was code for going to the bathroom, or he had some DEA business to attend to. Either worked for me.

"I'm going to stay here," Doghn said, staring pointedly at me. "I have a few questions for the conductor."

Good luck with that. Now that I knew this train would be moving soon, I didn't care if Doghn found out I'd been snooping in his room. *Fork-stealing freak.*

Terry and I took off, parting ways in Car 5. If he was going to check on his luggage, he was in for a surprise, though I was confident he had no reason to suspect me of stealing back the pot.

I located Jed in Car 8, talking to his girl. They both smelled a little ripe, but she smiled sweetly when she caught sight of me. "Hey, Jed, can I talk to you for a minute?" I asked.

"Sure."

He followed me into the diaphragm. There was steady traffic in and out, much steadier than there had been when the train was moving. I wondered what the passengers were up to, and I asked Jed as much.

"It depends," he said. "Car Five is where the drinkers go. They're more country music. If you want weed, you come to Car Eight," he said proudly, "and we lean toward the blues. The sleeper cars are snooty—no offense—so most of us stay out of there. I heard there's a family car now, where people with kids are hanging out and coming up with games to pass the time, and someone turned the Love Car into the Art Projects car. I heard that they're going to start distributing food in all of them, too."

It amazed me how quickly mini-societies set up in times of stress, focused around either protecting the family or partying. "Are you getting a sense that people are ticked off?"

He scratched his head. "Little bit, but mostly, everyone's bored and wants to get moving."

"Let me know if you hear anything different." I pointed at his walkie-talkie. "It'd be great if you kept that on."

"Sure thing."

"And Jed?"

"Yeah?"

"You gotta hide your pot better. Terry got his hands on it. You might be right about him being a cop."

Jed's eyes widened. "How'd you get it back from him?"

"Never you mind that." I thought back to the train layout, when I'd first searched for Aimee. "Have you been to the second-to-last car on this train, the one right before the caboose?"

"Car Fifteen? Yeah," he said, blushing. "That's where Eliza and I went for some privacy."

"Perfect," I said. "So you know where it is. There are also little cabinets lining the walls. That'd be a good place to stash your stash."

Jed spontaneously gathered me up into a hug. He smelled like weed, patchouli, boy sweat, and friendship. I hugged him back.

"Hey, you know that secret I wanted to tell you about?"

"Yeah," I said. "I've been meaning to ask you about it."

He opened his mouth at the same time a scream ripped through the car. His movement and the sound were so perfectly timed as to be unsettling.

The cry was incoherent at first, but as the fear raced down the aisle of the train like wildfire, it took on a clear message: "Someone else has been killed!"

Chapter 40

I tried to push toward the original scream, but panic clotted the aisles. People were rushing over themselves to escape. Was the murderer on a rampage? I tried to peek over the heads of the crowd, but I lost my footing and would have been trampled if not for Jed yanking me back up.

"Keep your walkie-talkie on!" It was all I had time to yell before I threw myself into the stream of terrified humans, flowing with them instead of against them. I let them carry me halfway through Car 9, away from the scream, until we reached the stairwell. I propelled myself down. I fell five steps, bruising my hip, before I caught my footing. The people at the base of the stairs could sense the panic, but word of the new murder hadn't hit them yet.

And I certainly wasn't going to tell them.

I shoved toward the nearest exit and slid it open, falling into the icy outdoors. The chill of it sucked my breath away, and the snow came up to my thighs. It was still falling, big thick flakes that beat against my head like moths. My visibility was limited, maybe at ten feet, and the deep snow slowed me down, but stepping outside was the only way I could reach the car where the scream had originated.

It wasn't that I wanted to come face-to-face with a murderer, mind you, but I couldn't in good conscience walk away. What if Aimee had resurfaced and was in danger? My options were fight or flight, and on a train, there were only so many places to run to.

Better to face this head-on.

I plowed ahead, lifting my feet high to clear the snowbanks, which were shallower near the train. The air felt above zero, but not by much. I wasn't wearing a coat, and while my boots were warm enough, they weren't tall. Snow leaked in around the cuffs, running in icy rivers to my stockinged feet.

I tried to peek in the windows to see if I could reenter the train, but the windows were too high. Despite this, I continued to try to see in as I trudged forward, heavy flakes melting into my collar, my fingers growing numb, the shouts from inside the train growing quieter the closer I drew to the viewing car. My plan was to reboard there.

My breath ragged, I pushed forward. The snow was so thick and I was so intent on seeing inside the train that I was almost on top of the body before I saw it.

It was Terry.

He clutched his throat, surrounded by red exclamation points of blood against the pure white snow.

Chapter 41

"Oh my god!" I grabbed for him, searching for a wound. "What happened?"

His eyes spun like a terrified animal's. I looked around in a panic. We were surrounded by blinding snow. I kicked at the train.

"Help!" I hollered. Glancing up, I saw people still in a panic, pressing against each other and the windows. "Please, get out here and help me!"

It was no use. They were too scared to see what was going on. I fired up the walkie-talkie and yelled at Jed to get to the viewing car as fast as he could and bring some big guys. Then I reholstered the device and returned my attention to Terry. I swallowed my stomach, steeled myself for the gore, and pushed his hands away from his neck, because that was where the blood must have been coming from. His throat sported a three-inch gash, a wicked red smile that was leaking blood. I quickly stripped off my sweater and dabbed at it as gently as I could. I almost fell over with relief when I discovered that it wasn't bleeding too heavily.

"It's long, but it isn't deep," I said. I sucked in a mouthful of icy air and realized I was trembling. I pushed my sweater harder against his throat. "Who did this to you?"

Terry started to shake his head and then thought better of it. "He was wearing a mask."

I glanced each direction and saw only never-ending snow. "Where were you?"

"Car Five. I was going to grab my duffel when he came at me from behind. I felt it," he said, swallowing audibly, "like a paper cut. You know how the pain is sharp and buzzing? But I didn't know what'd happened. I turned and saw his back. Then the blood started flowing."

"Was anyone else down there with you?"

"A couple people, but they screamed and ran."

"Any chance they got a look at the guy?"

"I don't know. Probably." He was growing pale.

I pulled a corner of the sweater away, no mean feat, given how I was shivering. The bleeding had all but stopped. "Can you walk into the train so we can get a better look?"

"As soon as I catch my breath."

I nodded. "Take your time."

Jed showed up minutes later, towing the hairy hermit who'd stopped me earlier in the day. They helped Terry into the lower level of the viewing car and into a booth. A staff member ran for the first aid kit and pulled on some gloves to clean the wound, butterfly bandage it, and wrap some gauze around the works. Both Doghn and the conductor located us before the first aid was complete. Terry told them what had happened.

"He's a professional, whoever he is," Doghn said at the end of the story. "To walk up those stairs, take off a ski mask before you reach the top, and blend in? That's no amateur."

I studied Doghn. His face was flushed. He appeared almost aroused by this new development. "And you?" I asked him. "Where were you when this happened?"

He drew back. "I was with the conductor the whole time."

The conductor coughed. "Not the whole time. I had to check into the engine car briefly."

Doghn scowled. "Where were *you*?" he asked me.

"With Jed." I scanned the car's lower level. A crowd had gathered, but no faces I recognized. "Where's Reed?"

"Why do you want to know?" Doghn asked.

Because I sensed that he was somehow connected to this. "Terry, was the man who did this to you wearing gloves?"

Terry shrugged, then winced. "Didn't see him well enough to know. Probably, though."

"Can you describe the other witnesses who were down here when it happened?"

"There were three on this level, maybe more on the stairs." He went on to list their features with a police officer's detail. None of the three sounded familiar.

"I think we should track them down and ask them what they saw," I said. "Particularly if someone was on the stairs while your attacker unmasked himself running to the second level."

The conductor shook his head. "I'm afraid I can't allow any of you to put yourself in any more danger. I'm putting the train on lockdown. Everyone is confined to their assigned seats. No one goes anywhere but the bathroom, and they don't go there alone."

"What?" I couldn't believe it. That was going to create a mutiny for sure.

"He's right," Terry said, coughing. "We're no longer looking for clues. Right now, the game is to stay alive."

Chapter 42

The staff, on the buddy system, was bringing twenty-four hours' worth of food to each person on the train, starting with the last sleeper car and working their way forward. I watched them travel past, sitting in my chair in a funk, Mrs. Berns across from me.

"You wanna talk it through?" she asked.

I didn't. Stress made me quiet. I did want to sketch it, though, so I yanked out a notepad and a pencil. Here's what I knew: Aimee, her mom, and her dad had boarded in New York. Her mom and dad had been nervous, or had at least grown nervous sometime after they left and before I met them. Reed had also been on at least since New York, as had Ms. Wrenshall. Mrs. Berns, Jed, and I had gotten on in Detroit Lakes. An escaped prisoner had boarded in Fargo immediately after murdering his colleague at the Fargo train station.

So had Terry.

That night, Aimee's mom, Sofia, was murdered next door. Ms. Wrenshall was awake when it happened, and Reed was in the hallway. One or the other of them was lying about whether she'd called Reed. Doghn claimed to have boarded in Glendive, and he'd get a lot of publicity if he could solve this crime. I'd thought I'd spotted Aimee at least three times since then, but it could have been a trick of my eyes. Since we'd been stopped in the Rockies and Terry, Doghn, and I had identified ourselves as investigators looking into this case, Terry had had an attempt on his life.

And Terry himself was a wild card, a man who claimed to be a PI but who'd stolen Jed's pot.

I scribbled as I thought, underlining, crossing out, and ultimately finding myself no better off than I'd been when I started. Why had Sofia Ramos been murdered? And if Emilio, Aimee's dad, wasn't the guilty one, as the attack on Terry suggested, why was he hiding? And what was the murderer afraid we'd discover in our interviewing process?

"Hello?"

My pencil lead snapped. I'd been pushing too hard. Across from me, Mrs. Berns snored. Ms. Wrenshall stood at our open door.

"Hello," I responded. I was on edge. Every corner seemed sharp, and Ms. Wrenshall's eyes were too wary. The whole train felt like a convoy of murderous looters.

"Can I still join you for lunch?" She held up a tray. We must have gotten our food delivered while I was obliviously scribbling away.

I closed the notebook. "Sure." I indicated sleeping Mrs. Berns. "Maybe in your cabin?"

Ms. Wrenshall studied her feet. "It's dirty. The porters aren't cleaning, you know."

"Yeah," I said, not having the patience for her eccentricity at the moment. "They have bigger things to worry about."

She nodded and turned away silently. I followed her next door. Together we cleared the pile of clothes off the second chair and both settled in, surrounded by the clutter and reek of stale cigarette smoke.

I pointed at the tray she'd set down. "What do we have?"

"Sandwiches, water, and chips."

It sounded good to me. She handed me a turkey and cheese and selected a roast beef for herself. That left six more sandwiches, three bags of potato chips, and seven bottles of water.

"Is that all for you, or are we sharing between cabins?"

"They haven't brought us food yet," she said, unwrapping her sandwich. "You live as long as I have, you always make sure to bring your own."

I peeled the clear plastic off my sandwich, sniffing at it. No telling how long she'd been hoarding it, but it smelled OK. I bit into it. My mouth watered immediately. I tried to remember the last time I'd eaten. The bite of roll seven hours earlier?

"So, what's your story?" I asked her.

She put down her sandwich, a smile creeping across her face. She still wore all the gaudy jewelry she'd had on when we first met, but she'd given up on the makeup. I found I liked her better without it. She had a strong face, sagging at the edges, with watery brown eyes and a big nose.

"Isn't that a little abrupt?"

I unscrewed the cap on a bottle of water and took a swig. "If you haven't heard, we're on this train with a killer. It's snowing outside like it'll never stop, and we're on lockdown. I'm past the pleasantries stage."

"All right," she said slowly. "Here's my story: I used to be rich. I'm not anymore. I had friends when I had money. Now I've got a grandnephew whom I've never met. He lives in Spokane. He doesn't know that I'm broke. I haven't decided if I'll tell him yet. I don't know if I can stand to find out I never meant anything to anyone."

She delivered this sad tale in a short, matter-of-fact breath, then tucked back into her sandwich.

I'd stopped chewing. My turkey hoagie suddenly tasted like shredded paper. "What about his parents, or their parents? You must have had a brother or sister, right?"

She nodded and reached over to open a sack of chips. They smelled like salty burps. "A brother. He stopped talking to me when I stopped paying his bills. I didn't want to support his alcoholism. He died of liver failure two decades ago. Left behind a son. That son died in a car accident and left behind a son of his own. Dylan Wrenshall. He looked me up a few weeks ago. We agreed to meet. I'm sure he still thinks I'm rich."

Her big wet eyes met mine, not a lick of self-pity in them. What was there was much worse: the utter, raw realization that she was alone. It wasn't fear; it wasn't exaggeration—it was truth. My throat felt tight. "You don't seem like a bad person."

That smile shadow found its way back onto her face. "You can be honest."

I put my sandwich down. "Honestly? You seem kinda high maintenance." I gestured at the room. "And messy. But also unique, and I like that. You've got this eccentric vibe."

She glanced out the window. "I used to be a painter."

"Yeah? Anything I'd be familiar with?"

She looked back at me, weighed me, and made up her mind. She placed her chips and sandwich on the tray and waded through the clothes on the floor to the narrow closet. She pulled out a portfolio and slid it open. It contained twelve photographs of paintings, each of them about 11 x 17. If the photos were even half as gorgeous as the originals, she was a woman of amazing talent. The art reminded me of a sharper Matisse, gorgeous jewel tones evoking landscapes and emotions.

"These are incredible." I meant it.

That sad smile again. "Thank you. Do you think my grandnephew will like them?"

Her unspoken question trailed behind that one—*even if I'm not rich?*

"He'd be silly not to," I said.

She nodded shyly and closed the portfolio, returning it to the closet. I felt the bond settle in between us.

"What do you think happened to the little girl next door?" I asked spontaneously.

The intercom crackled before she could answer. It had been used so little on this trip that I'd forgotten the train had one. Why *wasn't* the crew communicating more?

"Hello. This is your conductor, James Christmas. I'm thrilled to report that the snow cutter has been officially dispatched from Coeur d'Alene. It will reach us late tonight or early tomorrow, whether the snow stops or not."

The cheer reverberated the length of the train, muffled, but almost more powerful for it. "Although we will not need it, we have food and water to last us for seven more days. Unfortunately, our waste disposal is limited. As such, we are asking that no one use the restroom unless absolutely necessary."

A drowsy-faced Mrs. Berns appeared at the door, rubbing at her messy hair. "What? I have to curb my recreational peeing?"

"In addition," the conductor continued, "we're asking that you no longer charge your personal devices. This includes cell phones."

I didn't like the sound of that. I had no personal devices to charge, but hoarding electricity suggested that we might be stuck here longer than ideal or that our power supply was lower than promised. What could I do about it, though? The conductor had put us on lockdown. Any non–staff member found outside their car would be held in the conductor's office until we arrived at Coeur d'Alene, and the conductor'd been serious as a heart attack when he'd broken that news.

"I have to go to the bathroom," I said, rising.

"That's how it works," Mrs. Berns said, scooting to take over my spot and my sandwich. "They tell you what you can't do, and that becomes exactly what you must do. Didn't these people ever raise kids? They should think before they speak."

I thought back to the last time I'd gone to the bathroom. It had been only an hour ago. She might have had a point. My stomach was feeling the eensiest bit queasy, though, and I didn't know if it was the sandwich or the thought of being on this train without electricity and with a murderer. It'd be like the world's biggest coffin.

I steered toward our cabin before changing my mind and instead headed toward the communal bathroom. I reached for the door handle at exactly the same moment it opened toward me, and Aimee stepped out.

I reached toward her, my breath frozen.

I touched her. She was real.

"Aimee!"

Her eyes were shadowed, her face ashen with fear. Her tiny angel face was pinched, reminding me more of Noelle than ever.

"You can't trust anyone," she whispered.

Chapter 43

I pulled her into a hug. She stiffened in my arms, and I let her go immediately. "Sorry, hon," I said. "Are you OK? I've been worried sick about you."

Aimee's eyes were big and brimmed with tears. "I'm not suppose to be here. I'm not suppose to let anyone see me. I can't trust anyone. But I had to pee. I had to."

"You can trust me," I said, but I realized I had been seeing her as Noelle, not as the scared little girl she was. She deserved better. "You're hiding on the train, right? Do you need food? Water? Is your dad still with you?"

She shook her head so her hair fell into her eyes. "If you tell that you saw me, we don't get to go free. It's at Poorland that we get to be free."

Her five-year-old ears must have heard "Portland" wrong. "I won't tell anyone, honey, I promise. But I want to help you. Do you want to hide in my cabin? I can make sure no one finds you."

The offer terrified her. A war was being waged in her eyes. She finally spoke. "Have you seen Mr. Bunny? I wasn't suppose to leave, but I miss him. And I had to pee."

"Mira?" Ms. Wrenshall stood in her doorway, her expression concerned. "Who are you talking to?"

When I looked back, Aimee/Noelle had vanished. But I had *seen* her. I could still feel her tiny bird bones in my arms. "No one." I would keep my promise to her. "Just talking to myself."

Ms. Wrenshall nodded slowly, squinting at me. She appeared ready to ask me something important but instead said, "I don't suppose you have a light? Mrs. Berns said neither of you smoke, but you seem like a resourceful woman."

I didn't like how she was talking to me like I was delusional. "They won't let you outside to smoke."

"I wasn't going to ask them." She slung a purse over her shoulder and pitched her voice into the cabin. "You joining me?"

Mrs. Berns appeared at her side. "Sure. Best offer I've had all day."

I watched them slide past me and start down the stairs. My blood pressure was still spiking. Aimee must have gone down those stairs, too. I followed them.

"You want a toke?" Mrs. Berns said, waving a doobie in my direction.

"No," I said. "Just stretching my legs."

She glanced at me but said nothing. At the lower level, I scoured the cabins. Their doors were open, their inhabitants looking like startled zoo creatures when I peeked in. The communal bathroom was empty. I raced back upstairs and toward the rear of the train.

I didn't slow until I stood outside Doghn's closed door. I slid it open, my heartbeat pounding.

"Hello," he said. "I was wondering how long until you figured it out."

Chapter 44

He sat in the fore-facing chair, his stolen booty moved to the top bunk. He wore a white suit, reminding me of Kentucky Fried Chicken's colonel.

I consciously slowed my breath. "Figured what out?"

"That you'd need me if you wanted to know what's really going on. So, what do you want to know?"

He was right about me coming to him for answers, though I hadn't been aware of it until I stood facing him. "What do you know about Sofia Ramos?"

He twisted the left tip of his mustache. "What do you *want* to know about her?"

I closed the door behind me and had his throat in my right hand in two short strides. I leaned in close, smelling the not-unpleasant odor of mustache wax. "Everything."

In a move I recognized from tae kwon do, he reached around the top of my hand, grabbed the soft spot between my thumb and forefinger, and twisted until I was on my knees from the sharp pain.

I didn't make a noise, and I also didn't fight back, though one well-placed elbow drop would splash his nuts across the chair like windshield bugs. This was a pissing contest, though, and a certain kind of person will give you what you want if you let them feel like the winner. I suspected Doghn was that kind of guy.

"Like the fact that Sofia Ramos was a housekeeper from Brooklyn who told her employers she needed a week off to visit a sick aunt in Portland?" He twisted my hand a hair more, sending bolts of silver pain down my arm. I hoped I wasn't underestimating the turd.

"Ouch," I said. "And her husband?"

"I don't know."

I glanced over my shoulder. He was smiling, and he was lying. I began to prime my elbow. "You don't know *anything* about her husband?"

"Nothing." His smile grew wider, tipping his mustache up in a Cheshire Cat grin. "Except that she didn't have a husband. Or children." He twisted again. I couldn't hide the yelp this time.

I blinked away the pain. *So who was the man with her? And how did she know Aimee?* Thoughts of human trafficking and kidnapping raced through my head.

"That's not a whole lot of information," I said, hoping to goad him into revealing more. Unfortunately, my words had the opposite effect. Anger fell like a curtain across his face, and he began to twist my wrist with enough force to break it.

I was ready for it, though, and I turned with his momentum, sliding underneath my own hand, around, and up, putting me in the dominant position. My quick movement startled him, and he stood, bumping his head on the upper bunk. A knife clattered to the ground.

A vision of Terry standing in the snow, blood staining the white like a lurid raspberry sauce, clouded my eyes. I stepped backward.

"Why do you have a knife?"

"It's for my room cheese."

Room cheese? If there was a grosser term, I had yet to hear it. I felt toward the door, unwilling to turn my back to him.

"You don't believe me?" He stooped to pick up the knife and slide it back into his suit coat. "How's about this? It's dangerous times, and a man has to protect himself."

How's about that, indeed. Doghn was one creepy monkey. I stepped into the hall, glancing around, ominous shadows everywhere. When I saw no movement, I slid Doghn's door shut, my last view of him looking half-sad, half-conniving.

I couldn't get to my own cabin fast enough. I massaged my wrist as I speed-walked, coming up with a street plan as I went. I would find Aimee. I would search this train from back to front, starting at the weird storage bins in the car in front of the caboose. I would not stop until I located her, and I would not let her out of my sight until we were in Coeur d'Alene and I handed her over to the police. If staff tried to slow my search, I'd tell them the conductor had given me the command. If they found the conductor and he called me out as a liar, I'd . . . come up with a different plan.

When I reached our cabin to let Mrs. Berns know what was up, she wasn't there. I peeked out the window. She and Ms. Wrenshall were still outside, smoking any number of cigarette-shaped objects. I had my hand poised to tap on the glass when my walkie-talkie crackled.

"Yeah."

"10-40, good Mira, this is Smokey the Jed Bear. Are you a 10-40 on your end?"

"I'm busy. What do you need?"

Some more crackling, then Jed's voice came out as a loud whisper. "It's me. Jed."

"Got it. What's up?"

"You told me to keep my ear to the ground. I have, and word on the train is that a porter has disappeared. All the other porters are talking about it. They're pretty mad."

"Which one?" I asked. But of course I already knew the answer.

Chapter 45

Jed confirmed that Reed hadn't been seen since breakfast. This presented a major problem to the rest of the staff, who were already seriously overworked trying to prepare and deliver food to every car.

It was an issue for me because I had a strong suspicion that Reed was a murderer.

And so I did what anyone would do in my place: I took advantage of his absence to finally search his bunk. Accepting a note the comically serious-faced Jed slid into my hand as I passed his seat in Car 8, I made my way to the front of the train.

Walking through the other cars was like entering a honky-tonk war zone. People were arguing or laughing too loud. A fistfight was brewing in the viewing car between a guy who thought he had more rights than another guy to a candy bar discovered on the floor. And if they were in the viewing car, that meant I wasn't the only one violating curfew.

The conductor had lost control of his train.

I continued toward the staff sleeping car, my shoulders tight, my wrist aching from where Doghn had twisted it. If I acted like I had a purpose, I was less likely to be stopped, but I didn't like the lawless atmosphere surrounding me. If we didn't get moving soon, more people were going to get hurt.

A female porter with a whiskey-colored drink in her hand stopped me at the dining car.

"Where're you going?" she asked.

The smell of liquor was strong. I pointed over her shoulder. "The conductor asked for me. You OK?"

"Yeah, super. Great. Good." She swayed. "You know we don't get paid overtime if the train's late, right?"

I didn't. And if that was true, that meant the passengers were not the only potential mutineers. "So you're drinking the difference?"

She clinked her glass against an imaginary one. "Damn straight. And you can tell Mr. Christmas I said so."

She lurched to the side as if the train were in motion. I slipped past her, realizing I still held Jed's note. I shoved it into my back pocket. Two porters were talking in Staff Car 3, but I ignored them, torpedoing straight toward Reed's bunk. I yanked open the door, half expecting to find him inside.

He wasn't.

I hoisted myself up and crawled in headfirst, feeling exposed until I was fully inside the metal cage. The tiny cabin smelled neutral, verging on clean, like it had been recently bleached. It made my skin crawl.

I slid open one of three cupboards nearest to me. It held clothes. I pulled them out and unfolded them. They concealed nothing. The second cupboard was empty, which sent a trill of alarm through me. Who has three tiny cupboards in which to store their belongings and doesn't use them all? When I discovered that the third cupboard was also empty, I felt genuinely sick. Something was very wrong here.

It took every ounce of self-control not to shoot out of that metal tube like a cannonball, but as long as I had access, I had to look everywhere. Lightheaded, I thrust my arm under the mattress as best I could while still lying on it.

My hand slid across the cool metal of the gun first. I yanked it out and dropped it on the mattress like it was hot. It was an ugly, snub-nosed thing, lying there like a sleeping viper.

Leaning forward, I searched some more beneath the mattress, blindly moving my arm. I had nearly given up when I felt the slip of paper. I almost moved past it, thinking it was a tag, but it snagged on my finger. I gently pulled it out. It was a newspaper clipping. The article was dated February 8, which was five days ago.

Woman Scheduled to Testify Against Mob Boss Pierre Danza Disappears

Gisela Alvarez, 27, former girlfriend to accused drug runner and arms dealer Pierre Danza, initially agreed to testify against Danza, who is currently awaiting trial on 12 counts of racketeering and four counts of murder. According to the FBI, Alvarez did not appear for her February 7 deposition and her current location is unknown.

The son of Italian and Irish immigrants, Danza is known on the streets as the Gunner, having made a name for himself as a ruthless dealer in illegal weapons and heroin as well as money laundering. He is believed to be the leader of an organization called the West Side Donnys. He was untouchable until recently, when an FBI sting uncovered enough evidence to arrest him. Their initial case relied heavily on testimony from Alvarez. Her occupation is unknown.

Danza is believed to be the father of Alvarez's daughter, though paternity has not been established.

Below the article was a black-and-white photograph that paper creases had rendered nearly illegible. It featured a woman, her face almost obscured by hair, a girl of around five years old in her arms, the girl's back to the camera. Standing next to her was a short, dark-haired man in a suit coat, his expression grim. His face was the clearest of the three, his eyes black and angry. They were identified in the photo as Gisela Alvarez and daughter, and Pierre Danza.

I knew the woman as Sofia Ramos, murdered next-door passenger and mother to Aimee (if that was even the girl's name).

My head was spinning. Sofia/Gisela had been on the run from the mob, fleeing west with her daughter. That explained her nervousness. It did not explain the man, Emilio, who was traveling with them, who looked nothing like Pierre Danza. Was he her lover? Actually, I knew I should use past tense, as Gisela was no longer with us. Pierre sounded like a monster, but all that mattered was that I find Aimee before the bad guys did. She clearly understood the danger she was in, even if I had not.

Trust no one.

That was damn good advice. I glanced again at the newspaper clipping and committed the meager information to memory before folding it back up as I'd found it. I tucked the article and the gun approximately back where I'd discovered them, wondering at the ball of lies Doghn had fed me. He'd said Sofia Ramos didn't have a daughter. In fact she did, along with a nice chunky alias.

The thing was, I'd been certain Doghn had told me the truth. Sure, he had me twisted like a pretzel when he'd said it, but the truth had a timbre, and I thought I'd heard it. Either I'd been wrong, or someone had given Doghn bad info.

It didn't matter. The mob was obviously still after Aimee, judging by the attack on Terry. That meant the little girl knew something, or Pierre Danza wanted her back. I thought of his fierce black eyes in the photograph and shuddered. I would find that girl first. I'd let Noelle get stolen; I wouldn't make the same mistake with Aimee. I needed to get to her before Reed did. If he wasn't the chief executioner, he was helping somebody.

Why, I didn't yet know.

That thought was firmly in my head as I scooted out of the bunk, feetfirst.

It, and every other thought I'd ever entertained, fled as a cold hard hand clamped down on my ankle like Death's paw.

Chapter 46

"Chad!" I punched him in the arm, feeling a cold-hot wash of fear and relief. "Why'd you grab me like that?"

He rubbed his shoulder, his expression pained. "I was trying to help you."

I closed Reed's door. "Help me?"

"Yeah." He pointed at the bunk. "Help you get out."

I glanced up and down the aisle. "What're you even doing here?"

He broke into a smile. "I saw you walk past. Didn't you see me? Back in my sleeper car?"

I most definitely hadn't, but I'd been focused on my mission. "Sorry."

"No worries. I've been trying to catch up with you, but I kept getting stopped. Do you know there's people fighting over a bag of peanuts in Car Seven like it's their spare kidney? Jeez, some people buckle under stress. You know?"

I did. "So what'd you want?"

He leaned against the wall, or at least meant to, but misjudged the space and missed it. He fell forward, catching himself at the last minute. The guy was not suave. I noticed that he'd styled his hair differently, slicking it back a lot like Doghn did with his own hair. And was that the spidery hint of a new mustache on his upper lip?

"You know," he said, not acknowledging his goof, "just wanted to see how you're getting on."

Oh brother. I did not have time for this. "I'm fine. I better head back to my room. Thanks for your concern."

His face fell. "All right. Well, if you want to, you know, hang later, you know where to find me."

"Sure." *Weirdo.* What sort of guy mistakes an accidental crotch-diving expedition as an invitation? "Catch you later."

I didn't wait for his answer. Using my best waitressing skills, I glided all the way through the train, dodging a fistfight here, an argument over who was looking at whom wrong there, piles of empty containers and wrappers everywhere. The train was taking on a distinct smell. Somewhere between "used sweat sock" and "old eggs." It was not pleasant.

In Car 10, someone screamed, and I jumped. I turned to see that it was just a small boy getting a time-out. I thought I caught a glimpse of Chad behind me, on the other end of the raucous crowds, but what did it matter? He was just a kid looking for a connection that wasn't there. I made it to Car 11 unaccosted.

Our cabin was empty.

Ms. Wrenshall was not next door, and I didn't see either her or Mrs. Berns outside the window. It seemed no one was sticking to the lockdown. That would make my investigation both easier, because I could not be sent back to my cabin, and harder, because everyone would be in my way.

I left a note for Mrs. Berns and was about to travel to the rearmost car when I thought of one really good hiding place on this train that I'd been overlooking: Aimee's room! It had police tape over the door. Presumably, no one was supposed to go in or out until we reached our destination. I ducked into my room for a pair of knit gloves and donned them, being careful of my tender wrist. I'd do my best not to sully the crime scene.

Fingers covered, I slid beneath the police tape, closing the door behind me. The room was exactly as it had been when I'd peeked in right after the body was taken out, but then again, it had been this clean even when it had been occupied. The curtains were closed, so I stood still, allowing my eyes to adjust. When they did, I dropped on hands and knees, peeking under the bed and in cracks and crevices.

Nothing.

I worked up one level, examining under the mattress and on shelves. Still nothing. It was while straining to reach the back of the closet shelf that I felt it—something with some give, something soft.

I pulled it out.

It was Mr. Bunny, his fur patchy, his ear bent, one eye loose. He looked sad and well loved. My heart tightened as I thought of Aimee cowering somewhere on this train without him. The tears began to slide down my cheek.

I was wiping them away with the back of my hand when the door slid open.

Chapter 47

The man I'd known as Emilio Ramos—and Aimee's dad—stood there. He appeared more startled to see me than I was to see him. He also looked different. It took me a moment to realize it was his hair color. It had been dark before. It was now blond, at least the parts of it sticking out of his ski cap. The brassy color did not complement his olive skin.

He snatched Mr. Bunny out of my hand. His mouth opened and then closed, drawing attention to the complete hairlessness of his face. The rest of him looked haggard, but he'd made time to shave? I couldn't read his expression, but I didn't feel like I was in danger.

And then he was gone.

He'd come for Aimee's bunny. That meant he was with her, and he was probably taking care of her. I took off after the man, watching his shadow slip down the stairs. I might have caught him if the train hadn't picked that moment to lurch forward with such force that I was thrown from my feet, cracking my head against the stairwell and creating blue color blitzes in front of my eyes.

What was going on? I stayed still for a moment, tasting my pain, before I pulled myself to my feet. I limped gingerly down the stairs, holding my head with my hands, wondering if I was imagining the cheering and the fact that it felt like the train was actually moving.

Another lurch confirmed it: the train was in motion. I was able to grab a railing this time so I didn't fall. By the time I reached the lower landing, there was no sign of the man with Aimee's bunny.

I stuck my head inside the nearest cabin. "Did you see a man just come down here?"

The pair of men inside smiled back at me. *"Ja."*

"Do you speak English?"

"Nein," they said apologetically.

I went to the next cabin and got the same answer, though in English. Everyone was too busy chattering about the train moving to have noticed anything else. The air held the feeling of a giant festival, a mix of celebration and anticipation. I could go forward, or I could go backward, or I could stay in place and search the car I was presently in. Each option had pros and cons.

The train gave another careening pitch. We all grabbed something solid. The train was either being pushed or pulled, and it wasn't smooth sailing. Given what I knew about driving a car out of a snowbank, I figured that once we broke free of the packed snow, we'd cruise smoothly.

Until then, we were in for a bumpy ride.

And I needed to find Aimee before we reached our next stop. Reed and whoever he was working with would be trying desperately to locate her before she disappeared for good or, worse, went to the police with what she knew. I wondered why she hadn't talked to them back at Glendive. But of course she was so young, and as she said, she didn't know whom to trust. Well, I needed to figure out who was on my team, and quick, because I couldn't search this whole train alone. Mrs. Berns and Jed could, of course, be trusted, and since his attack, I had to gamble that Terry could be, too. With four of us looking, it would go faster.

Mrs. Berns still wasn't back, and Jed and his girlfriend weren't in their seats. That meant I didn't find anyone for my posse until the viewing car. Terry, a little red seeping through the bandage on his neck, was nursing a gin and tonic as people partied around him, jumping on furniture, beating their chests like Tarzan, and generally acting in a way that I hoped embarrassed them tomorrow.

"Terry! Have you seen Mrs. Berns or Jed?"

He shook his head infinitesimally and quietly sipped his drink. A bra flew through the air like a slingshot, followed by a matching set of panties.

"I need your help, OK? I think that girl, Aimee, is still on the train. I think she's in danger, and I think whoever wants her is the person who attacked you." I grabbed his arm. "Terry? Are you listening? I think I know where the girl is."

And I really thought I did. I'd pieced together all my sightings of her, and they all happened in the train's back half. She, and the man she was with, had managed to disappear like smoke on the lower level. Cupboards lined the walls down there, and I had a hunch they all led back to the storage car, forming a train-length ventilation system.

But Terry was not interested. He was the picture of calm, a bulky ship standing firm in the storm. "Good luck with that."

"Please! Just come look with me. If she's there, great. If she's not, what have you wasted?"

"My time, if I'm lucky. More likely, my skin." He pointed at the patch of red staining his bandage and blooming like a flower. "You see this? It was fine until the train started swaying like a drunk. That's my throat. Someone tried to slice my *throat*."

"Yeah, I get it. And that someone is still on this train. Do you want them to get Aimee?"

He shrugged.

It was all I could do not to yank at his hair. How could he not care? That more than anything told me he wasn't a DEA agent. He really was just a punk private investigator, maybe a cop in a previous life, for sure a pot-thieving scaredy pants now. So I'd meet him at his level.

"Think of all the publicity we'd get if we cracked this case."

He sat up a little straighter. A woman wove through the car with a crying baby, the smell of old diaper wafting behind them.

"That'd drive up some good business," I continued. "Besides, I know for a fact there's weed hidden in that back car."

He looked at me dead-on now. "How do you know that?"

207

"You'll have to come and see. Come on. Please?"

An uproarious cheer drowned out my pleading as our train stopped the careening and began *chug-chugging* forward like it'd never stopped. Beads of sweat broke out on my face. It was now or never. I pulled Terry's hand, ignoring his protests.

I led him through the crowd. After we made it through two cars, he stopped protesting. We were in Roomette Car 10 when the announcement came on, James Christmas sounding perkier than he had the entire ride.

"As you are likely aware, the snow cutter successfully reached us. They've cleared the entire track from our location to Coeur d'Alene. We should reach that stop in approximately forty-five minutes."

The cheers were truly deafening this time. All around us, people hugged and high-fived. Terry burrowed forward, head down, shielding his neck.

Chad was still nowhere to be seen. Same with Mrs. Berns and Ms. Wrenshall. We passed Doghn's cabin. His door was closed. I wasn't certain whose team he was on, so I didn't slow, even though Terry paused to toss me a questioning glance.

We were in the second-to-last car, the storage car where I was certain Aimee and the man were hiding, when Terry spoke.

"You don't think Doghn can help us?"

I appreciated him waiting until we were past Doghn's car to ask. "I'm not sure about him. Same with Reed, that first porter you interviewed. There's something off about both of them."

Terry scowled. "You're certainly suspicious enough to be a PI. I don't know about Reed, but I can tell you Doghn's not a bad guy. A little puffy, for sure, but he's decent."

Terry might think differently if I told him about the wrist twisting. But really, what did I care what Terry thought of Doghn? I needed his help finding Aimee, and then I'd never have to see either of these other PIs again.

"I think they're in one of these," I said, pitching my voice low. I pointed at the cupboards behind the racks of luggage. If Aimee and the guy she was with knew I was close, they'd run and hide again.

Terry wordlessly tucked in closer, understanding my need for caution. We opened the first cupboard together. I was validated to find that it was three feet deep and as high as the train car. Definitely enough room for people to hide in, though this one was full to the top with luggage. I stretched so I stood taller than the luggage, stuck my head into the cupboard, and peered to the right. A glimmer of light leaked through, suggesting that a person could in fact travel the length of the car, unseen, inside these cupboards.

We moved to the next storage compartment, pushing aside luggage to access it. This one was less full than the previous, but there were still no signs of anyone hiding.

"You know," Terry said, "it's amazing what someone will do to get away from the mob."

I nodded. It was true. Why hadn't Aimee and her mom just gone into the witness relocation program? I supposed if you trusted no one, you trusted no one. My hand was reaching toward the third cupboard when a thought niggled at me.

Trust no one.

It made sense if the mob was chasing you. So why were the words suddenly resonating, even as I slid the panel open, revealing the cupboard's contents? This one also contained luggage, but it was pushed to the side.

A woman and a child huddled in the middle.

Chapter 48

The thoughts collided like cars, resounding painfully in my head:

I had only Terry's word that he'd boarded in Fargo.

The ticket stub from Chicago in his duffel.

Terry giving Jed the heebie-jeebies.

Me never, ever telling Terry about the mob.

Then, in the moment of silence right before it became terror and pain, everything clicked. Doghn had *not* lied about Sofia Ramos. She likely *had* been a childless housekeeper in Brooklyn, and she had been poisoned in the cabin next door to me. She had been *posing* as Gisela Alvarez, so Gisela could pose as a man and further protect herself and her daughter.

I didn't know what their relationship had been—sisters? Some bond deep enough for Sofia to risk and then give her life so Gisela could escape with Aimee, one step ahead of the mob.

Except not now, because I'd brought the devil to their doorstep. They cowered in the cupboard, Aimee holding Mr. Bunny and a now-undisguised Gisela holding Aimee, their faces pure masks of terror.

Terry was the one hunting them.

He must have sliced his own throat.

It was a sick, terrible strategy, but it'd worked. It had thrown the heat off him, at least as far as I was concerned. The ruse that he didn't care where Aimee was hidden had been a nice touch, as well. But he'd blown it all by letting on that he knew about the mob connection. My only hope for saving Gisela and Aimee from my blunder now was in pretending I didn't know Terry was the bad guy.

"Aimee!" I tried to make my voice sound excited, but I couldn't hide the quaver. Terry's eyes zeroed in on me, and they were as flat as bits of coal. He knew.

He reached for his waistband.

I saw a flash of silver.

Aimee screamed.

I punched Terry's throat. Blood began to flow freely.

"Run!"

But the woman and girl couldn't run. Terry had one hand over his throat, the other holding a gun trained on Gisela. I shoved him, and we both fell to the floor. He was a big guy, though, and he had the advantage. He picked me up like a rag doll, kicked at the exit door to open it, and dragged me into the bladder separating the cars.

Amy and Gisela were trapped behind us, unable to move either direction in their cupboard because of the luggage, and I was about to be erased.

The train was now traveling at normal speed, and apparently we were rounding curves, because Terry's footing was uneven. He almost lost his balance twice. Shoving his gun into his waistband, he pulled the emergency exit cord. A whole panel of the bladder fell away, revealing mountains close enough to touch.

I gasped at the air's icy chill, and the terror of how fast we were moving. My hair blew back from my face, and the wind sliced at my skin. One easy pitch, and I'd be out of the train. If I was lucky I'd survive the fall, making it a toss-up whether I'd bleed or freeze to death first. The skinned-alive feeling of absolute terror consumed me.

I kicked and screamed with everything I had. Except it didn't do any good. Terry had gone into the no-pain zone. He lifted me in the air. He propelled me forward. His arms twitched as he flexed.

And then, in a flash, we were both thrown to the floor as a force struck Terry.

"Mira!"

It was Jed. I was so relieved I could cry, but that emotion quickly turned to horror as Terry roared to his feet, slamming Jed against the opposite wall. His head made a sickening cracking sound before he melted to the floor. Jed lay limp as a doll, unconscious. I jumped on Terry's back, digging my fingers into the open wound at his throat.

He gurgled, and I dug deeper.

Outside, the quality of the light changed. Rather than mountains, a limitless blue sky stretched across the horizon. Terry picked up my friend. Jed's eyes were closed, a trickle of blood leaking from his temple. His beautiful brown, curly hair was matted with red. It was excruciating to see his face so pale and motionless.

I needed to save him.

I ground a finger into Terry's eye, but he continued into the open area where the diaphragm had been, the icy winter air rushing around him, the mountains fallen away, leaving only a vast, empty space. The train lurched, but he didn't lose his balance.

He tossed Jed into the endless blue.

Chapter 49

I opened my mouth and screamed from my deepest place, but no sound came out. Terry grabbed my throat from behind and squeezed. His hands were unforgiving chunks of meat, and none of my squirming would release me.

I gasped for breath, my heart pounding against my lungs, both threatening to burst. He grunted and tightened his grip until all the fight drained from me. My vision narrowed, black closing in, until it was just a pinprick, and still I couldn't fight back.

Jed was dead because of me.

I heard rather than felt my body drop to the ground with a thump, near the edge of the train but not quite over. Below, a valley stretched out for miles. The winter wind flayed the skin from my bones. I wanted to grab at something solid, but my hands weren't listening to me.

From the sideways position, I watched Terry's boots clomp toward Gisela and Aimee. He was either swaying treacherously, or I was losing consciousness. The train lurched again, tossing a piece of luggage to the floor. It missed my head by inches, falling outside and into space.

Was that blood on Terry's boots?

Did it matter?

Yes. Yes it did. Because it meant he was hurt.

I screamed again, my yell silent, but it was enough. My vision expanded, at least partially, and I pushed myself to my knees. I put a hand to the wall. The cold winter air poured over me, seeking me, wanting to lure me into the freezing wilderness with Jed. I looked toward it. The endless blue was still out there. The mountain valley we were traveling over must have gone on for miles. My heart cried for my friend, but my head didn't have the luxury.

I grabbed at a pipe to pull myself to standing. It came free in my hand, likely loosened when Terry or I had fallen against it. Swaying with the train, I pushed forward. Terry had his back to me. He had trained his gun on Aimee and Gisela with one hand and was trying to wrap his coat around his neck to stop the bleeding with the other.

Once he got that under control, he would pull the trigger.

That was his plan, anyhow.

Mine went more like this:

I swung that pipe with the strength of everyone I'd ever loved, and everyone who'd been taken from me before their time.

It whistled through the air like the song of justice.

When it connected with the back of his skull, the melon-popping sound was almost as satisfying as the crunchy, wet feel of it sinking into his brain. Terry fell to his knees and then straight back.

But he wasn't dead. He was breathing.

Jed *wasn't*. He was dead.

I held the pipe over my head. I thought of bringing it down on Terry's face. I thought of pulling Terry's unconscious body to the edge and tossing it over.

You know what stopped me?

Jed was out there. He was on the other side. And no way in hell was I going to let this bastard be with my precious friend.

Chapter 50

Reed was on the scene within minutes, Doghn shortly after. They found Gisela and Aimee holding me. I was too broken to cry.

When we reached Coeur d'Alene, the police and an ambulance were waiting to whisk Terry away. Officials had already sent a helicopter to search for Jed's body before dark fell, but based on my description of where he'd been tossed from the train, they weren't hopeful.

It sounded like Jed had fallen into the Silver Valley from a ten-mile stretch of railroad bridge that rose several hundred feet above the ground.

Medical personnel diagnosed me with a concussion and a sprained wrist.

I didn't care.

Reed explained that he was a federal marshal tracking Gisela and Aimee. He said that the feds couldn't force them into police protection, but they could stay close and try to catch Pierre Danza's goons in the act. His best guess was that Terry worked for Danza and had boarded the train as soon as they'd discovered Gisela's location, probably in Chicago. He'd chosen poison as his weapon so it was less likely to be traced back to his boss.

It was Pierre's bad luck that Terry had killed the wrong person. Sofia Ramos had been Gisela's housekeeper and close friend back in Brooklyn. Terry hadn't known that. The two women looked enough alike that he'd believed she was Gisela.

Chad was the one who'd told Jed where to find me. Apparently, Chad had been keeping a close watch on my whereabouts. After he sent Jed after me, he sent Reed, and then Doghn. Turned out the kid had good instincts. I was lucky to be alive.

I didn't have the energy to nod as Reed filled me in. I just sat in the back of the ambulance. It wasn't until Johnny showed up that the tears came. He'd been waiting in Coeur d'Alene, frantic, since he'd gotten word that the train had been trapped in a snowstorm with a murderer aboard.

"Oh, honey," he said, gathering me into his arms.

The EMTs stepped back. Reed disappeared. I melted.

"I killed Jed," I whispered.

Saying it out loud was too much. I started sobbing, and Johnny held me, murmuring soft words, not letting go. He told me I hadn't killed Jed, that I'd never hurt him, and I wanted to believe it, but I knew better.

Mrs. Berns joined us, and the three of us wept.

When I was wrung dry of tears, my face swollen, my heart empty, I convinced the EMTs that I would be fine. When they protested, I asked if they could force me to stay. They couldn't. I let Johnny take my hand as we returned the blanket wrapped around my shoulders. The three of us were walking toward Johnny's rental car, Mrs. Berns holding my other hand, when I spotted them.

Gisela and Aimee stood near Johnny's car talking to Reed, but their conversation stopped when they saw me approach. Aimee ran up and hugged my waist. Before I knew it, she'd shoved Mr. Bunny in my hand and ran back to her mom.

I held the animal in the air. "I can't," I said. It didn't sound like my voice.

"Please," Gisela said, her eyes also big with tears. She stepped forward but stopped herself. This wasn't over for her. It probably never would be. Her entire life would be devoted to jumping at shadows and worrying for her daughter. "You saved us. Please. Aimee needs to thank you. Let her."

They turned away, walking toward an unmarked car, mother with her arm around her daughter, their heads leaning close. Reed spared me one last glance before following them. What else was there to say?

People left the train in droves. I expected most of them would never board another. A pink coat caught my eye. It was Ms. Wrenshall, standing still amid a moving throng.

Her makeup was flawless, and she appeared both strong and vulnerable as she scanned the crowd. I realized I'd never know whether she connected with her grandnephew and, if she did, whether he deserved her.

I clutched the Velveteen Rabbit to my chest and wept for things lost.

Chapter 51

I stood outside his door, a light snow falling on my shoulders. It was a February snow, more ice than fluff, but lacking teeth. Mrs. Berns and Johnny had offered to come with, but I'd turned them both down. I needed to do this alone.

I'd gotten Noelle's last name from my mom. It was funny—she'd always been Noelle to me. Five-year-olds don't care about last names.

My mom had told it to me in a hushed tone. *Noelle Flanigen. I haven't thought of that poor girl in years. Why are you asking?*

I had called my mom from a bedside phone in a cheap motel somewhere in eastern Montana. I'd made Johnny pull over once I'd made up my mind. I think he and Mrs. Berns were happy to hear me finally talk. Once I had Noelle's last name and last known address, I needed a computer. The hotel manager had been reluctant to let me use his, but a whispered conversation with Johnny changed his mind.

Using the research database I subscribed to for investigative work, I tracked Oscar and Ursula Flanigen. They'd moved to Saint Cloud immediately after Noelle's abduction, and then to Willmar, and then divorced. Mrs. Flanigen had either changed her name or fallen off the face of the earth, because I couldn't track her after that.

Mr. Flanigen had stayed in the Willmar house, where he still lived.

I brought that information back to the hotel room and sat on the corner of the bed. My whole world felt shrunken, no bigger than a box around my head. When Mrs. Berns appeared in my sight line, I couldn't give her my attention. She shoved a brown package in my hand anyway. It was the box Kennie had asked me to deliver to Seattle.

"What do I do with this?"

"Open it." Mrs. Berns looked like I felt—sad, deep-in-her-bones sad.

"It's not addressed to me."

The slightest toss of her shoulder was the only physical response she could muster. "Kennie said you're supposed to open it. She told me to tell you that when we hit Portland, but that ain't gonna happen."

She disappeared into the bathroom. Johnny was out getting us food. I opened the box.

Inside was a note. The handwriting was flowery, full of unnecessary swirls and flourishes, just like Kennie Rogers.

I figured you'd need this after spending a week on the train with Mrs. Berns. Don't ever tell anyone I never did anything for you. And stop judging people so quickly. —K

I pushed aside the tissue paper under the note. Inside were a dozen Nut Goodies. I cried again, my tears rolling over the red-and-green wrappers and pooling at the bottom of the box. That's when I remembered Jed's note. I pulled it tenderly from the jeans I hadn't changed. The scratchy handwriting read like a message from beyond:

Mira Bo-beera: I wanted to tell you my secret, but you're so busy. Don't feel bad about that. You help everyone, and that's cool. Anyhow, my secret isn't that big a deal, and I figgered I'd write it in a note and we could talk about it later. Here it is: I want to move to Colorado to be a snowboarding instructor. Do you think it's stupid? Do you think my parents will be mad?

The air went out of the room. Johnny found me on the floor. He helped me to the bed. He read both notes. He held me until Mrs. Berns finished in the bathroom, and when she did, we drove through the night to reach Willmar, a medium-size town a half an hour from where I grew up, Johnny promising the whole way that his internship would wait for him. When we arrived at the house, a neat little one-story painted white with black trim, Mrs. Berns and Johnny parked the car at the coffee shop up the block and waited for me.

I knew I needed to see Oscar Flanigen and ask him the question, but I couldn't bring myself to push the doorbell. The snow continued to fall. I was a statue. Tiny drifts formed on my shoulders. I might have stood there until I was buried if not for the gentle cough behind me.

I turned, disturbing my private snowfall.

He looked exactly like I remembered him, but older.

Noelle's dad.

I fought back the tears. I'd already cried enough for two lifetimes.

The words came out in a child's rushed monologue. "Mr. Flanigen? I'm Mira James. I knew Noelle. We were best friends the summer she disappeared."

His face tightened, and it was a terrible thing to see, but it lasted only a moment. He collected himself, nodded, and led me inside by the elbow. Over tea, he caught me up on his life. He and his wife had divorced because their marriage couldn't survive their grief. She died in a car wreck a year later. He believed she'd been driving drunk, though it hadn't been proven.

He ran for a seat in the state legislature and won. He'd led a quiet political career, characterized mostly by his tireless work on behalf of child safety. He raised their two remaining children on his own. One was a pediatrician in Willmar. The other was a marine biologist in Hawaii.

They were happy.

Noelle had never been found. There were sightings every few years, when the news replayed a special recorded after her abduction, but for the most part, the world went on without his beloved daughter. He assumed she was dead, had believed so for years.

His story took more than two hours. He paused every few minutes, staring off as if looking for someone, and then he'd return his attention to me. He asked me about myself. He was happy that I was a librarian. He was also not surprised I was becoming a PI.

"Makes sense," he said, as if he heard it every day.

"What do you mean?"

He refilled my teacup. "You had something traumatic happen to you when you were five. Someone was kidnapped right in front of you. Now you're trying to fix that wrong. You can't, though. You know that, right? You can't bring her back."

A single tear leaked out. I wiped it away. "I want you to know that I'm sorry. I could have yelled. I could have fought that man off. I just let him take her."

He'd been staring off in one of his moments, but my words brought his gaze back to mine, his expression startled. "What?" If not for the gruesome topic, he looked as though he would have laughed. "Honey, you were five years old. Five. Do you remember that age? Shoot, you were a baby."

He leaned across the table and put his hand on mine, his expression concerned. "You haven't felt responsible for her being abducted, have you? Not all these years?"

My tears answered him. Dangit, I needed to figure out how to get control of myself. He didn't hold me—I sensed he hadn't held anyone since his divorce—but he also didn't look away from my tears. We sat like that for several minutes, me a puddle and him a rock.

When I felt I could control myself again, I reached into my bag. I'd intended to tell him the story of Aimee, but it didn't feel like the right time. Maybe he and I would cross paths again. For now, though, I had a rabbit to give him. He looked confused when I pulled the doll out, but that quickly turned to melancholy.

"Noelle used to have a doll like this," he whispered. "It was her favorite."

I nodded. There was nothing else to say. I kissed him on the top of his head, thanked him for his time, and let Johnny drive us back to Battle Lake.

Chapter 52

Jed's funeral was held two days later. The church was so full that speakers needed to be set up in both the lobby and the parking lot, despite the cold temperatures. People told stories and laughed, and held each other and cried. We celebrated the life of someone pretty incredible.

I held it together until Jed's parents spoke. They helped each other to the podium, and the church went silent as the congregation became one huge, aching heart. Jed's dad was a salt-of-the-earth guy and not a public speaker. He let his wife step to the microphone.

"I—" The screech of feedback made her stop speaking. The pastor rushed over to adjust it, and she leaned forward again. "I want to say thank you all for coming. Jed was . . . he was my boy. I know you loved him. We did, too."

That's all she could get out before the sobbing overtook her. Her husband held her, and I thought he'd lead her away. Instead, he leaned toward the microphone, his voice deep and hoarse. "My son taught me about being happy, and about always treating people well. We'll miss him every day of his life, but it's our job to make sure the best parts of him—his spirit and his innocence—never die. And I want to especially thank those of you who were his friends. You made his life better."

He made eye contact with me. His eyes were so full of sorrow, for Jed and for me, that it was hard to hold that gaze, but I did. And then he did something that I'll forever be grateful for: he smiled. It was small and sad, a shadow of his regular, boisterous grin, but it told me that he understood.

There was not a dry eye in the church. As the choir sang "You'll Never Walk Alone," I glanced around at the good people of Battle Lake, the bighearted citizens who'd welcomed me into their town, chaos and death on my heels, and who still accepted me despite how many times I'd turned their lives upside down.

I had a single thought: it was time for me to leave these people alone. They were incredible and kind. They were also big weirdos, it was true, but there were no better people.

They'd always looked out for me.

And that was why it was time for me to move on.

But first, I'd celebrate the life of a wonderful man and friend, and I would drink wine with Mrs. Berns, split a Nut Goodie with Kennie, and sleep in the arms of Johnny Leeson.

Acknowledgments

February Fever is the tenth in my Mira James mystery series. My kids, friends, family, editors, publicist, agent, and the person who built my computer all helped in this endeavor, but here's the truth: this book wouldn't have been written without you. I would have given up on the series long ago if not for readers who take time out of their busy lives—and often money out of their pockets—to buy and read my books. (If you checked this out from the library, that's great, too. I love libraries.)

In fact, if not for you, I'd probably have given up on writing at least five years ago and pursued a career that paid better and had fewer rejections, like acting, oil painting, or being a scarf-acrobat for Cirque du Soleil. So thank you. It is your attention that turns this pile of words from a doorstop into a book, and for that, you have my gratitude. May your kindness find its way back to you ten times over.

About the Author

Photo © 2023 Kelly Weaver Photography

Jess Lourey writes about secrets. She's the bestselling author of thrillers, rom-com mysteries, book club fiction, young adult fiction, and non-fiction. Winner of the Anthony, Thriller, and Minnesota Book Awards, Jess is also an Edgar, Agatha, and Lefty Award–nominated author; TEDx presenter; and recipient of The Loft's Excellence in Teaching fellowship. Check out her TEDx Talk for the true story behind her debut novel, *May Day*. She lives in Minneapolis with a rotating batch of foster kittens (and occasional foster puppies, but those goobers are a lot of work). For more information, visit www.jesslourey.com.